P9-DKF-925

THE
MARVELOUS
MIRZA GIRLS

THE
MARVELOUS
MIRZA GIRLS

SHEBA KARIM

Quill Tree Books
An Imprint of HarperCollinsPublishers

Quill Tree Books is an imprint of HarperCollins Publishers.

The Marvelous Mirza Girls
Copyright © 2021 by Sheba Karim
All rights reserved. Printed in the United States of America.
No part of this book may be used or reproduced in any manner whatsoever without
written permission except in the case of brief quotations embodied in critical
articles and reviews. For information address HarperCollins Children's Books, a
division of HarperCollins Publishers, 195 Broadway, New York, NY 10007.
www.epicreads.com

Library of Congress Control Number: 2020945258
ISBN 978-0-06-284548-1

Typography by Erin Fitzsimmons
21 22 23 24 25   PC/LSCH   10 9 8 7 6 5 4 3 2 1
❖
First Edition

For Anand, who brought me to the jinn.

PART ONE

New Jersey

one

Air Quality Index: No Clue.

DURING THE SPEECHES AT her high school gradu-
ation, Noreen picked at dirt on her sneakers and thought about
her dead aunt. Today was the first anniversary of Sonia Khala's
funeral, and Noreen would have preferred to stay home, bake
Sonia Khala's favorite blueberry scones, and eat them on the
hammock while listening to Sonia Khala's three musical beloveds
(Nusrat Fateh Ali Khan, Marc Anthony, and Prince), but her
mother, Ruby, had insisted, saying, imagine how my sister would
feel if she knew she was the reason you skipped your graduation.

Having researched notions of barzakh, the period between
death and resurrection, Noreen had learned it was widely
accepted that souls awaiting the Day of Judgment in Paradise
(where, if there was a Paradise, Sonia Khala's soul would certainly be) could have knowledge of the actions of the living.
Better not to risk it, given how much Sonia Khala had loved the
academy, with all its towers and traditions. Had she been alive,

she would have flown out for Noreen's graduation and decorated the house with balloons and a big cheesy sign made by her nine-year-old twins, Amir and Sohail, illustrated by Amir with a silly rhyming couplet by Sohail. Somewhere on the sign, Amir would have drawn her portrait. The last time, he'd gotten the shape of her eyes exactly right.

He'd stopped drawing since his mother died.

Noreen had worn running sneakers under her lacy white graduation dress so she could go far and fast on a moment's notice. She used to hate running, but her adviser had suggested rounding out her high school resume with a sport, and she'd joined cross-country because it didn't cut anyone. Though Noreen was not athletically inclined and considered second to last a victory, running grew on her. It was like writing; she approached it with a modicum of dread but was always glad to have done it, and, unlike her unfinished scripts, she always completed a race. She hadn't been able to write in the past year, but she ran four to five times a week. It took her out of her head, provided a respite from the grief and the doubts and the dark.

At the podium, valedictorian Purima Sen was addressing her fellow graduates, fifty-three white-clad girls poised at the brink of their futures. "As you go through life, do not take no as an answer, but a challenge. Because if you put your mind to it, nothing is beyond your reach, whether it's the stars or a Nobel Prize."

Every year, the same solemn speeches, *go forth, bright young women, and achieve greatness in the world, courage kindness girl power Nobel Prize blah blah blah.* Even Sonia Khala, when she was high school valedictorian, must have uttered the same sincere, inspirational hokiness, while a thirteen-year-old Ruby sat in the audience between their parents, rolling her eyes as their mother cried and their father filmed every last moment on his giant camcorder.

Why all these false promises? Why not speak the truth? That getting hit by a bus, dying quickly of a disease, dying slowly of a disease, even sunbathing at the unlucky moment an epic tsunami powered by climate change swept the whole island, all of those things were more likely than any of them winning the Nobel Prize for anything? Or at least quote Chris Rock—*you can be anything you're good at, as long as they're hiring.*

The speeches ended; the distribution of diplomas began. Noreen made sure to smile at the congratulations of her teachers, some of whom had watched her grow from quiet, awkward middle schooler, mustache over braces, errant eyebrows, and a roving band of small but vicious pimples, to high school graduate with a far more manicured face, quiet still but less awkward. Coach Novak, for example, had witnessed Noreen's transformation from girl who tried to dodge dodgeball to reluctant runner to breast cancer 10K participant. She was saying goodbye to the school where she'd spent her formative years, met Abby, and started a humor zine (after the debut issue, half the junior class had come to her with some version of, "Noreen, I didn't realize you were so funny!"), and though she was moved by the finality and poignancy of this academic rite of passage, her aunt was rotting under six feet of dirt, of which Noreen had thrown three fistfuls, and since then everything—laughter, hope, nostalgia—came steeped in grief.

"Greetings, high school graduate! Care to spike your lemonade with some of Mama Wu's finest bourbon?" Abby wrapped her arm around Noreen's waist, pulling her close as she dug inside a canvas bag for her flask, a skull and crossbones poison symbol etched into the leather. Noreen refused the booze and rested her head on her best friend's shoulder.

"How you doing?" Abby asked.

"Better than I expected, honestly," Noreen said.

"Did your grandparents come?"

"Nah. They were going to but my grandmother couldn't get out of bed this morning, first anniversary and all, and my grandfather didn't want to leave her."

"Got it. Where are Ruby Auntie and Adi Uncle?"

"Hitting up the jerk shrimp skewers before they disappear."

"Did somebody say shrimp skewers?" Abby despised fish but could eat half her weight in crustaceans.

"Jumbo. Better get some before they're gone."

"I'm on it. Want one?"

Noreen shook her head. A few seconds later, her stomach gurgled. "Hey, get me one too," she called out to Abby, girl on a mission in her fuchsia Doc Martens boots and a tight, white silk

4

dress. Poor outfit for running, but excellent for the ass.

Then whoever had appointed themselves DJ—Coach Novak, probably, who always opened their school dances and was the reason every student at Covington School for Girls could perform the electric slide in their sleep—decided it was time to switch up the dulcet harp instrumental.

One, two, one two three huh!

Prince.

You had to be kidding.

She'd pretended through the ceremony, but she couldn't pretend through Prince.

Noreen threw her drink at a trash can, missed, kept going, turned back a moment later because grief would not make a litterer of her, dammit, disposed of the cup properly. She waved at Abby and her mother, hitched up her dress, lengthened her stride.

"Raspberry Beret." Of all the songs in the world.

Her feet hit asphalt.

Go.

See Noreen.

See Noreen run.

Watch her long, dark hair fly as she pushes uphill against the wind. Note the grimace on her face, taste the salt on her lips. Feel her muscles fire, her heart expand and contract. Hear her inhale, exhale. See how it helps her forget, memory replaced by breath.

* * *

On their last happy visit to the Bay Area, Noreen and Ruby had convinced Sonia Khala to rock out to Prince behind the wheel of a sports car. It was early December, sunny, sixty degrees. They'd stopped by the BMW dealership because Sonia Khala was interested in trading in her SUV for a newer model with improved safety features. Noreen and Ruby went straight to the center of the showroom, where a sleek blue sports car rotated on a platform strung with paper snowflake cutouts. "Feliz Navidad" played through the speakers.

"Do you think we could get Sonia Khala to test-drive this?" Noreen said.

Sonia Khala had once said if she didn't have five things going on at once, she felt bereft. For their visits, she prepared a daily itinerary, with backup options in case of rain. She spent her "free" time fundraising for Muslim refugees, engaging in political protests, volunteering every Satuday in a soup kitchen, and overseeing tutors and signing up the boys for extracurriculars to help them along the path to Yale. Ruby joked that Sonia Khala was "half martyr, half Tiger Mom." Even her band, an international group of pathologists who donated all show proceeds to charity, combined pleasure with purpose. Whenever Noreen and Ruby visited, they tried to get her to do something spontaneous, for no other reason than the hell of it.

"Hey, Apa," Ruby said. "Come here."

Sonia Khala looked up from the window sticker on a silver SUV. She pushed at the bridge of her glasses, an old habit from her Yale undergrad days, when her glasses had been loose and her head bent over books, and walked over.

"What do you want?" she said. "You usually call me Apa when you want me to do something."

"We want you to test-drive this sports car," Noreen said.

"Oh my goodness," she said. "I hope you're joking."

This could be an episode, Noreen thought. Risk-averse aunt test-drives fancy sports car, hijinks and hilarity ensue, all's well that ends well (at In-N-Out Burger).

"Come on, Khala," Noreen said. "YOLO."

"What?"

"You only live once," Ruby explained. "When does your comfort zone become a prison?"

"Even if I did have any interest in driving a race car, which I don't, we don't have time. Sohail has his violin lesson at one and right after Amir has aikido and we have to be at that cheese-tasting benefit by five."

"Haven't you ever wanted to drive a sports car?" Ruby asked.

"Have you ever heard of Newton's laws of motion?" Sonia Khala said.

"Mom, maybe we should drop it," Noreen said.

Ruby nodded. "True. You're too nervous a driver, Apa. A sports car might overwhelm you."

"And she doesn't like to try new things," Noreen said.

"False, on both counts." Sonia Khala folded her arms over her backpack-sized purse. "I did Zumba last week. Have either of you tried Zumba?"

"I don't like dancing to instructions," Noreen said.

"If you're not a nervous driver, how come you won't play music with words in the car?" Ruby said.

"Because I find words distracting while driving," Sonia Khala said.

"But you'll listen to NPR," Noreen said.

"That's information. Knowledge is power."

"Come on, Apa." Ruby nudged her elbow. "If you don't want to do it for you, then do it for us."

Sonia Khala looked at Noreen, then Ruby. "All right. I'll do it, though I won't drive fast, and only if you two come to Zumba with me tomorrow."

"Ooh, barter," Noreen said. "I like."

"Done." Ruby rubbed her hands together. "This is gonna be fun!"

"What if someone sees me?" Sonia Khala asked.

"They'll say, hey, isn't that woman rocking out in the sports car the bass guitarist from that awesome eighties cover band that raises money for charity? And people say pathologists aren't cool," Noreen said.

"I better wear my sunglasses, then." She took her sunglasses out of her purse, which was stuffed with smaller zipped purses to keep things organized. "The boys chose these, but they're a little too Jackie O, hai na?"

"Good afternoon, ladies."

Enter Sharlene, a Black woman in her forties who'd greeted them when they'd come in. Noreen made a note of the silk bow at her shirt collar, tied with perfect symmetry.

"I'm Sharlene, the manager. I'm so sorry about the wait. How can I help you this fine December day?"

Sonia Khala removed her sunglasses. "I'm interested in trading in my SUV," she said.

"Maybe for that blue sports car," Ruby said. "She'd like to test-drive it."

Sharlene took in Sonia Khala's wrinkle-free slacks and scuffed loafers, the thick, frayed leather tie of her mom purse. Seeing the two sisters together, you'd think Ruby was the rich one. "Looking for a change?"

"We heard adrenaline delays menopause," Ruby said.

Sharlene laughed. "Is that the secret now? Well, this model goes zero to sixty in 3.9 seconds."

"My SUV can do it in a little over five," Sonia Khala said. "What difference does a moment make?"

"Everything," Noreen said. "Right, Sharlene?"

"I've got an SUV and a sports coupe myself," Sharlene said. "It's a different feel, different aerodynamics. And different reactions from other people."

They all four looked at the sports car, the hood rotating away to the "fa la la la la la" of "Deck the Halls."

"I'd like to try it," Sonia Khala told Sharlene. "Just to see what it's like—I don't think I'd ever actually purchase a sports car. Is that possible? Trying it, I mean?"

"I don't see why not. Come with me."

Noreen and Ruby high-fived each other.

"You two," Sonia Khala said as they followed Sharlene to her desk. "Do I need to get a Mirza girls rider on my life insurance?"

"It's all in fun," Ruby said. "No one's dying."

"Amen," Sharlene said. "Also to that point, this car has some state-of-the-art safety features, which I'll explain on the ride."

Ten minutes later, Noreen and Ruby were squished in the puny back seat (they hadn't quite thought this through), Sharlene in front with Sonia Khala, who was waiting to take a right out of the lot.

"All clear," Sharlene said.

Sonia Khala recited bismillah and took a slow turn, stopping well before the red light.

"Don't be afraid to give it a little gas," Sharlene said.

"Okay. Any other tips?" Sonia Khala said.

"Relax," Sharlene said. "Enjoy the ride."

Sonia Khala rolled her shoulders back. "YOLO," she said, with an earnestness so endearing that Noreen wished she could bottle for whenever the world felt too cynical.

Mere minutes later, Sonia Khala was relaxed enough to accelerate up the ramp, then, after a second, breathy bismillah, cut all the way across to the left lane with a *Yippee*.

Noreen leaned forward to look at the speedometer. *Seventy-five!* she mouthed to her mother.

Ruby made a roaring sound. "Excuse me, cheetah, who are you and what have you done with my sister?"

"Actually, cheetahs can't roar," Sonia Khala said. "Unlike a lion, the cheetah's hyoid bone is one piece rather than two, making them physically incapable of roaring."

"I did not know that," Sharlene said.

"My sister used to read the Encyclopedia Britannica for fun, back when it was books," Ruby said. "Before Siri, there was Sonia."

"Not anymore," Sonia Khala said. "After all those IVF hormones and being pregnant with twins, I've forgotten half of what I knew. Back in my heyday, I would have at least made it to finalist on *Jeopardy!*"

"I still remember," Sharlene said, "when I was pregnant with my first and I was buying something at Walgreens and gave the guy a twenty from my purse and he looked at me funny and I realized I'd handed him a panty liner."

"Speaking of words that begin with *P*," Noreen said, "Sonia Khala, you ready for some tunes?"

"For you, my beloved niece," Sonia Khala said, catching her eye in the rearview mirror, "anything."

"Sharlene, can you please connect my phone to this twelve-speakered radio with its powerful 360-watt amplifier?" Noreen asked.

Sharlene laughed. "You looking for an internship?"

Like their mother, the twins also loved Prince, and each had their favorite song. "Raspberry Beret" was Sohail's, and when it began to play, they all cheered.

"Girl, this is my jam." Sharlene started singing along, prompting a collective gasp at the deep, bright timbre of her voice. *Fine December day indeed,* Noreen thought.

Cruising at a cool sixty-five in the middle lane, they sang and shimmied and laughed.

Even as it was unfolding, Noreen knew this would be a memory she'd hold precious and dear, one that would bring her great joy with every remembrance, the exhilarating high of being (relatively) fast and free with the two people she loved best and one she would never forget.

After Sonia Khala died, Noreen learned that buttressing this joy had been the implicit promise of more such moments. Now that Fate, or Allah, or the Incredible Unfairness of the Universe had stolen this promise, the memory had become a painful reminder, of what had been lost, and what would never be again.

two

AS NOREEN RAN ONTO her street, she had to duck behind a shrub because Tammy, their garrulous down-the-street neighbor, was getting into her car. If Tammy saw her, she'd make her stop for a glass of lavender lemonade. Noreen very much enjoyed the lemonade; the accompanying questions, not so much. *Heavens, why are you running in such a pretty dress? Wasn't today your graduation? Did you get your diploma? Does your mother know where you are?*

A needle tickled Noreen's nose and she sneezed, but Tammy had left the driveway. Noreen waited for her car to turn the corner, then sprinted the last leg home. She stopped to check the mail and joined Adi Uncle and her mother, who were waiting on the porch with a towel and water. Adi Uncle was her mother's best friend and Noreen's godfather. Ruby and Adi Uncle had been so close for so long they could often read each other's minds and almost always guess the direction of the joke (though not always the punch line).

"Good time," her mother said.

"Would have been better but I had to hide from Tammy." Noreen tossed the mail onto the hammock, yanked up her dress, set her foot on the lower rung of the porch railing, stretched her hamstrings. Though she'd shaved yesterday, her calves were already stubbly. Beads of sweat dripped from her forehead to the floor. The white lace armpits of her dress were now yellow. This was why she never wore white. If she ever got married, she'd dress like a desi bride, in some vivid shade of red.

Adi Uncle and her mother watched as she toweled off, their smiles belied by the concern in their eyes.

"I'm fine, everybody," Noreen said. "You may have seen a girl running from her own graduation, but they're casting for *Runaway Bride 3* and I thought I'd give it a shot."

Adi Uncle laughed. "Was there a *Runaway Bride 2*?"

"If there was, it was terrible," Ruby said.

"Not if it had Julia Roberts," Adi Uncle said. "Nothing with Julia Roberts can be terrible. That smile is worth at least two stars."

Ruby disagreed, and Adi Uncle did a Google search. Julia Roberts's movies had been ranked from best to worst and worst to best and by critical and audience acclaim. As her mother and Adi Uncle debated the lists, Noreen climbed into the porch hammock, her springtime place of refuge, unless Tammy was out on a stroll, in which case it put you at a disadvantage. She closed her eyes, lulled by the breeze and the sway of the hammock and the familiar rhythms of her mother and Adi Uncle, listening as they argued and laughed, argued and laughed.

Yes, they decided, Julia Roberts had acted in some pretty terrible films, but relatively few considering the breadth of her career.

She walked in through the out door, out door.

"Hey," Ruby said.

Noreen opened her eyes.

"You okay?"

"I've heard Coach Novak deejay for years and she's never played 'Raspberry Beret,'" Noreen said.

"Maybe it's a good thing," Adi Uncle said. "Maybe it was Sonia Khala's way of being there. You know how much she loved signs."

This was true. Where others might see coincidence or luck or everyday happenstance, Sonia Khala saw signs. If Ruby and Noreen protested that she was reading too much into it, she'd quote the Quran, the final word on the matter.

Verily there are signs for those who reflect.

Maybe Adi Uncle was right. Maybe Prince was a sign.

"Of everyone of my life," Noreen said, "she was the most excited about my graduation. Not that you two aren't, but you know how she is—how she was . . ."

She is. She was. The past tense could still jolt, but if she were to use the present, Sonia Khala *is*, then where *is* she?

"She always was a sucker for a cap and gown," Ruby said.

"I'm glad I went, though," Noreen said. "I'm glad you made me go."

"And where do you want to go to dinner?" Adi Uncle said.

"We were thinking we don't have to go all the way to Brooklyn," Ruby said. "We can stay local, go to the Thai diner."

"It's the weekend, we'll have to wait," Noreen said.

A few years ago, their local, old-school New Jersey diner had been bought by a Thai family who had turned it into a Thai restaurant but retained the décor. The food was delicious, more typical Thai dishes combined with regional dishes from Isan, and they ate there once a week, at least. A few months ago, to their great annoyance, the *New York Times* had discovered it and now there were often lines out the door.

"Or we could get takeout and eat at home," Adi Uncle said.

"No. Sonia Khala would want us to go celebrate in the city. I want to celebrate."

"I agree," Ruby said. "Let's do it."

As Noreen got up from the hammock, the mail spilled onto the floor. On top was a card, addressed to her, written in Leila's cursive.

She felt Ruby looking at her and met her eyes.

"You can open it later," her mother said.

But now she'd seen it, and it was better to get it over with than wonder if this time would be any different.

She tore the envelope, read the card.

Dear Noreen, Congratulations on graduating high school, and all the best for College. With Love, Leila and Farhan

Inside the card was a check for $501.

She preferred her father's handwriting to Leila's, whose cursive had too much flourish, an excess of loops and curlicues. And why was *college* capitalized? Though, to be fair, for years it had been a main motivating force in her life, worthy of a capital letter. All the late nights and practice tests and extra-credit assignments and Amnesty International petitions and cross-country meets, all in service of *College*, those four years of transformative learning and personal growth, where she would take screenwriting classes and find forever friends like her mother had found Adi Uncle and travel and maybe even try improv because it was supposed to make you a better writer. The thought of performing in front of others made her toes clench, but if not college, then when?

And now, now she couldn't write, wasn't sure what to say, and the idea of *College* was more exhausting than exhilarating. Noreen was also reluctant to leave her mother; it was one thing to grieve separately, another to grieve all alone.

Not that her mom would let her stay. She'd insist otherwise, say, *Come now, Nor-bear, you have to go, explore a new world. Time for your next adventure.*

"You okay?" Adi Uncle said.

Noreen held up the check. "Dinner's on me."

"Hell, no," he said. "You deposit that into your savings account. Dinner is on me."

three

GRADUATION DINNER BEGAN WITH oysters and a bottle of prosecco. Noreen wasn't one for alcohol, or pot. In varying degrees, both brought her down, then pummeled her with dark thoughts—you'll never write anything worthwhile and anyway your writing sucks, your mother could die, Adi Uncle could die, you could die, if you were funnier/smarter/prettier/a better writer maybe your father would want to know you.

But the dinner was a celebration in her honor, and she felt obliged to sip from her mother's proferred glass, and as Ruby and Adi Uncle reminisced about a dingy summer sublet they once shared in Williamsburg before it became hopelessly hipster, she considered her aunt in present tense, the window in the coffin. In her afterlife research, she'd read about the theory of the torture of the grave, that right as your grave filled with the last of the dirt, your spirit returned to your body, and Munkar and Nakir arrived. Munkar and Nakir were demon angels, blue-faced, black-eyed, with wild hair and mile-wide shoulders. They came to test your faith, interrogating you with tongues that breathed fire. If you failed, your grave became an oppressive, stifling space with a small window overlooking hell, and worms would slowly consume your flesh, causing excruciating pain. In this manner, you would await the Day of Judgment. But if you passed, your grave became spacious and comfortable, a penthouse suite for the dead, with a floor-to-ceiling view of the garden of Paradise.

Sonia Khala prayed and fasted, and she was good and kind. The torture of the grave, it couldn't possibly be true, but if it was, if it was, then Noreen was certain Sonia Khala would pass the test, would be enjoying her Egyptian linens and Paradise views. But, Noreen thought, what if she didn't want to look upon jannatul firdaus? What if instead she wanted to see her sons, her husband, Noreen onstage today, accepting her diploma? What if she was thinking, fuck the gardens and rivers of Paradise. Show me my kids.

Except Sonia Khala didn't curse. The fictional character based on Sonia Khala that Noreen wrote—used to write—swore once in a while. She should change that. Anyway, her mother, both real and fictionalized, swore enough for a whole tribe.

"Nor-bear? Whatcha thinking?" Ruby asked.

Come back to the present. Smile. Crack a joke. Graduation dinner with the two living people you love most.

"About how much you swear." Noreen glanced at her plate.

"Man, I like oysters but sometimes it's better not to look too close."

"I used to hate oysters—they looked so moist," Adi Uncle said, cringing as he said *moist*. He selected the smallest oyster remaining on the ice. "But now I love them. Do you think they have oysters in India? I don't know if I'd trust them, though, if they did."

"India?" Noreen repeated. The look exchanged between Adi Uncle and her mother was subtle and fleeting, but Noreen knew them well enough to both notice it and understand. "What's going on? What have you not told me?"

"I thought you did tell her," Adi Uncle said to Ruby.

"There's nothing to tell," Ruby said.

"Oh, yes there is," Noreen said. "Come on. As long as no one's dying in a few months from cancer, I can handle it." Terrible joke. Grief and prosecco was not a good look on her. "Sorry—but seriously, spill it. You know this is one of my pet peeves."

Her mother drummed her fingers against the table. "The foundation is interested in supporting projects in India, and they asked me if I'd be willing to relocate to New Delhi for a few months to do a kind of assessment report."

"Assessment report?"

"They want me to meet with different NGOs, see which types of projects have good outcomes, what the different challenges are."

"Wow. Cool. Are you going to go?"

"They can send someone else. It's bad timing. You're starting college. And neither of us is exactly in our best state."

"That's your precondition for going to India?" Noreen said. "That both of us be in our best state? How do you even define that?"

"Exactly," Adi Uncle said.

If they'd been home, her mother would have gotten up and started pacing. Instead, she bounced one leg under the table and began to rearrange the empty oyster shells across the bed of ice. "I don't want to leave you; it's your first semester of college. What if you need me?"

"Don't worry about me," Noreen said. "I'll be fine."

"I can understand why you wouldn't want to go," Adi Uncle said, "but you've wanted to live abroad since I've known you. Remember how upset you were when we both got accepted to study abroad and your parents wouldn't let you go?"

"I'm not moving halfway around the world while my daughter is still grieving!"

The couple next to them paused their conversation. Ruby cleared her throat, smoothed the napkin over her lap. Adi Uncle reached over to rest his hand on her knee. The table stopped vibrating.

"I really am fine," Noreen said. "I'm learning to dance with a limp. Wait till you see my moves at my wedding."

Noreen's therapist had once quoted a writer, comparing grief to having a broken leg that doesn't heal right and still hurts when it's damp outside, but eventually you learn to dance with a limp. It was a weird analogy, but it had stuck.

"Love the happy face!" the waiter said, referring to what Ruby had done with the oyster shells. He was a lanky hipster in a red bow tie and carried three appetizer plates, one balanced on his forearm. Adi Uncle always over-ordered.

The waiter set the plates down, describing each one in unnecessary detail. As they ate, Noreen remembered how, in the car on the way to Target, she'd once asked Sonia Khala if she had any regrets, and Sonia Khala said she wished she'd visited India, before it became difficult for people with Pakistani heritage to get a visa. *Where would you want to go?* Noreen had asked.

Delhi, of course. I'd pay my respects at Hazrat Nizamuddin's shrine. I'd go to a lot of places outside of Delhi too. Taj Mahal, Fatehpur Sikri, Ajmer Sharif, Rajasthan. Bombay, Shahrukh Khan's house of course, bhel puri on Chowpatty Beach. I'd spend the most time in Delhi though. You know my naani grew up there, before Partition, but she wouldn't talk about it much, I think it was too painful to remember that life, I wish you'd met her, I wish she hadn't died before her grandkids were born. She did tell me once about the monkeys, how they were so naughty and bold. If you left food out on the balcony or windowsill they'd come and steal it, and leap from balcony to balcony, roof to roof. She said she was both frightened of them and in awe of how they could cross whole neighborhoods without touching the ground.

Noreen had a vision. In India, she would allay her grief by

realizing some of Sonia Khala's unfulfilled dreams. In India, she would start writing again.

"Did you know it was a dream of Sonia Khala's to visit Delhi?" Noreen said.

"What are you getting at?" Ruby asked.

"Why don't we both go? Could we get visas?"

"Not a hundred precent sure, though it helps if your foundation was started by a multimillionaire with connections. But, hello, what about college?"

Noreen shrugged. "I'll write to Wesleyan and request to defer a year. A girl in my class did it. I heard they usually grant them if you have a good reason. And what better reason than fulfilling a dream of my deceased aunt? And, to your 'best state' point, if white people go to India to figure their shit out, why can't we?"

Adi Uncle raised the prosecco bottle. "Hear hear!"

"Adi!" Ruby said. "This conversation is not settled yet."

He set the bottle back down, winked at Noreen. "College will still be there in a year," he said. "The Mirza girls hit Delhi—that's a once-in-a-lifetime adventure."

"Exactly," Noreen said. "Adi Uncle's right—college isn't going anywhere. We have to do this. We need to. It'll be an adventure. What happened to *When does your comfort zone become a prison?*"

"It'll be her gap year," Adi Uncle said. "All the Aussie kids do it."

"But—ah, who am I kidding?" Ruby waved her hand. "You had me at adventure."

"Yes!" Noreen said.

They raised their glasses.

"To the Mirza girls in Delhi."

"To the Mirza girls in Delhi."

"To the Mirza girls in Delhi."

Ruby took a sip and turned her head, burping into her shoulder. "Oh, man," she said, wiping the corners of her mouth. "Mom and Dad are not going to be happy about this."

From the Mixed-Up Screenwriting Files of Ms. Noreen Mirza

INT. THAI DINER - EVENING

NOOR and her mother, RUMANA, are seated in a booth in a crowded New Jersey diner, a small jukebox on one end, a plate of raw papaya salad and a plate of fresh spring rolls between them. Rumana is drinking a beer.

                    NOOR
     What do you think of Mall Apocalypse
     as the theme of me and Anne's next
     zine?

                    RUMANA
     Ooohh. Is there a zombie fashion show
     at the food court?

                    NOOR
     Maybe—shit.

                    RUMANA
                What?

                    NOOR
        Naani and Nana just walked in.

                    RUMANA
                (swiveling her head)
        Here? They can't be here. The Thai
        diner is my safe space.

                    NOOR
        I don't think they got that memo.

                    RUMANA
        Duck so they don't see you!

                    NOOR
        Too late.

ZOHRA, age 71, and JAMSHED, age 74, wave and
walk toward them.

                    RUMANA
                (frantic)
        My beer!

                    NOOR
        They know you drink.

                    RUMANA
        Knowing and seeing are two completely
        different things.

Just in the nick of time, Rumana hides her beer
bottle on the floor underneath the table.

                    NOOR
        As'salaam alaikum.

                    RUMANA
Look who's here! Salaam, shalom.

                    ZOHRA
Salaam, beta. Do you come here often?
It's so close to your house. We
thought of calling you.

                    NOOR
Oh, we're here like once—

                    RUMANA
        (shooting Noor a look)
In a while. What brings you guys here?

                    JAMSHED
I read the review in the *New York
Times*.

                    RUMANA
Goddamn *New York Times*.

                    ZOHRA
Rumana, don't swear.

                    RUMANA
That's not even—sorry.

The owner, **PREEDA**, age 51, comes over to their
table.

                    PREEDA
        (to Rumana)
Would you like another bee—

                    RUMANA
Beetroot salad? No, thank you.

                    PREEDA
But we don't serve—

                    RUMANA
Preeda, these are my parents, Jamshed
and Zohra.

                    PREEDA
Oh, so nice to meet you! Rumana and
Noor are two of my favorite customers.

                    RUMANA
My parents want a drink, but nothing
with alcohol. They don't drink. It's
against their religion.

                    ZOHRA
Our religion.

                    RUMANA
Against our religion.

                    PREEDA
Aah, okay. How about some Thai iced
tea?

                    RUMANA
Perfect! Three of those.

                    JAMSHED
        (pointing at the shopping bag
        next to Noor)
What did you buy?

                    NOOR
A dress for my formal.

                    ZOHRA
Formal? Formal like a dance? Rumana,

you're letting her go to a dance?
Jamshed, aap sun rahe hain? Do you
have anything to say about this?

Jamshed stays focused on the menu.

> ZOHRA
> You know when a girl and a boy dance
> together, Shaitan dances with them.

> RUMANA
> I hope Satan enjoys hip-hop, because
> that's what the kids dance to these
> days.

> NOOR
> Don't forget the electric slide.

> ZOHRA
> This is not a joke!

> NOOR
> Relax, Naani, my date is a girl.

> ZOHRA
> A girl?

> NOOR
> My best friend. Anne.

> JAMSHED
> The Chinese girl?

> NOOR
> Half Chinese, yes. We're just going to
> get some inspiration for our school
> humor zine. I can guarantee you I
> won't be dancing with any boys.

                              RUMANA
Boys suck.

                              ZOHRA
Noor, you know we have trust in you.
You are a good girl. You've taken
after your Saira Khala. You even have
her eyes.

                              NOOR
I think I have my dad's eyes.

Preeda returns with the Thai iced teas,
breaking the moment of tension.

                             PREEDA
You ready to order?

                            JAMSHED
Yes, we will share the pad Thai with
chicken—does it have pork?

                             PREEDA
No, no pork.

                             RUMANA
Why would the chicken pad Thai have
pork?

                              ZOHRA
You never know. When we went to
Beijing, everything had pork.

                            JAMSHED
We had to eat veg the whole time we
were there.

                    ZOHRA
    I had too much gas.

                    JAMSHED
    She almost floated over the Great Wall
    of China.

A moment of silence before they shake their
heads and laugh, Zohra smiling in spite of
herself.

four

NOREEN WAS GLAD THEY'D decided to wait until after dinner to tell her grandparents about moving to India, because in honor of graduation Azra had cooked Noreen's favorites: nargisi kofta, eggs encased in spiced minced meat and simmered in a masala gravy, chicken biryani, and aloo gobi. She and her mother couldn't truly relish the meal; not with the specter of imminent family drama hovering above them, whispering, *Guess who'll be eaten next.* They both still ate two helpings, because, well, good food was good food.

Then dinner ended, followed by a bowl of kheer for dessert, and then Ruby told them, and so came the storm.

"Tell them this is crazy," Azra told Jameel. "Tell them how crazy this is."

"This is crazy," Jameel said.

"How can you do this to us?" Azra said. "Ruby, tum toh had karti ho. Right when I think you can't do anything worse, you break my heart all over again."

"I have to go for work," Ruby said. "It's for my career."

Azra snorted. "Career."

"But what about Noreen? Why does she have to go?" Jameel asked. "This is a very bad decision, Noreen. You need to complete all your studies so you can make money. Travel comes later, after you have earned it. A 401K does not fund itself."

How to explain it? To her grandparents, education and work were a matter of duty, necessity, stability, and respect, not emotional fulfillment. Choice meant choosing your medical specialty. If school or work didn't make you happy, what did it matter, it wasn't supposed to make you happy—happiness comes from having kids who grow up to choose their own medical specialty.

She chose the explanation they were most likely to understand.

"Sonia Khala never got an opportunity to spend time in Delhi," Noreen said. "She wouldn't want me to miss mine. Especially not when Mom and I can go together."

"Sonia would tell you to go to college," Azra said.

"No, she wouldn't," Ruby said.

"Achcha? Now you speak for the dead?"

"You're the one—forget it."

"You know they hate Muslims in India. Do you know what they are doing to Muslims there?" Azra said.

"We're not exactly winning any popularity contests over here."

"It's not safe for women to be alone there."

"We'll be careful," Noreen said.

"Why should we help pay for Noreen's college if she's not going when she should?" Azra said.

Ruby reached down and squeezed Noreen's hand. "You don't have to worry about it. I make a good salary at the foundation; I'll figure it out."

"You'd be earning three, four times as much if you'd become a doctor," Jameel said.

"I won't sleep one night when you're gone," Azra said. "After all we have been through, Ruby, please."

"We're going," Ruby said. "We *want* to go. We'll be fine, and you'll be fine, I promise. It'll all be fine."

"I'll faint," Azra said, and slumped against the back of her chair. Jameel stood to help her and she leaned into his side as he rubbed her shoulder. They looked smaller now than even six months ago, and Noreen wished there was a way to do this without hurting them. They'd never seen Azra actually faint, but still.

"We will be fine, Naani," Noreen said. "It's only for a short time. We'll be back before you know it."

Azra shook her head. "Your mother has always done stupid things, but you, you've always studied hard and been good. How can you abandon your studies?"

"I'm not abandoning my studies, I'm only delaying them a year," Noreen said. "And I'll be engaging in experiential learning."

"What the hell is that?" Azra said.

"Learning through experience," Ruby said.

"It's good for aspiring writers to have life experience, more things to write about, draw upon," Noreen said.

"This is a mistake," Jameel said. "Think of your future. You need to work toward a real career."

"That's exactly what I'm doing," Noreen said. "I have thought this through, promise."

"Allah, it hurts to even stand," Azra said, grimacing in pain but refusing Jameel's help in getting up. "I don't know how much longer I have left on this earth. Lekin main aur kya bolon?" She dabbed her tears with the hem of her dupatta. "Ruby will do whatever she wants, like always. The things we have suffered no parent should go through, and still you make us suffer more. If you really loved us, you would not do this."

Ruby, almost to the kitchen with the stack of plates, spun around. A drumstick, sucked clean of cartilage, fell at her feet.

"I'm sorry you don't think we love you," she said, "and I'm sorry that Allah left you with the wrong daughter, but this is important to Noreen and me, and I hope one day you'll understand."

Azra replied with a small wail and went to lie down on the couch across from the TV. Ruby stomped off to the bathroom. Jameel excused himself to pray Isha. Noreen cleared off the rest of the table, retrieved the bone from the floor.

When Ruby returned, she tried to talk to Azra but Azra refused to speak, so she came to the kitchen to help Noreen clean up. Together, they loaded the dishwasher, scrubbed the pots, wiped the table and counters, swept. On the muted TV, two political commentators, a Black woman and a white man, debated health care reform on CNN. You could see how the man kept interrupting, cutting the woman off each time she tried to answer a question.

When they'd finished cleaning, Noreen went to say good-bye to her grandmother. A commercial was playing now, for some arthritis medication that had enabled an elderly couple to hike and garden and dance at their grandson's wedding. Azra lay gazing at the ceiling, her hands folded over her stomach, feeling sorry for herself because while her elder daughter had followed the right path, her younger was a divorced single mother who'd always made foolish decisions, was making them still. You'd think, after losing one daughter, she'd care less about what others might say and more about enjoying precious time with the ones she loved, but Azra's fixation on honor and shame was so deeply ingrained that to change it would require a radical rethinking.

"Because of you," Azra still told Ruby, "in front of others, I can't hold my head high."

Though these scenes were the most dramatic of all, brimming with tension and conflict and high stakes, none of them made it into Noreen's scripts. She'd tried once but couldn't get beyond the first page. Each line felt like a betrayal of her family's pain and dysfunction. How many times had her grandmother put the fear of appearances into her, chastised her to never speak to anyone of what happens inside your house? She'd die if Noreen wrote about it, even as fiction.

Noreen touched Azra's shoulder. "Khuda hafiz, Naani."

Azra sighed out a "Hai mera malik" and turned her face.

As Noreen and Ruby were putting on their shoes in the foyer, Jameel joined them, holding a card in his ink-smudged right hand.

"For you, beta," he said to Noreen. "Happy graduation. Go ahead, open it."

In the card, he'd written, *Congratulations on your achievement. May this be one of many. Put $501 in savings and invest $2,500 in index funds that track the stock market. Always spend less than you earn and remember compound interest. Love to our high school graduate, Nana and Naani.*

Inside was a check for $3,001 dollars.

"Nana, you didn't have to do this," Noreen said. "But thank you."

"I'm sorry we missed your graduation," Jameel said.

"It's fine," she told him, but he was looking at Ruby.

"You know she doesn't want you to go because she loves you," he said. "She'll worry day and night about something happening to you."

"Something could happen to me here, too," Ruby said. "I can't stop living my life because Sonia passed away."

"Ruby . . ." Jameel shook his head, deciding against whatever he'd been about to say. He preferred to avoid conflict, even if this came at a cost. "Chalo. Take care, huh? Text me when you reach home."

Noreen's heart ached as she hugged her grandfather goodbye. Though of couse she worried about Azra, she worried about Jameel more, because of all of them he had the hardest time talking about emotions. At the Muslim cemetery in San Jose, after Jameel had thrown the first fistful of dirt over his daughter's casket, the man no one had ever seen cry sank to his knees and began rocking back and forth and wailing. Ruby got down and put her arms around him and as they swayed together, he cried into her shoulder and said in Urdu, "When she was born I recited the azaan in her ear and now I am throwing dirt on her grave? How can this be? How can this be?" and by then practically everyone was sobbing with him.

He didn't cry again after that, and didn't want to talk about it. The closest they'd come was a few months back, when, as Noreen was leaving the bathroom, she saw Jameel at the other end of the hallway, catching his breath, one hand braced against the wall, the other on his chest.

She ran to him, terrified he'd had a heart attack. "Are you okay?"

"I'm fine."

"Your chest?"

"What?" He looked down at his hand pressed to his heart.

"No, not like that. I forgot."

"Forgot what?"

"Arre, one of my friends messaged a link to an article about Mughals, and you know Sonia liked the Mughals, so I was about to forward it to her, and then I remembered. But I'm fine now. See?" He held both hands up, stepped away from the wall. "All good."

She wanted to say, *It's okay, I understand, deep down I was wailing along with you at the funeral, and since then I've been going through the motions but really I'm a mess, can't write, can't sleep,* but instead she held his elbow and walked him to his study. He asked her if she'd thought more about her college major. *If you are certain you can't do premed, then you must choose a major with good career prospects, like computer science or economics. Writing is a hobby; you can always do it on the side. John Grisham was a lawyer first. Lots of doctors have also written books.*

After they'd given Jameel a second hug for good measure and left the house, Ruby let out a groan, tapping her forehead against one of the columns that flanked the front entrance.

"It's all right," Noreen said.

"I shouldn't have said it. The wrong daughter thing. Even if I feel it sometimes, I shouldn't say it. Years of therapy, but the second I cross that threshold, I become forty-seven going on sixteen."

"When we get home, you can send Naani an apologetic text."

"Yeah." Ruby smiled wide and waved at Jameel, who stood at the window, watching to make sure they got out okay.

"Hey, you have a penny?" Noreen said. "I want to make a wish."

"Yeah, here. Give me the car keys. You make wish, I pick song. Any requests?"

"Something good."

"Always."

The water fountain was in the center of the circular driveway, in line with the front door and surrounded by rose beds. Water cascaded down its three tiers of scalloped white marble. The small bulbs that lined the interior made the water glow gold, green, and red, but her grandparents only switched them on for parties. At least a hundred pennies lay scattered across the bottom, the twins' wishes, mostly. They used to visit twice a year, and, having inherited their mother's superstitious streak, insisted on making a wish every time they left the house.

Noreen folded her palms over the penny.

Please take care of my family. Please let Naani overcome her anger and shame. Please make those wishes of Amir's and Sohail's come true, well, the reasonable ones. Please help Nana catch his breath.

A lot of weight for a single coin.

Noreen kissed and then threw the penny. It flew upward, a copper flash in the portico light, then dove into the water and joined the others, each wish indistinguishable from the next, impossible to know which would be forsaken, and which fulfilled.

EXT. - RUMANA AND NOOR'S PORCH - NIGHT

TRACY rings the doorbell, twice. She is wearing
a leopard print jacket and holding a reindeer
print gift bag. Rumana opens the door, Noor
coming up behind her.

> TAMMY
> (holding up the gift bag)
> I come bearing gifts!

> RUMANA
> Tammy! You didn't have to.

> TAMMY
> Oh, it's just a little care package to
> send you off to India.
>
> Here.
> (gives the bag to Noor)

> NOOR
> Thank you. That's so kind.

> TAMMY
> Go ahead, take a look.

Noor pulls out an *US Weekly*.

> TAMMY
> In case you're missing the celebrity
> gossip.

Noor takes out a packet of Pepto-Bismol
tablets.

                    TAMMY
These saved my life when I got Montezuma's
Revenge in Cancun. Though in India I
guess they'd call it something else.

                    RUMANA
Yes, I'd imagine.

Noor takes out a bag of twelve four-crayon
packs.

                    TAMMY
I know there's all those poor children
over there living in the garbage, so I
figured if you see them, you could give
them those. My church wanted to send
so much more stuff for the poor kids,
but I told them you wouldn't have room.

                    RUMANA
That's very sweet of you.

Noor takes out a gallon storage bag packed with
cookies.

                    NOOR
Please tell me these are your lemon
drop cookies.

                    TAMMY
Of course.

                    NOOR
Yay! Thank you!

                    TAMMY
There should be two more things—have
another look.

Noor takes out two lipstick cases.

                    NOOR
     Lipstick?

                    TAMMY
     Pepper spray disguised as lipstick.

A surprised Noor almost drops them.

                    TAMMY
     I thought you should have it, you
     know, because of all the rapes.

                    RUMANA
     I'm sorry?

                    TAMMY
     All the rapes in India. I keep seeing
     it in the news. Did you know New Delhi
     is the rape capital of the world?

                    RUMANA
     Ah.

                    TAMMY
     It's made me worried, honestly. You two
     sweet girls over there alone. The way
     they treat women! It doesn't seem too
     civilized over there.

                    RUMANA
     India doesn't have a monopoly on the
     mistreatment of women. One in four
     female undergraduates will experience
     sexual misconduct by the time she
     graduates, so we should also worry
     about American college campuses.

                    TAMMY
     Is that so? Still, I'd feel better
     knowing if you're out at night over
     there, you have your phone in one
     hand and pepper spray in the other.

Noor starts to say something, but Rumana puts
her hand on her shoulder.

                    RUMANA
     Thank you for your concern, Tammy.
     And for the thoughtful gifts. We'll be
     careful, promise.

                    NOOR
     Yes, thank you.

They hug Tammy goodbye and watch her walk away.

                    RUMANA
     She means well.

                    NOOR
     I know—but the stuff she says
     sometimes. It doesn't seem *civilized*?
          (frowning at the lipsticks)
     We aren't taking these with us, right?

                    RUMANA
     Of course not. Gimme a cookie.

She puts her arm around Noor as they both bite
into the cookies and look up at the night sky.

                    NOOR
     Mmmmm. Worth every racist bite.

PART TWO

New Delhi

Hi, everyone. My name is Noreen, and yes, it's true, this is my first time. That woman clapping is my mother. She's my number one fan. When I was young, she praised me so much that when people would ask me, "What's your name?" I'd say, "Amazing." This is also my first time in India. Thank you, thanks a lot.

I love to read, so to prepare for coming here, I read a bunch of novels set in India. Now, reading can give you some knowledge and familiarity, but it doesn't really prepare you for what it's actually like here. You know what did help prepare me? Flying Air India.

five

Air Quality Index: 298. Very Unhealthy.

THIS PARTICULAR POLLUTED MORNING in her new room in her new flat in New Delhi, Noreen Mirza had written two sentences.

Zohra lies on the couch, eyes closed, arms folded over her stomach, like a scowling corpse. Noor stands over her, hesitant.

It was all she could manage; she may have journeyed halfway across the world, but physical distance and psychic distance were two separate things.

So much for New Year's resolutions.

She closed her laptop and checked the AQI app on her phone. In the week since they'd landed, today was the first that the air quality index was below 300, the formerly ashen sky now a pleasant periwinkle. Their visas, when finally issued, were valid for only three months, which meant no grand India tour, and the delay in processing meant Noreen and Ruby hadn't arrived until late December, a time of peak pollution in Delhi. When their Air India flight began its descent, Noreen had pressed her face to the window but could see nothing through the smog except gray, ghostly outlines of roads and rooftops. Their first day here, jet-lagged and coughing, they'd gone to the market and bought three air purifiers, one for each bedroom and one for the living room. They'd also bought pollution masks at the market, but they didn't have a tight seal and she'd read if the mask didn't fit exactly, it actually made you breathe in more air, causing more insidious particles to enter your nose and mouth and coat the inside of your lungs, poisoning your bloodstream. Plus, almost nobody here wore masks, even at AQI 300.

It was time, Noreen decided, for a brisk walk. Running was impossible here; breathe too hard and you'd choke. She did most of her walking in the large, leafy main park of her colony, which was what they called her walled and gated neighborhood. Noreen found this term ironic, given how hard India had fought for its independence. The park was in the center of the colony, surrounded by houses on all sides. She pushed through the squeaky metal turnstile at the entrance, picked up her pace. In early morning, the park was frequented by old folks, doing a round or two of the paved path along the perimeter, some slow, some relatively fast, like their downstairs landlady Geeta Auntie, who was seventy-eight but sprightly and, on Sundays, even drove herself to take her girlfriends to the movies. But now it was afternoon, the old folks were taking their post-lunch nap, the park empty except for an uncle and his trainer. The uncle, bald but for a U-shaped strip of hair on the back of his head, was doing jumping jacks in the corner of the park with the bright orange exercise equipment: a body-powered elliptical that reminded her of a tall, skinny insect, a body-weight chest press, something resembling an adult seesaw. The personal trainer, dressed in shiny red track pants and a white undershirt, his waist cartoonishly narrow compared to his massive chest and biceps, stood with legs spread and fists on hips and counted down the uncle's jacks. When he saw Noreen, he joined in the last ten, flexing his biceps on the way down, ending with an overhead clap. *Eight—clap! Seven—clap! Six—come on, you can do this!* At six, the uncle huffed to his knees and refused to get up. The trainer ordered him to do push-ups, squatting next to him and slapping the ground with each count, giving Noreen a view of his butt crack.

Must be nice, she thought, to be a guy in India and not care if your crack is showing. Except for some markets, in Delhi outdoor public space belonged to men. Her colony was no different. The streets were lined with two-, three-, four-story houses, separated by boundary walls and entrance gates. Many of these houses were divided into flats, and almost every household employed servants, a good percentage of whom were male drivers and security guards. It wasn't their fault that it was their job to wait outside, but it meant there were a lot of men hanging out on the street. In the one-minute walk from park to home, she passed a total of seven men and no women: three drivers chatting in plastic chairs between two parked cars, uniformed security guards at two different gates, an ancient man riding a rusty bicycle, a pizza delivery guy leaning against his scooter and swearing into his phone, a young man walking his employer's doberpoodle. Inside the colony, she didn't feel unsafe, but she did feel judged, and watched.

From the street, she saw their maid, Sarita, had hung their laundry on a clothesline on their front terrace, including two of her mother's lace thongs, and made a mental note to shift their underwear inside.

As she pushed open the gate of their house, Geeta Auntie called out hello. She lived on the ground floor and was often in her front garden. Right now she was hovering over the maali, their gardener, her gray hair twisted into a chignon. She gestured for Noreen to wait.

"Theek se kaam karo," she admonished the maali, who was planting flowers in a row of red clay pots. She summoned Noreen to join her on the patio, where there was a wicker coffee table and three chairs and her husband, Yash Uncle, sitting in his wheelchair. He'd had a stroke, which slurred his speech, and he rarely spoke, but Geeta Auntie made sure to include him in the conversation, and he'd often nod at the appropriate moment.

"Beautiful day, hai na?" Geeta Auntie said.

"Beautiful," Noreen said. Everything was relative, and when it came to the pollution, Geeta Auntie was one of the complacent ones. When they'd moved in and asked her if she could recommend an air purifier, Geeta Auntie had said, "Oh, we don't use them. They're mainly for foreigners. We've been in Delhi fifty years; our lungs are used to the air."

"Kya piyogi?" Geeta Auntie asked her. "Chai is already coming, but would you like something else? Fresh lime soda?"

The thing about desi culture was, even if you didn't want what was offered, you might as well take it, because anyway you'd be trapped in ten rounds of *No, I can't, Please, you must.*

"I'd love a fresh lime soda," Noreen said. Fresh lime soda, which was fresh-squeezed lemon and soda water mixed with sugar and salt, was her new favorite drink.

Geeta Auntie waved her hand. "Raju, idhar ao."

Raju hurried over. He was basically Geeta Auntie's butler, but without the stiff manners or uniform. Noreen smiled and returned his *"Namaste, ma'am,"* still getting used to being greeted with such deference by a man more than twice her age.

"Noreen, would you like yours sweet, salty, or mixed?"

"Mixed," Noreen said.

Geeta Auntie issued instructions to Raju and sat down next to Yash Uncle. She was wearing a faded, oversized Rice University sweatshirt. Her youngest son, now married with kids and living in Ann Arbor, had gone there for engineering. "Did you have a nice New Year's?"

"I was asleep before midnight," Noreen said.

"Still jet-lagged?"

"Not anymore, thankfully."

"And your cough?"

"Much better," Noreen said, and immediately coughed.

Geeta Auntie handed her a tissue. "You should drink haldi doodh morning and night. Happy with the flat?"

"The flat is lovely."

"No Delhi belly yet? Motions good, not too loose?"

"Yes, things are running relatively smoothly in that department."

"Very good."

Raju brought out a tray with biscuits and a bowl of pistachios and two small plates. The biscuits had dark chocolate and a crown on one side.

Geeta Auntie pushed the biscuits toward Noreen. "I know you like chocolate, so I had Raju pick these up from the market."

"Thank you. That's very kind."

Noreen put one cookie on her plate, and, at Geeta Auntie's insistence, another. Raju returned with their drinks, and Geeta Auntie reminded him he'd yet to give her the receipt from yesterday's shopping. Though he'd gone back inside the house, Geeta Auntie lowered her voice when she said, "Raju has been with us for twenty years. This house can't function without him. We've become too dependent on him, which is not good. If he takes advantage, what can I do? He knows we cannot afford to lose him. Ek aur biscuit le lo, you are too thin."

Too thin was something no one had ever called her in

America. As Noreen took a third biscuit, she noticed Yash Uncle looking.

"Would you like one, Uncle?" she asked him.

"Oh no, he's not allowed." Geeta Auntie wagged her finger. "Naughty fellow. You know that's against the rules. Achcha, tell me, Noreen, have you made any friends yet?"

The directness with which people here asked questions still threw her—are you married, how much is your rent, is that a pimple on your chin, what is your salary, how old are you, where is your husband, who is your father, how much did that cost, are you having good motions?

"I don't make friends easily." That wasn't accurate; the friends she'd made she'd made easily. "I mean, often."

"Nonsense. A young woman like you should be enjoying with other youths. Doston ke saath mazay karo. You have your whole life to work and only a short time in Delhi. I want to see you all smiles."

Noreen laughed. "Did my mother put you up to this?"

"No. Why?"

"Oh, Adi Uncle, my godfather, he sent me this boy's number, the son of a friend of a friend, and my mom has been bugging me to message him."

Geeta Auntie stirred a golden teaspoon of sugar into her chai. "What's his name?"

"Kabir."

"Kabir what?"

"No clue."

"You haven't contacted him? What are you waiting for?"

"I don't know." For starters, she didn't know the guy. Adi Uncle didn't even know the guy. "I guess to be settled."

"And now you're settled. WhatsApp him."

In India, WhatsApp was the primary means of digital communication. People didn't say, *I'll message or text you,* they said, *I'll WhatsApp you* or *I'll send you a WhatsApp.* Her mother said people even conducted their entire businesses—scheduling appointments, taking orders, requesting payment—over WhatsApp. People here were in dozens of different WhatsApp groups, based on family, friends, shared interests. Noreen had made one with Amir and Sohail. So far, it was mostly funny cat memes.

Geeta Auntie pointed at the phone in Noreen's hand. "Abhi kar lo."

"WhatsApp him right now?" Noreen said.

"Why not? Right, Yash?"

Yash Uncle nodded.

"I don't know what to say," Noreen said.

"Aren't you a writer? Write something."

A challenge. She unlocked her phone. Kabir was in her contact list; she'd done that much.

Dear Kabir, she typed, **I got your number from my godfather Adi Uncle who hung out with your mom's friend Zara in**

LA. Was that too complicated? Was Zara even the right name?

Her phone vibrated.

"Holy shit," she said, forgetting the company she was in.

"Kya hua?" Geeta Auntie said.

"Kabir literally just messaged me."

"Fate!" Geeta Auntie said with a quick side-to-side nod.

"Or coincidence."

Geeta Auntie clucked her tongue. "Coincidence is simply the coward's word for fate."

Verily there are signs for those who reflect.

Sonia Khala and Geeta Auntie would definitely vibe.

"So," Geeta Auntie said, "what did this Kabir write you?"

Hi Noreen! Heard you're new in town. Would be happy to show you around, if you'd like. Cheers, Kabir.

Though the message itself was innocuous, Noreen's cheeks flushed as she read it aloud. "Should I wait to respond?"

"No, no, reply at once. Write something like . . . *Hello, Kabir, that sounds lovely, thank you. What is your schedule like?*" Geeta Auntie pronounced schedule with a soft "c."

Noreen hit send. "You're pretty good at this."

"My best friend is a recent widow and I've been helping her with online dating. Don't worry, Yash!" Geeta Auntie slapped Yash Uncle's thigh. "I only have eyes for you."

Kabir was online, and the two blue check marks indicated he'd read her message. Nothing to do now but wait. Noreen frowned at her phone. If she didn't know the guy, why was she anxious?

"Fikr mat karo. He'll write back." Geeta Auntie brought her palms together underneath her chin, her gold bangle sliding down her arm. "You know, I have a good feeling about this Kabir. The two of you, you have a kismat connection."

six

Air Quality Index: 311.

Hazardous.

"SERIOUSLY? ONE WORD FROM Geeta Auntie and now you have a date?" Her mother was in a bathrobe, and as she bowed to adjust the towel around her head, Noreen admired her cleavage. She wished she'd inherited her mother's proportions, her ability to gain weight in flattering places.

"It's not a date," Noreen said. "Plus it's impolite to refuse your elder. Plus Geeta Auntie won't take no for an answer."

Her mother went into Noreen's bathroom to wash off the rose-tinted facial peel that had dried patchily across her face and neck. "I need to make her my partner in crime. So when are you meeting him?"

"Next Thursday. He's out of station on a film shoot this week."

"Out of station?"

"I guess that's what they say here for out of town."

"What?"

Noreen waited for the sink to stop running, then repeated what she'd said.

"Out of town for a shoot? Is he a filmmaker?"

"Dunno."

"Do you know where he's taking you?"

"A place called Firoz Shah Kotla."

"What's that?"

"The ruins of a fourteenth-century palace built by this sultan called Firoz Shah."

Her mother returned, turning her face side to side. "Have my wrinkles disappeared? Is my flesh plump and dewy?"

"You look like you always do, which is great," Noreen said.

When her mother told people she was forty-seven, they were genuinely surprised. The Mirza girls had good genes; Azra looked a good ten years younger than her age. But Ruby had been fretting more about both her age and her mortality. It didn't help that Sonia Khala had died right before her fiftieth birthday, that in the near-enough future, she'd be older than her older sister ever was.

Ruby patted her cheeks. "Padmini told me my crow's feet would be fifty percent less visible after one use."

"Who's Padmini?"

"The woman who sold me this ancient Indian beauty secret, at a steep price."

"Who named it crow's feet anyway?" Noreen said. "That's such a shitty term."

"Some man, no doubt. For the record, you know you're beautiful, and you'll always be beautiful, at forty-seven and fifty-seven and a hundred and seven."

"Do as I say, not as I do."

"You try being a good role model all the time." Ruby snapped her fingers. "Since you have a date, I should give you yours."

"My what? Where are you going? And it's not a date!" Noreen called after her.

Ruby had forgotten to close the door behind her. Noreen's air purifier glowed red and made a whirring sound as it worked to remove the new particulate matter entering the room. Leaving her bedroom door ajar for even a minute made the air purifier color indicator change from blue (air quality good: breathe easy, and hope this thing actually works) to violet (air quality moderate: killing you softly) to red (air quality poor—life span shrinking).

Noreen shut her door. Several minutes later, the indicator was blue again and Ruby returned dressed in the pajamas Adi Uncle had gifted her last Christmas; soft, organic cotton printed with a geometric pattern of stylized marijuana leaves. Stoner couture, her mother called it. She tossed a small object next to Noreen on the bed.

"Are you serious?" Noreen said. "You brought the lipstick pepper spray?"

"You can throw yours away, if you want," her mother said.

"Where's yours?"

Ruby hesitated. "In my purse."

"Really? Does it make you feel safer?"

"No. You know my purse—I'd pull out a tampon, a grinder, a bottle of Advil, and ten Sephora samples before I got to the pepper spray."

"So why even have it in there? I feel like if I keep it on me, I'll end up spraying the WRONG thing at the WRONG time, and best case I'd be able to laugh about it later."

"Noreen Mirza," Ruby said, ruffling her hair, "not everything is one of your episodes. Now show me his pic again."

Kabir's WhatsApp profile pic was of his reflection in the water. Though artistically blurry, you could make out his thick, wavy hair, large eyes.

"What do you think?" Noreen asked.

Ruby whistled. "I'd say, Hotness Quality Index: Very Healthy."

seven

Air Quality Index: 257. Very

Unhealthy.

INDIAN STANDARD TIME MEANT if someone said
I'll be there at nine, they'd come at nine thirty, earliest, maybe
ten. If a party started at eight, it meant don't arrive before nine.
Their first week here, Ruby had made the mistake of showing
up for a dinner party five minutes after the invited time, and the
hostess had been in the shower.

So when Kabir said he'd pick her up at ten and hadn't arrived
by ten fifteen, Noreen knew not to worry. She was at the mirror,
fixing her eyeliner and humming the *Thank you, India* chorus
from the Alanis Morissette song "Thank U," which her mother
must have played fifty times while they were packing. The liner
on her right lid had come out thicker than the left, but then she'd
overthickened the left and was thickening the right to match,
when she was startled by Sarita's knock on the door. Sarita,
whose services were included in the rent, had been cleaning and

cooking for the various tenants of this flat for the past five years. She was an excellent cook, but the last tenant was a German man who told her not to bother because he didn't like Indian food. What a waste, Noreen had thought when she'd told them this, to live in India and not like Indian food.

"Hi, Sarita," Noreen said.

"Kabir bhaiyya aaye hain," Sarita said, announcing Kabir's arrival.

Ten twenty. Kabir was early.

The eyeliner on the right was now a peak instead of a line. Better to remove all of it. She told Sarita to tell him she'd be out soon, referring to herself in the wrong gender. Though her Urdu had improved since coming here, vocabulary and grammar often came a beat too late. Yesterday, though, she'd spoken a sentence in one seamless go, pronoun, verb tense, object, gender, all correct. The accent, well, that was hopeless.

She knew Sarita would offer Kabir chai, and Kabir would likely say yes because desis were a chai-blooded people. Noreen still drank coffee with breakfast, but had chai midmorning and after lunch. Sarita would make a pot, give her a cup, drink the rest.

Initially, it had been weird, to have someone coming six days a week, making you chai, serving you breakfast and lunch, washing and folding your clothes. Those first few days, Noreen would ask Sarita if she needed help and she'd laugh. Her mother, who'd visited Pakistan a few times as a kid, had fallen easily into the role of house madam, politely instructing Sarita on what to cook or do. "This is how it works here," she'd explained to Noreen. "So be respectful, pick up after yourself, and enjoy the chai. We'll give her a generous bonus when we leave."

Noreen wiped off her eyeliner, ran a brush through her hair, tied it back, let it loose again. On her way out, she knocked into her space heater, which fell over with a crash. Hopefully she hadn't broken it; with no central heating, at night it got so cold inside their flat that you needed a thick shawl or multiple layers to keep from shivering. She winced, rubbing her thigh; the tendency to bruise easily and become clumsy when anxious was one of her many winning combinations. Before opening the door, she took a few deep breaths, did worst case best case.

Worst case—he's a dick. Best case—you make a friend.

A Mughal miniature painting of Emperor Akbar with a hawk perched on his shoulder hung on their living room wall. Kabir was examining this painting, his back to her. He was dressed in a short black kurta top and coral felt pants that were baggy at the thigh and tapered at the calves. His hair was black, wavy, thick. Between the pants and the hair, he reminded her of Aladdin, or rather, *Ala'uddin*. When she'd said it like that in kindergarten, the kids had made fun of her, even though she'd pronounced it the way Aladdin's own parents would.

"Hi," she said.

He turned around, and she half expected to see an exaggerated curl across his forehead. No curl, but his eyes were big and brown. It was rare she met someone with eyes larger than hers.

"Noreen? Hi," he said. "I was admiring the painting."

"Emperor Akbar," she said. "Not that I know anything about the Mughals."

"You probably know more than you think," he said.

"I doubt that."

"What city is the Taj Mahal in?"

"Agra."

"You see? You know more than at least fifty percent of the world's population."

She laughed. "Seventeen percent of the world's population is in India."

"Well, it's only a matter of time before they try to erase the Taj Mahal from the history books here."

Sarita was peeking from the kitchen door, bemused. Kabir's pants had made an impression.

"It's nice to meet you, Noreen," he said.

She liked how he'd said her name. She liked his accent as well. People back home made fun of Indian accents, but she found his sexy, the way he drew out some words, treated nearly every syllable like it mattered.

"Nice to meet you, Kabir."

He switched his mug of chai to his left hand and extended his right. The solidity and formality of the handshake calmed her. Yes, he was scruffy cute, but if she could touch him without imploding, she could manage a non-embarrassing conversation.

"Thank you for picking me up," she said.

"Apologies if I came too early," he said. "I know Americans are fairly punctual."

Attractive and thoughtful. "Yes, that's been an adjustment."

The top three buttons of his kurta were open, offering a preview of the dark chest hair beneath. Liam, her fling from last summer and the only guy she'd dated, if you could even call it that, had a stellar body but literally two hairs on his pecs, a companion for each nipple. She'd found this unsettling. When dating, she preferred to be the one with less chest hair.

"I like your nails," she said. His fingernails were painted ten different colors, as were his toes.

He displayed his hands. "My nieces were over. They're seven, twins. They like to give me makeovers. I told them I was meeting someone new today and this is the outfit they chose. I'd forgotten I even had these pants. I bought them in Sarojini Nagar years ago, when I was apparently considering a career in the circus."

Given how much people stared here, she loved that he walked out the door dressed by his nieces, that he didn't give a shit. She felt like she spent much of her time outside wishing she could disappear. Granted, he was a guy, but still.

"I was thinking more Aladdin," she said, pronouncing it American-style, "but I can see circus. I have cousins who are twins. Boys, though. They're nine. So far they're more into magic tricks and video games than makeup."

"There's still time." Kabir set his chai down on the coffee table, a rectangular plate of glass supported by the back and upturned trunk of a white ceramic elephant. The elephant was adorned with multicolored jeweled anklets, a jeweled headdress, and cascading necklaces of pearl. Noreen and her mother had nicknamed her Hathi Blingbling.

"So what do you know about Firoz Shah Kotla?" Kabir asked.

"I read up on it a little. I know it's a palace built in 1354 by Sultan Firoz Shah Tughluq. It has an Ashokan pillar that dates back to third century BC that he brought from somewhere else and had installed at the palace."

Conversation, not book report.

"Did you read about the jinn?" he asked.

"Sorry?"

"Jinn."

"Jinn?"

"Do you know what jinn are?"

The last time she'd spoken the word *jinn*, she'd been with Sonia Khala. "Yes, but what do jinn have to do with Firoz Shah Kotla?"

"People believe that jinn live inside the ruins of Firoz Shah Kotla, and that they can intercede on their behalf, so they ask things of the jinn, just as you do at the grave of a saint, except here you do it by leaving them letters. I like to take visitors there because, unlike Humayun's Tomb or Qutub Minar, it's usually someplace they haven't been. But I have to warn you it can be a little intense."

"Like how?"

Kabir stroked his jaw. The stubble that spread from his Adam's apple to the hollow underneath his cheekbone lent him a certain gravitas that helped balance out the pants. "It's really the underground chambers that are intense, a bit dark and spooky. That's where I leave my letters, but we don't have to go there; there are other, sunlit places to leave them."

"You're talking actual letters?"

"Yes, actual letters. People bring multiple copies and stuff them into cracks in the wall at different altars. It's hard to imagine until you see it."

"Sounds fascinating," Noreen said.

"So you'd like to go, then?"

"Definitely."

He nodded. "Cool. Now the next question is, would you like to write a letter?"

"To the jinn?"

"Yes."

"What is it supposed to say?"

"There are no rules. It's simply a letter addressed to the jinn. Most people talk about their lives, what's been on their mind, what's been bothering them. They ask for things they want. A better job, a child, to marry the person they love, to cure a loved one's illness, whatever it may be."

"Does anyone read them? Humans, I mean."

"Not really. If you leave them in the underground chamber,

it's too dark, and at the end of each day they're collected and burned."

"It's been a while since I've written." They were standing across the coffee table, and she wondered if she should invite him to sit on the sofa, which was white and stiff and so unyielding Noreen had proclaimed it the Most Uncomfortable Sofa in the World.

"What did you used to write?" he said.

"Oh. I've done a few zines with my best friend, and I was working on these scripts."

"Scripts? Film?"

"More TV—do you know this show *Gilmore Girls*?"

"No. Tell me."

"It's this show about a single mom and her daughter who are best friends. If you live in America, and you're a daughter living with a single mom who you are very close to, someone's going to compare you to *Gilmore Girls*. For a while I resisted watching it, but I finally did."

"And?"

"And . . . it's a good show, mostly. I couldn't relate to a lot of it. My mother and I are close, but we want to have our own best friends, not be each other's. And my mom was just shy of thirty when she had me, not sixteen. And the show is really white, and we're brown. I could relate to some of it, though, like the mother having tension with her own mother—sorry, you probably don't want to know all this."

"I do." Kabir had a seat on the most uncomfortable sofa in the world and looked up at her, his mug cradled between his hands. "You were talking about the show."

"Yes, so, after I watched it, I kept examining my own life, like, if I were to make a show inspired by my life, what aspects, what moments, what tensions would I want to include? And where could I derive the most humor? And I started writing scenes, fictional but drawing heavily on my own life. But it's been a while since I worked on a script, or anything creative. I thought coming to India . . . anyway." She cleared her throat; she'd been talking too much. She waited for Kabir to interject, break the silence, come back with something about himself, but those sweet brown eyes remained fixed on her with an almost grave attention.

"You thought coming to India?" he said finally.

"Oh, I don't know what I thought. Hey, do the jinn speak English?"

"Good question. Most of the letters are written in Hindi, a few in Urdu, but I assume they'd understand English."

"Interesting. Do you think they have an innate ability to understand all other languages or do they have to pick it up by hanging out and listening to humans who speak that language?"

"Another good question," he said, and she could feel her heart-glow warming her chest. "The jinn of Delhi could certainly pick up English, depending on where they hung out, so either way you can write your letter in English."

Sarita came out to see if they needed more chai or a snack.

"Would you like to write a letter?" Kabir asked Noreen.

"I would."

"Then I'll have some more chai. Would you like some as well, Noreen?"

She could listen to him say her name all day. "I'm okay," she said. "I'll go write this letter, then."

"Take as long as you need," he said. "And don't worry, no one will read it except you."

"And the jinn."

"And the jinn."

Back in her room, she stared at the blank page of her notebook and remembered the night Sonia Khala had explained jinn to her. They were having dinner at Azra and Jameel's house during one of her visits. Amir and Sohail were in the den, playing Lego video games, and she was with the adults at the table. They were eating mangoes desi-style, making a hole in one end, putting it to their mouths, squeezing and sucking out the juicy flesh. Azra told them that her cousin's granddaughter had become possessed by a jinn in Pakistan and had an exorcism, and Noreen had asked, "What are jinn, exactly?"

"They are a separate kind of being," Sonia Khala explained. "The Quran says humans are made from dust, angels from light, and jinn from smokeless fire. The Quran also says there are good jinn and evil jinn. People like to blame evil jinn for all types of things—illness, weather, theft—but we know very little about them beyond their existence. Islamic philosophers and scholars have had many theories about the nature of jinn over the years, but they are impossible to prove."

Azra wiped mango juice off her chin. "I heard a jinn once," she said. "I was reading Quran in the masjid in Medina and suddenly I heard another voice reading in my right ear, as if sitting right next to me. But when I looked to my right, there was nobody there. Who else could it have been but a jinn? The Muslim jinn have the same Quran as us."

"There are Muslim jinn and non-Muslim jinn?" Noreen asked.

"The Quran does say this," Sonia Khala said.

If only she could call Sonia Khala and tell her what she was about to do. *You're writing a letter to the jinn?* she'd say. *Oh my goodness. Put in a word for Amir and Sohail, would you? For their good health and happiness. And maybe Yale. Harvard's okay too.*

How to begin? Dear Jinn? Esteemed Jinn? O Jinn! Blessed Jinn? She considered asking Kabir but didn't want to lose her momentum. Also she had a feeling he'd say it didn't matter as long as it was respectful. She could always fix it later. Hopefully the jinn didn't mind corrections.

> *Dear Jinn,*
>
> *This is my first time writing a letter to jinn so forgive me if I err; I'm from America and I don't know all the customs. I was told that people leave you letters asking you to intercede on their behalf. My Sonia Khala is dead and awaiting the Day of*

Judgment either in Paradise or in her penthouse coffin. Not sure if that's true, though you may know better, but if our souls do live on and you could ask for blessings for hers, I would be extremely grateful, because she was a really special person. She would have loved to come visit you, leave her own letter. She always wanted to visit Delhi, which is the main reason I came, not that I've done much with my time here. Yet. Also please ask for blessings for Amir and Sohail, and Imran Khalu.

Also if you could put in a kind word for my mom and Adi Uncle and Abby and my grandparents and the rest of my family and friends and the whole world really, you probably know how bad things are getting out here. As for myself, I'd like to start writing again. And make a friend (I'm by no means a social butterfly, but it's lonely without any friends). And maybe you could help me find whatever else I came here looking for and haven't realized yet, or help it find me.

Kabir said we can also write what's in our heart. I've been thinking about regret. Not sure if that's an important emotion in the jinn world, but it's huge with the humans. For example, now that Sonia Khala is gone, my mom regrets not being close to her sister earlier; for much of her life their relationship was benign estrangement. She tries to protect me from her sadness because she knows I'm sad too, but I know it tears her up sometimes. After meeting my dad, I pretty much wrote him off, but all that's happened has made me think—what if he got hit by a bus, would I regret not having tried at all to get to know him? Though it's

*not like he's shown any interest in getting to know me, and we
live twenty-eight miles from each other as the crow flies. But I
see my mother struggling with regret, and we only have this one
wild and precious life. I know he was a liar and a cheat, so what
makes me think he would suddenly be a decent father? Is there a
way of assessing the path of least regret? Not sure if you do this
kind of thing but maybe you could send a sign?*

*Also I should ask for blessings for Kabir because he's the rea-
son I'm even writing this. And he seems pretty cool.*

Thank you!

Sincerely,

N

It felt so good to write again, even something as strange as
this. And if she was one for Sonia Khala's signs, or Geeta Auntie's kismat, she'd say it was a good omen that Kabir had been in
her life less than an hour and she'd already written two pages.

In the living room, Kabir chuckled as he messaged on his
phone, and Noreen felt a jealous pang toward whoever was making him laugh. Seeing her, he stood up, the phone disappearing
inside his deep pocket. He gestured at the letter between her
folded palms. "Success?"

"I think so. Hey, is it okay if I signed with my initial? Will they
still know it's me?" She was amused by her matter-of-fact tone,
as if writing a letter to jinn was an ordinary act (though she was
beginning to realize that often the difference between what was

ordinary and extraordinary was a simple matter of perspective).

"I guess we can assume that they'll know it's you," Kabir said.

She hesitated. "And what if I'm not sure I believe in jinn?"

"You believe enough to leave a letter for them. Isn't that what matters most?"

Noreen nodded. "Okay, then."

"Chalo phir—do you understand Hindi?"

"Some," she said. "My grandparents speak a lot of Urdu at home. But I'm constantly doing things like using the wrong gender for a word."

"Ah, gender is a construct," he said.

"Not in your language it isn't."

He laughed. "Touché."

They paused at the front door, bending at the waist to put their sandals on. Kabir smelled like fresh earth and something else, floral and vaguely familiar.

"Ready?" he asked.

She realized she'd been holding her breath, filling her lungs with him.

"Ready," she said, and followed him out the door.

eight

Air Quality Index: 248. Very Unhealthy.

THE AYAT AL-KURSI AND a small disco ball hung from the rearview mirror of Kabir's car. After starting the engine, Kabir touched his heart, then the Quranic verse, then gave the disco ball a spin. She could tell from the unconscious manner with which he did it that it was a ritual of his.

"My naani and nana have almost the exact same one hanging in their car," she said. "Not the disco ball, the Ayat al-Kursi. I'm guessing you're Muslim, then?"

"My naani is," he said. "The rest of my grandparents were Hindu; my parents were Marxists, now atheist narcissists."

Noreen laughed. "And you?"

"Well, I definitely have an affinity toward Islam. I grew up on my naani's tales of jinn, went with her to the grave of every Muslim saint in Delhi. She gave me this Ayat al-Kursi when I got my own car. My mother keeps telling me to take it down."

"Why?"

"I'm sure you know what the maahaul is over here. She worries that if I'm in the wrong place at the wrong time and someone sees a verse from the Quran hanging in my car I'll be beaten up, or worse. And though she's right, I can't bring myself to remove it."

"I'm so sorry," Noreen said.

"No need to apologize, it's not your fault."

They'd reached a clogged intersection and she looked out her window and gasped. To her right, sandwiched between a bus and an auto rickshaw, was a large elephant. It carried a bundle of branches on its back, the leafy fronds fanning out like wings. On top of the branches a mahout balanced cross-legged, a goading stick in his hands.

"Elephant!" she said.

Kabir laughed. "Elephant."

The light turned green and they left the elephant behind. She enjoyed watching Kabir drive, his confidence amid the chaos of Delhi traffic, the subtle line of sinew in his forearm as he shifted gears. He started giving her a tour, pointing out neighborhoods and metro stops and markets and famous paratha stands. When he said, *Over there is the dargah of the Sufi saint Nizamuddin Auliya*, she told him how Sonia Khala had always wanted to pay her respects at his tomb, and he replied, *Let's make a plan to go there, then*, so casually, like they were already friends, with a cemented relationship and a certain future, and though Noreen feared her voice would betray the electric tremor of her heart, she managed a nonchalant *Sounds good* in response.

In Firoz Shah Kotla's large, grassy parking lot, there were only two other cars, many more motorbikes, a smattering of auto rickshaws, and one cycle rickshaw whose owner dozed in the seat. His bare, calloused feet stuck out one end, the rest of him cocooned inside a shawl.

"I'll go get tickets," Kabir said.

She tried to give him money. Like a good desi, he refused. Like a good desi, she insisted he take it, and he refused again. She acquiesced, watched him walk up to the ticket booth. He had a nice stride, relaxed but not too slow. Last summer, she and her friend Liz from the ice cream parlor would sometimes walk in the town park after a day shift, which proved a challenge because though Liz talked a mile a minute, she took thirty minutes to move a mile.

It was only after he returned that Noreen thought to ask, "Hey, did you buy me a foreigner or Indian ticket?"

"Indian," Kabir said.

Noreen shook her head. "You and my mother."

"What? You are Indian."

"Not for the purposes of this ticket."

At monuments and other tourist attractions, foreigners paid fifteen times more than Indians, and her mother always bought them the Indian tickets. Ruby and her desi friends joked about how cheap their own parents were, but they'd all inherited versions of desi frugality. Ruby claimed no self-respecting ABCD, which stood for American-Born Confused Desi, would pay the foreigner price, but she was also more confident about passing.

"It worked when your mom bought the tickets, didn't it?" Kabir said.

"Yes, but my mom does the talking," Noreen said.

"So I'll do the talking, na? If it's really bothering you, I can go back and exchange it."

"No," she said, embarrassed for making a fuss. "Let's go."

As it turned out, the ticket collector, sitting cross-legged in a white plastic chair and sipping chai from a white plastic cup, was far more interested in Kabir's coral pants and painted fingernails than Noreen's national origins.

They passed through a gap in the thick boundary walls onto a path lined with what had once been grand columns but were now stumps of jagged rubble. Some of the buildings had entire walls missing; others had collapsed, an avalanche of mortar and stone. Green pigeons, alone and in flocks, pecked at the grain tossed on the ground by visitors.

Kabir opened his arms. "Welcome," he said, "to the fifth city of Delhi, founded 1354."

"Okay."

He laughed. "You don't seem impressed."

"No! It's not that. I'm not really a visual person. It's hard for me to visualize what these ruins used to look like."

"Let's try this. Close your eyes. Now imagine a tree, with a narrow trunk and long, thin branches reaching up to the sky, and shiny, heart-shaped green leaves. Can you picture it?"

"Yes."

"See? You are visual."

"But that's different," she said. "You're directing me."

"Close your eyes again. Now, imagine you are a noblewoman, coming to the royal palace to deliver a petition to the sultan."

"A petition?"

"A request you want the sultan to grant," he said.

"Like what?"

"Like . . . maybe you want him to recognize your title to a disputed piece of land."

"Okay."

"You're looking out the velvet curtains of your palanquin, which is being carried by four footmen—two in the front, two in the back. You're approaching the main gate of the palace, which would have looked imposing and ornamented, the boundary walls covered with white limestone plaster and decorated with colorful carvings and paintings. After you pass through the gate as we just did, you'd be carried through this columned passageway, lined with guards dressed in close-fitting coats and pointed cloth caps, with long swords tucked into their waist sashes. Then you'd enter the waiting hall, a grand building lined with colonnades, and your servants would lower your palanquin as you waited to be granted admission into the main palace. Now, look again."

She looked with new eyes at the passageway where the

guards once stood. In her mind, they'd worn stern faces, their close-fitting coats a deep purple. She pointed at what remained of a building ahead, a few arches visible in the pocked rubble. "That's the waiting hall?"

"Yes."

"How do you know all this?"

"When I was in college, my friend did these heritage walks. One day he got sick, and asked me to fill in, and I fell in love with Delhi's ruins," he said. "I find them magical. A few are quite wild. I feel a sense of peace in them, a connection to the Delhi my naani remembers, before it was torn apart by Partition. Like, there's this nala, a stream, in South Delhi, and when my naani was young they used to picnic next to it, and now it's filled with toxic sewage. Looking at it, smelling it now, you couldn't even imagine . . . anyway, I'd love to go back to the fourteenth century, visit this palace, wander around Delhi then."

"See, I'd like to visit the future. Mostly to know if we're still alive. But hearing you describe it, the fourteenth century might be cool, too."

He smiled. "Sometimes I think I'm attracted to ruins because I find the present so depressing. There's so much hatred in India now, other places too. Sometimes I wonder if we're one seismic event away from collapse. But I digress. Shall we enter the main palace?"

She liked that when he asked her a question, he always waited for the answer. "Yes."

On one side of the waiting hall were the remains of a recessed arch, the stone a dark black. This blackened arch, Kabir explained, was the first altar to the jinn. Every day for years, people lit incense and small diyas, clay lamps shaped like small bowls with a flame balanced on the lip, and set them on the arch's bottom ledge, the resulting smoke scorching the surrounding stone.

A barefoot woman, a red, penny-sized bindi on her forehead and a pale green dupatta draped over her hair walked up to the altar, lit an incense stick from the flame of a diya, and added it to the others burning on the ledge. Then she removed the stack of letters tucked in her armpit, went on tiptoes, and left one copy in the dark wall of the arch. She bent her head, said a brief prayer, and continued on.

Noreen counted eight other letters, tucked into the wall's crevices and crannies. All of them had been photocopied with a passport photo in the top corner.

"Why the photocopies? And the photos?" Noreen whispered.

"Not sure if you've had to deal with this yet," Kabir said, "but if you try to do anything in India—open a bank account, get a phone line—you need to attach passport photos to your paperwork. The people who come here treat the jinn like a government agency, sort of like a ministry of jinn. Also, the more jinn you appeal to, the better your chances of getting what you seek, so people bring multiple copies of the same letter to leave at different altars."

"A holy bureaucracy?"

"You could say that. And remember this is originally where people came to seek justice at the royal court. Even peasants were allowed to present petitions to the sultan. I guess it's a continuation of that tradition."

Noreen took a closer look at the letters, the serious faces in the corners.

"And the jinn—are they supposed to be visible?"

"Not in the way you think," Kabir said. "Some people claim to feel or hear or see something, but I never have."

Like Azra, Noreen thought, who'd heard the jinn chanting in her ear.

"And people believe that some of the animals here—the cats, the birds—are jinn that have shifted shape," he added.

She glanced at the pigeon inside a cannonball-sized hole in the rubble, scratching its wing with its beak. "You think that's true?"

"I don't know. How could you ever prove it, one way or the other?"

"I don't know."

A man dressed in a starched white shalwar kurta and white lace skullcap approached the altar with great purpose, a stack of letters in his right hand, a garland of marigolds dangling from the crook of his elbow.

"How many altars are there here?" she asked.

"A lot."

If Sonia Khala came here, she'd stop and recite a du'a at every one. She'd offered prayers at churches, synagogues, the redwood forest. Allah is everywhere, she used to say.

"Where did you go?" Kabir asked.

"Sorry?"

"You were lost there for a second."

"Oh," she said, both embarrassed and flattered he'd noticed. "My mind wandered for a sec. Where do we go next?"

"Well, we could go see the Ashokan pillar, or we could first go underground and leave our letter. But like I said, it can be kind of intense down there, so we could also leave our letter in one of the aboveground altars instead. Or at the Ashokan pillar—it's said the most powerful jinn lives inside it."

She gestured across the palace grounds. "That's the pillar?"

"Yes. See the building it's on top of? The sultan commissioned it specially to serve as a grand base for the pillar. It used to have eight domes on its roof, and a stone lion at each corner, with the pillar rising from the center."

What remained of the building reminded her of a three-tier wedding cake, each rubble tier smaller than the next. She could make out some arched doorways and windows, but it would take a detailed description from Kabir to visualize its former glory. Topping the ruins was the polished stone pillar, narrow and nondescript, at least from afar, the domes and lions and whatever else long gone. They'd caged the bottom of the pillar, Kabir said, to keep people from touching it.

"Let's leave our letters where you usually do, underground," she said.

They crossed the palace grounds, which had been converted into a park: wide lawns and shrub-lined pathways, dotted with ruins and trees. Not a single edifice—the royal court for nobles, the royal court for the public, the harem, the grand mosque— had survived intact. Some of the buildings, Kabir told her, were in such a state of decay they couldn't even be identified. The ruins were spread out and the park was peaceful. Birds twittered from leafy trees, squirrels scampered across the grass. Though Kabir said it became crowded Thursday nights, it was afternoon and there were so few people everyone had ample space. Strolling through this part of the park, you wouldn't even know this place was supernatural.

They reached the masjid. It'd been stripped to stone, its walls badly broken, but impressive nonetheless, the raised courtyard large enough to hold prayers for ten thousand, the domed entrance and surviving arched doorways and colonnades hinting at its former splendor. Kabir explained that powerful jinn lived in the underground chambers beneath the masjid, and each chamber had its own altar. Before you could climb up to the courtyard or down to the chambers, you had to remove your shoes. This was still an active masjid, where humans performed Friday prayers and, it was believed, jinn prayed along with them. None of this information was on the official informational signs from the Archaeological Survey of India, which anyway were so dull Noreen had stopped reading them.

Next to the stairs, a man on a prayer rug thumbed through prayer beads and minded people's shoes for a small fee. Nearby, at a row of fat black water tanks with taps, two men in bright yellow skullcaps performed ablutions.

"Are you ready?" Kabir asked.

Noreen glanced down the stairs. It didn't seem so different from the rest of the ruins: blackened stone, crumbling brick, a series of archways. Anyway, she thought of herself as someone who didn't spook easily. Unlike her mother, she watched horror movies without a pillow at the ready, was more amused than frightened by a Halloween haunted house. Real life worried her more than the supernatural; she'd rather take her chances with a powerful jinn than a white supremacist with a gun.

"I'm ready," Noreen said.

They left their chappals with the shoe minder and went down the stairs, into an underground passage made up of a series of rooms with pointed archways on all four sides. The arches to their left opened to the outside, allowing in some light. The arches to the right led into small cave-like chambers. The back of every chamber held an altar to the jinn. At the second chamber they passed, she glimpsed a shadowy figure at the altar, a lit diya in their hand.

Kabir stopped at the entrance to the fourth chamber. "Would you like to leave your letter here? Or there are more altars if you'd like to keep going."

"Is there a special one you go to?" she asked. He shook his head. "Let's go in this one, then."

A few feet into the chamber, the daylight receded to pitch black. The altar was a nook on the back wall, illuminated by three diyas, and they paused in the chamber's dark middle to take it in. So many incense sticks had been burned here that the ash had spilled over, forming a cascade of ash so craggy and thick that people had stuck new incense sticks into it like quills. A few of these were still lit, tendrils of sandalwood smoke rising from the tips and dancing up toward the diyas' flames, which burned slim and steady in the stagnant air. Someone had managed to hang a garland of marigolds from the smoke-charred ceiling. All around the altar, people had left red rose petals and tucked their letters into crevices in the wall, or set them atop the ash.

"You go first," Noreen whispered.

She followed Kabir out of the dark, staying a few feet behind to observe. After unfolding his letter and leaving it where petals had made a red valley between two mounds of ash, he bent his head and recited a prayer. When he was done, he stepped back and she took his place, resting her letter on top of his. Theirs were the only two letters that were handwritten, and without photos, the others all black-and-white photocopies with passport-sized photos in the corners. She looked at the letters, lingering on the ones written by women, their small, serious faces looking back at her. Though she couldn't read their words, she knew they'd break her heart; she could feel the collective weight of longing of all those who'd come before. So many people, so much anguish. How powerful did a jinn have to be to fix this much suffering?

She needed to say a prayer. The only recitations she could think of were one of the four Qul suras from the Quran. Feeling a little self-conscious because Kabir was watching, she bowed her head and cupped her hands and began to recite the shortest Qul, but had to stop after the first line because the air had become too smoky and thick with pain. She was breathing in other people's grief, could feel her own rise to meet it. Then she remembered Amir and Sohail at the memorial service, holding hands, and she couldn't pray, couldn't think, couldn't breathe.

"Noreen?" Kabir said. "Are you all right?"

She shook her head.

He reached for her. "Let's go."

A young girl and a pregnant woman entered the chamber, and Kabir and Noreen moved aside to let them pass, holding hands in the dark. They stepped through the arch, back into the empty, half-lit passage. As they walked back through the passage, a strange sound followed them, high-pitched staccato squeaks. In the last room, the sound became deafening. She looked at Kabir, alarmed, and he pointed upward, where hundreds of misshapen black icicles hung from the domed ceiling.

Not icicles, she realized. Bats.

Directly over her head, a bat stirred and unfurled its wings.

Noreen took off in a sprint, out of the passage, up the stairs, into broad daylight, toward the other end of the park. A year ago, this would have been a breeze. Now she wasn't sure if she could make it to the boundary wall without collapsing. How had she gotten so out of shape?

Halfway across the park, she slowed to a walk, exhaling sandalwood, inhaling pollution. A few moments later, Kabir ran past her, then collapsed on the ground, starfishing his long, lean limbs.

"I need to get back to playing football," he said, still catching his breath. "You're quick. Are you okay?"

"Better now. That one bat scared me."

Kabir patted the grass. "Let's chill here for a bit?"

"Sure."

She lay down next to him, let her body sink into the ground. Dust coated the soles of her feet, and she had grit between her toes. At some point, they'd have to go back for their chappals.

"You want to talk about what you felt back there?" Kabir said. "You don't have to."

But she wanted to share, to let her guard down. He'd already seen her frightened, he had a sense of it, and anyway she'd tired of pretending. And maybe it was Geeta Auntie's kismat declaration, but she felt she could trust him.

"I do want to talk about it, though I don't know how to describe it exactly. I know they collect and burn the letters, but all the pain and longing inside those letters, and inside the people who wrote them, that doesn't totally disappear, right? Some of it stays behind, I could feel it, and then when I was trying to say a prayer I had this painful memory of Amir and Sohail, my khala's kids, the twins I mentioned to you earlier, and I felt like I was suffocating."

"What was the memory?"

She watched as one of the last leaves fell from a nearby tree. "My khala died of pancreatic cancer a year and a half ago."

"I'm so sorry."

"It's okay—thank you. They held a memorial for her; it was a benefit, too, all the proceeds going to Sonia Khala's favorite charities, and she used to play bass for this eighties cover band called The Nuclear Clefts, it's a pathology joke, since the band was all pathologists. Anyway, the band played at her memorial."

"That must have been very emotional," Kabir said. "For her band to play without her."

"Yeah, it was, and then they ended their set with '1999' by Prince, because she loved that song, and everyone starts singing along, and a few people start crying, and I look over at the twins. Sohail has tears running down his face and Amir is trying hard not to cry because he wants to be brave for his brother, and they're both holding hands and singing along. As I stood there watching them, something broke inside me. Down there, at the altar, that's what I felt in all those letters to the jinn—all those people saying, *I am broken, I am broken, help me become whole.*"

"Wow," Kabir said. "That place really spoke to you."

"Yeah, I guess it did."

The birds were louder now, calling out to each other across the ruins.

"You know," he said, "none of the others I've brought here felt the things you did."

"Seriously?" Noreen couldn't imagine going down there and not having that reaction.

"I've brought a fair few people here, and they've found it spooky, or cool, or interesting, but you're the only one who felt the emotional resonance of the place. Thank you for reminding me what a powerful place this is. You're a special person, Noreen."

"Special, me?" She was moved by his words, uncertain how to respond. "I mean, aren't we all?"

She was sounding like an idiot.

"Sorry if I've embarrassed you," Kabir said. "I tend to wear my heart on my sleeve."

A slinky calico cat paused in front of them to lick its paw. Kabir leaned past Noreen, beckoning the cat with his hand. He had a fraying red thread tied around his wrist, its two loose ends reduced to wisps. She realized that though she remained very attuned to where his body was in relation to hers, she was much less nervous around him. It was as if they'd been through something together and come out the other side.

The cat deigned to sniff Kabir's fingers, then continued on its way.

"You think that cat is a jinn?" Noreen said.

Kabir grinned. "You're a believer now."

"I mean, I wouldn't rule it out completely. Also, thank you for bringing me here. And I'm sorry for all the serious conversation," she said. "I can be fun too, promise."

"What are you talking about? This is the most fun I've had in weeks." She tossed a fistful of grass at him, and he laughed. "It's true!"

They smiled at each other. He was so close now she could see the full length of his lashes, the way his stubble grew in a little swirl beneath his left ear. She decided to claim it, her own private Milky Way.

"So should we see the rest of the monument?" she asked.

"We could. I was also going to suggest we could see the rest another day and go get some ice cream."

"I love ice cream!" she said, with such enthusiasm that a family picnicking nearby turned to look. It was true, though. Even spending an entire summer scooping the stuff had not diminished her passion.

"Brilliant!" Kabir said. "So do I."

Though the probability of two people both loving ice cream was high, as they walked back toward the masjid to retrieve their shoes, Noreen imagined Geeta Auntie nudging Yash Uncle. *You see, Yash? I told you it was fate.*

The experience of flying Air India teaches you some basic rules that will help you navigate and understand India.

Rule Number One: Standing in the back of the line is for suckers. I learn this the hard way, because I'm a sucker. When they announce general boarding, my mom and I go to stand at the back of the line, but instead of moving forward, we keep moving backward. Soon we realize this is because everyone is cutting the line. Then this Uncle ji cuts right in front of us, even makes eye contact with me while he's doing it, and then he calls over his wife, his three kids, and his parents to join him. I'm like, "Mom, should we say something?"

She's like, "No, it could start a fight." So I say nothing.

Then, this young man cuts in front of Uncle ji, and Uncle ji says, "Oy, what are you doing? Can't you see there's a line?" I'm like, what kind of fucked-up moral logic is this? It's fine for you to cut in front of me, but how dare he cut in front of you? And that's how I realize Rule Number Two to understanding India: Things are only unfair if they are unfair to you. If something's unfair to a thousand people but makes your life better, what's the issue? No issue. Once you get this, everything starts to make a lot more sense.

nine

*Air Quality Index: 292. Very
Unhealthy.*

THE NEXT FOURTEENTH-CENTURY monument Kabir took her to was Hauz Khas, a complex of various ruins—picturesque domed pavilions, the sultan's grand tomb and a once-renowned madrasa—built along a large reservoir. It was also, as Noreen jokingly dubbed it, the PDA Capital of Delhi; inside the madrasa's columned doorways overlooking the lake's green, placid waters, young couples giggled, whispered, embraced. At one point, Noreen told her mother the next day, it felt like every ten feet they were interrupting yet another lovers' tryst, an experience both awkward and heartwarming.

"Makes sense," Ruby said. "A lot of kids here live at home until they get married, so they need to meet elsewhere. And you can't get much more romantic than lakes and domed pavilions."

"A little crowded for my taste," Noreen said, "but definitely a beautiful place to canoodle."

The doorbell rang.

"Hold that canoodle." Her mother grabbed her wallet and threw on a shawl.

Curious, Noreen followed her mother to the door, behind which was a man in a knock-off T-shirt that said *Abidas* underneath the striped flower logo, his tight acid-washed jeans belted low to accommodate what her mother referred to as the "uncle ji gut."

"Amit?" her mother said.

"Yes. Your good name, ma'am?"

"Ruby."

Amit unbuckled his scraped motorcycle helmet and took off his backpack. He bent down to unzip it, asking in Hindi, "You wanted four reds, right? Chile or France?"

Her mother had mentioned something about a wine bootlegger. Indian wine wasn't very good, but foreign wines were subject to huge import duties, which meant a bottle you'd pay ten dollars for in the States cost thirty or forty here. Hence, the wine black market and Amit the bootlegger.

"How much are they?" Ruby asked.

"Chile is six hundred rupees, France is one thousand," he said.

"How about you give me France for seven hundred and fifty," her mother said.

"No, madam. Not possible."

"Fine. France for eight hundred."

"Sorry. Fixed price."

"Eight hundred and fifty."

"Fixed price."

"Mom," Noreen murmured.

Her mother operated on the assumption that 80 percent of the people in India were trying to cheat you, especially when they realized you were foreign, and acted accordingly. Noreen hated the combative nature of haggling, the drama of pretending to walk away because the price was too high even if you'd already decided to buy something. She was a "fixed price" girl all the way, and didn't understand why her mother couldn't let the auto rickshaw wallah have the twenty extra rupees, even if it was more than he'd charge a local. But she'd given up arguing with her mother, for whom not getting ripped off was a matter of pride.

"Okay, okay," Ruby said. "Give me two Chile and two France."

Amit carefully removed four dusty wine bottles. Noreen thought that, if she were ever to write any scenes set in Delhi, she'd make him a recurring character. His appearances would be brief, but he could establish a humorous rapport with the mother character, or dispense good advice, or maybe turn up at inopportune moments.

"You do realize you were bargaining for goods you were purchasing illegally?" Noreen told her mother after Amit had left.

"We're in India! You think I'm bad, you should see your naani haggle. The bootlegger would have given her France for five hundred just to be rid of her."

Noreen laughed. "I totally see that. Well, except for the Naani buying wine part."

Ruby held up the two bottles she'd wiped clean of dust. "Which should I open, Chile or France? New World or Old World? Or, as some of my fellow NGO wallahs would say, High Income Countries or the Global South?"

"Global South for five hundred, please," Noreen said.

"Excellent choice, madam. Is that what you're wearing tonight? Looks great."

Noreen tugged at her loose shift dress. "I think so. Is it too plain for an opening?"

Kabir had invited both of them to an art opening this evening at a nearby gallery.

"Black is forever chic. And from what I can tell, Kabir would still love you if you went in your pajamas. Maybe you should borrow his Aladdin pants."

"Funny."

"Hey, do we have a corkscrew?" Ruby said as she rifled through the silverware drawer. "We've been here three weeks and I'm still learning my way around this kitchen."

"Very *Downton Abbey*," Noreen said.

"Funny. Come here and help me look."

As they searched the drawers and cabinets, Noreen longed for their sunlit kitchen at home, its small island with three cushioned barstools where they would rehash their day, or the previous night. Sometimes Ruby would sit up on the counter and swing her legs as they talked. The months after Sonia Khala's death, they'd both find themselves in the kitchen in the middle of the night, and Noreen would take out the ice cream, Ruby the bowls and spoons. Sometimes they'd reminisce about Sonia Khala, sometimes they'd talk about anything but, sometimes they'd honor her by listening to one of her favorite qawwali songs.

Their Delhi kitchen had one small frosted window, dark counters, and battered wood cabinets. Other than the bright red gas cylinder and the orange cord that connected it to the four-burner gas stove on the countertop, the space was narrow, dim, utilitarian. Her mother said this was because the kitchen was traditionally the realm of servants and women, and so its aesthetics mattered less. Next to the door was a low plastic stool where Sarita would sit on her breaks, even though they kept telling her to please relax in the living room instead.

They found a corkscrew behind some rolling pins. Ruby poured herself a glass of wine and they retreated to the living room, skipping the most uncomfortable sofa in the world for the two ugly but more butt-friendly armchairs.

"What time did Kabir say he was getting there?" Ruby asked.

"Eight."

"You know you smile every time I say his name?"

"I do not."

"Kabir Kabir Kabir."

"Mom!"

"Girl, you are crushing hard."

"We've only hung out three times!" Noreen said.

"And your point is?"

After seeing Kabir, she'd pace, review things they'd said, laugh again at something funny, recall gestures he'd made, play out what may have happened if she'd said X or done Y, imagine what might happen when they saw each other next, masturbate. The half-life of every hang with Kabir was at least twenty-four hours. Yesterday, after visiting Hauz Khas with all its young lovers, she'd entered serious Kabir La-La Land: a romantic walk through wild ruins; a passionate first kiss; falling madly in love; breaking up because she's leaving, after which they're both lonely and aching, until, one crisp autumn evening, he shows up at Wesleyan to surprise her. Maybe as she's leaving the library. Or maybe at a campus concert. Or right as she's about to make a big decision. It would also have to call back to something from their relationship, she wasn't yet sure what.

"I may have a small crush," Noreen said.

"You always did prefer being understated. Every time I'd dress you in that sparkle heart onesie you'd immediately puke on it."

"Haha. Fine. maybe I am crushing hard. The thing is . . ."

Ruby swirled her wine. "The thing is?"

"It feels too perfect. It must have felt perfect with you and my father, right, until it wasn't. And I know you thought it was perfect with Miles, until it wasn't."

Her mother set her glass down over Hathi Blingbling's jeweled head. "Nor-bear. The fact that my relationships ended doesn't mean that yours will. And my relationship with your father was never perfect—we were young and clueless."

"But isn't that what I am?"

"You were never clueless. I was so busy rebelling against my parents that it took me longer to grow up. You see how I still am with my folks. Your personality, your life, your circumstances . . . you may be of me, but you are not at all me."

"I know. But I'm still scared."

"That's normal. Forget the Disney bull about how love is all happy songs and roses. Sure, part of falling in love is euphoria, but part of it is so terrifying it makes you want to shit your pants."

Noreen smiled. "On that lovely note, I'm going to go put on some makeup."

Back in her room, Noreen repeatedly messed up her eyeliner and worried she'd upset her mother. She didn't want Ruby to blame herself for Noreen's relationship anxiety; if it was anyone's fault, it was her father's, and also maybe the internet's. Everything she read online said girls who felt unloved by their fathers went on to have shitty relationships with men as though it was a given. Her only relationship so far had been with Liam. He was the kind of chiseled gorgeous that turned people's heads, and he possessed, as Abby put it, mad bedroom skills; the summer before college, he'd had an affair with a much older woman who'd given him an education in pleasuring the female sex. Nearly every day for a month, he'd given Noreen orgasms and made her feel beautiful naked. In between sex, they'd watch TV and eat takeout and talk some, though not a lot. There was never any long-term potential (he dreamed of starting his own hedge fund, he wore ironed polo shirts, he didn't read books), but when he returned to Wharton and stopped texting, she still felt heartbroken. Later, when she kept seeing the same girl on his Instagram, her heart broke a little all over again. One day, her mother said, the hurt will fade, and you'll understand he came into your life for a reason, and that it's better it ended when it did.

It's true, Abby had agreed, one day you'll look back and think, Wow, that was some sexual awakening.

But, however you looked at it, her relationship with Liam hadn't been *shitty*. Would that keep, or was it beginner's luck?

"I need you to tell me the truth." Ruby stood in the doorway, her back to Noreen. She'd also chosen a black dress, hers almost knee-length but more fitted. "Can you see my double butt?"

"Your *what*?"

"Look." Ruby squeezed the bottom of her bum. "The cellulite has gotten together and formed a small shelf under my cheeks, like a little double butt."

"I see only one beautiful butt."

"You sure?" She turned around, adjusting the top of her

dress. "And do you think this cleavage is sexy yet age appropriate?"

"I would call that more glimpse than cleavage. And fuck age appropriate. That's the patriarchy talking. Now me." Noreen held two different earrings to her ears. "Dangly earrings or flower studs?"

"Dangly, for sure." Ruby pointed at the fat novel, *The Palace of Infinite Salt* by Inder Chaudhury, that lay open on the paisley bedspread. "Isn't that a male writer?"

A few days after arriving in Delhi, Noreen had decided that while here, as a counter to being surrounded by men almost anywhere she went, she'd only read books written by women.

"I'm making an exception," Noreen explained, "because Inder Chaudhury is Kabir's dad."

"Ah." Ruby flipped to the author photo. "Handsome. Check out these blurbs. *A tour de force of Indian literature. A haunting exploration of masculinity and the postcolonial condition.* He's pretty famous, huh?"

"In India. Kabir says he's been published in the US and UK but never became big there. Apparently, he's bitter about it, but he has a novel coming out this spring that his agent thinks will finally make a name for him in the West. Oh, and Kabir said his parents might come tonight, and if we meet his dad, not to bring up social media, because he'll go on a rant, or Salman Rushdie, because it'll make him grumpy."

"Sounds like a charming fellow. And why would I randomly

bring Salman Rushdie into a conversation? Salman Rushdie, Peter Gabriel too?" she said, humming "Cape Cod Kwassa Kwassa" by Vampire Weekend.

Noreen laughed. "And one more thing—"

"Oh my gawd, so many *rules*—"

"Do NOT tell Kabir any embarrassing stories from when I was a kid."

Ruby feigned surprise. "Of what embarrassing stories do you speak? I know none."

"Like how I used to eat my boogers in courses."

"Noreen! I'm offended. I would not share that story until you were married. Or at least engaged."

"Or how I cried when you told me the Pirates of the Caribbean weren't real."

"Aaarrrr, I had to! You made me stand in line for that ride five hundred times in a row. In *July*."

"Or how you potty trained me by letting me watch old Morrissey videos while I sat on the toilet. You love to tell people that one."

"Oh!" Ruby clapped her hands. "Do you remember when you were like, Morrissey loves ice cream like me, and I was like, what do you mean, and it turns out you thought 'Everyday Is Like Sunday' was 'Everyday I Like Sundaes.'"

"As far as I'm concerned, it will always be that."

"Sing it, sister. Anything else I should be aware of?"

Noreen considered. "If his mom is there, Kabir says she

can be a little intimidating."

"She's the painter?"

"Yup. She's been doing a lot more installation work lately, though she became famous for her miniatures. I'll show you one I like a lot." Noreen pulled it up on her phone.

The miniature was called *Zohra's Ascent*. In it, a girl sits on Buraq, a winged horselike creature with a woman's face and a shimmering peacock feather tail, and together they rise toward the sky. Dark curls spiral down her back and her face is hidden within a graceful, golden flame. With the double-edged sword in her hand, she fends off the men grabbing for Buraq's back legs. When you looked closely, you saw the men had different bodies and poses but the same exact face.

"It's beautiful," Ruby said. "And intense. What's she like?"

"Kabir said both his parents are pretty narcissistic, so don't expect them to show much interest in you unless they think you can be useful to them. But he also said his mother should be nice enough, as long as she thinks you're smart."

"She does not suffer fools gladly?" Ruby said.

"Apparently not."

"Ahoy matey!"

Noreen groaned. "If you do meet her, please don't talk pirate."

"Aye. You ready? Should I order le Uber?"

"Yup."

"Done. Okay, quick recap. Things I must not say." Ruby counted on her fingers. "Salman Rushdie, any so-called embarrassing stories about you, batten down the hatches and hoist the poop deck. Shit, you've taken my conversation gold."

Noreen laughed. "Hoist the poop deck? I think it's man the poop deck. What is a poop deck anyway?"

"The deck where you take a dump while watching Morrissey videos, obviously."

"Google it."

"Must we turn to Google Baba for everything?" Ruby said. "I'll save that question for the next sailor I meet."

"Okay, but I don't think Delhi has a Fleet Week. We're, like, a thousand miles from the ocean."

"You weren't acting like that when you ordered the tandoori pomfret the other night."

"Believe me, I paid for that decision."

Ruby's phone buzzed. "Chalo, Madam," she said, draping an embroidered black shawl that had been folded over her forearm over her chest and shoulders. "Our chariot awaits."

They went to meet their Uber, Ruby on a roll, saying, in the Queen's English, "I do not suffer fools gladly, and neither, I've heard, does Sir Salman Rush—I mean, He who shall not be named, except, of course, when manning the poop deck . . ." and would have gone on had Noreen not begged her to stop.

ten

Air Quality Index: 301.

Hazardous.

NOREEN AND RUBY CRANED their necks at the giant phallus composed of auto parts: bumpers, fenders, headlights, radiator grilles.

"This is the weak link of the group show," Ruby said.

"Word," Noreen said.

"I do not suffer fools—"

"Mom." Noreen caught her distorted reflection in a banged-up side mirror. "Can we move away from this monstrosity?"

A dramatic floor-to-ceiling wall of glass divided the warehouse-style gallery from the patio, and from inside they could see the crowd gathering at the patio bar.

"Time for libations," her mother said.

Noreen was more excited about the kabob stand set up on the large lawn, where three men flipped skewers of meat, paneer, and vegetables over a fire, a cloud of coal and masala-scented smoke hovering above their tall chefs' hats. She would have headed there first except she didn't want to have kabob breath right when she met Kabir. That was more of a 10:00 p.m. situation.

As Ruby braved the bar crowd, Noreen hung back and observed. Most of the guests were desi, with quite a few white people mixed in. Some of the men looked like they hadn't put a comb to their hair in weeks, though a few were quite fashionable. She liked that men here weren't afraid to dress in color. Almost all the women were dressed up: bright textiles, bold patterns, intricate embroideries. Even the ones in head-to-toe black had at least one eye-catching accessory, like the woman next to her, who was explaining to her friend, a pale white woman with a shock of red hair, dressed in a richly embroidered, voluminous caftan, that her striking, multistrand necklace of carnelian, cowrie, and bone had been made by a tribal woman in a remote area of Nagaland.

Noreen made a note to google Nagaland.

Her mother returned with drinks and as they walked to the quieter end of the patio, Noreen noticed a portly uncle checking out her mother. He had long sideburns and a crappy comb-over, wore a wool coat with bright yellow-and-red patchwork patterns and was smoking a cigar while talking at a woman in a silver sari, her shimmering backless blouse held together by a single, slender string.

"You have a fan," Noreen said.

"Who?" Ruby asked.

Silver sari lady received a phone call, and the uncle made a beeline toward Ruby.

"You're about to find out," Noreen murmured.

"Good evening," the uncle said. "I don't believe I've had the pleasure of your acquaintance."

"No, I don't believe you have," Ruby said.

"I'm Akash Chakraborty." He said his name like it meant something, though they'd no idea what. And he spoke with a plummy British accent that Noreen imagined the colonial British rulers using when they pronounced the natives restless.

Fuck this guy, Noreen thought.

"I'm Ruby; this is my daughter, Noreen," Ruby said.

"Mother and daughter!" Akash said. "But you look like her sister!"

"Never heard that one before," her mother said.

"Really? I'm shocked. Your name is Ruby, you said? The sun."

"I'm sorry?"

"Do you know what the navaratna is?" This was not a question, of course, but a self-invitation to mansplain. He leaned in, both Ruby and Noreen turning their cheek from his sour cigar-whiskey breath. "The navaratna is a piece of jewelry consisting of nine sacred jewels that represent the cosmos, a talisman, if you will. The ruby is always in the center, because it represents the sun."

"My name is actually Rubin—"

"In fact, one test of a ruby's authenticity is to hold it to your eye and look at the sun. The sun should appear as bright as it would to the naked eye."

"I think we—"

"Are you an artist, Ruby Sun?"

"No, I am not." Her mother had forgone sarcasm for the tight, polite tone she used when telling telemarketers to get lost.

"Nor am I," Akash said. He moved in closer to her mother. "I am, rather, an aesthete."

"An ass what?" Ruby said, and Noreen swallowed her laugh.

"An aesthete. A lover of the arts. I'm also the founder of Mangata." When he realized this did not register, he repeated it in full. "The Mangata Arts Festival."

"That sounds nice," Ruby said.

"You must come to the festival, Ruby Sun," Akash said. "We have the best after-parties on the circuit."

Beside her, Noreen felt her mother startle, then stiffen. As Akash launched into a story about last year's festival closing party, Ruby took a step backward, gripping Noreen's elbow to bring her along.

Akash had been busy name-dropping people they didn't recognize, but when he said, "I thought the party couldn't get more wild, but then Salman Rushdie decided to—" Ruby choked and sprayed red wine out of her nose, a few drops landing on the lapel of his hobo-chic coat.

"Sorry!" she said. "Inside joke. Here, take this."

Akash refused the napkin, balled up from Ruby's fist. "No, no, it's fine, I need to get it dry-cleaned anyway."

"Hey!" Kabir called out as he shouldered his way through

the lively group of French people next to them. "Sorry I'm late."

Noreen still caught her breath at those soft, sweet brown eyes. Look at them too long and she risked falling in completely, a one-way ticket to La-La Land.

"Kabir!" Akash said. "If you two know him, you must know his mother, Meena. I was one of her first patrons. It still surprises me how long it took for others to recognize her genius. Now I'm waiting on the son, eh, Kabir?"

Kabir winced as Akash clapped his back.

"I need to use the ladies' room," Ruby said.

"Me too," Noreen said.

"I'll show you where it is," Kabir said. "Nice seeing you, Uncle."

"Sorry about that," he said when they were out of earshot. "Akash Uncle can be quite the pompous ass."

"He put his hand on my waist while he was talking to me." Ruby did a disgusted shimmy and brushed off both sides of her body.

"That's why you jumped and moved back," Noreen said. "I was wondering."

"You need to stay an arm's length away from that guy," Ruby said.

"I'm really sorry," Kabir said. "Are you all right?"

"I'll be fine," her mother said. "Akash wasn't the first, and he probably won't be the last."

"But that doesn't make it okay."

"No, it doesn't. Although the fact he said 'Salman Rushdie' almost made it worth it."

"Mom!"

"What? Is it a secret?"

Kabir smiled. "I'm guessing Noreen gave you the intel on my parents."

"A little." Ruby extended her hand. "It's nice to finally meet you, Kabir."

"And you."

"Hey, Kabir!" A young woman with purple hair came at Kabir with open arms, her hair a shade lighter than her purple sari, its striped pallu pleated in front and cinched at the waist with a black braided belt.

"Hi, Dee!" Kabir said, hugging her. "Kaisi ho?"

"I'm good, yaar. Been working my ass off in the studio."

"These are my friends, Noreen and her mother, Ruby."

"Hello." Dee smiled at them. "Have you seen the art? What did you think?"

"I thought the graphic paintings were great," Ruby said.

"The landscape photos from Ladakh were cool, too," Noreen said.

"Did you see Saurabh's work? The penis made of dented auto parts? It's like the artistic equivalent of a teenage boner."

They laughed.

"Oh! There's Akash. I need to talk to him before he gets too drunk." Dee knocked back her remaining wine, summoned a waiter, set her glass on his tray. "Nice meeting you. Kabir, let's catch up soon."

"Wait," Ruby said. "Does she mean that Akash?"

"Yes. She's creating a large mixed media mural for this year's Mangata Festival," Kabir explained.

"So she has to play nice," Ruby said. "Lovely."

"I think that woman is gesturing at you from the other side of the glass," Noreen said.

"That's my mother, and there's my father," Kabir said. "Do you mind if we go say hello?"

"Of course not," Noreen said.

Kabir's mother, Meena, looked like a beautiful witch, her long silver hair parted straight down the middle. Her eyes were hazel, as large as Kabir's, the lower lids darkened with kohl. She wore a crisp black kurta with a burnt-orange geometric scarf, its knotted ends hanging to her knees.

Unlike Kabir and Meena, Inder had a wrestler's build, the lower buttons of his tailored Nehru vest straining over his paunch. He was the shortest of the three, his salt-and-pepper hair even thicker than his son's.

When Kabir introduced them, Inder nodded at Noreen and shook Ruby's hand, looking at her face, then her chest, then her face again. Meena nodded hello and asked Kabir, "Who all is here?"

"Well, Noreen and Ruby had the pleasure of meeting Akash Chakraborty," he said.

Meena made a *pfffff!* sound. "I'm sure he was his usual

charming self." She gestured at the installation in front of her, a saffron-colored auto rickshaw lying on its side. Two brown prosthetic feet stuck out from underneath, decorated with mehndi from ankle to toe, slim silver rings on both second toes. Attached to the top of the auto was a large wing made of wooden rolling pins held together by delicately braided rope. The installation was titled *Rise of the Right Wing*. "What do you think of the current work in the boy toy corner?"

"Why is it called the boy toy corner?" Ruby asked.

"In the group shows, this corner is usually reserved for whichever artist David is fucking."

"Who's David?" Ruby said.

"The owner of the gallery," Meena said. Even as she spoke to them, her eyes kept roving, checking to see who else was around. She could, Noreen thought, at least be a little subtle about it.

"His last lover had talent," Inder said. "I quite liked his lithographs."

"And my parents will end the night in the back room, finishing all of David's scotch," Kabir said to Noreen and Ruby.

"Oh, come on, Kabir," Meena said. "You know I say it to his face all the time. I'll certainly tell David exactly what I think of *this*. Really, the older he gets, the further his standards fall."

"It's not as though his cup brimmeth with options," Inder said, but Meena was looking past him.

"There's Renuka," Meena said. "Come, Inder, let's go say hello."

"Abe yaar—and be forced to listen to another reprimand on how I need a social media presence? When I published my first novel, she was still in nappies."

"And now she is the new editor in chief of your publishing house." Meena rolled her eyes at Ruby and Noreen as if to say, *these men.*

Inder turned to Ruby. "What do you think?"

"About listening to younger people?" Ruby said. "I think they have some great ideas. Noreen inspires me to be a better person every day."

Everyone looked at Noreen, who managed a smile in spite of feeling both annoyed at her mother for shifting the spotlight onto her and petrified by the possibility of Meena asking her an incisive follow-up question, to which she'd respond with some nervous, bumbling answer and destroy all hope of gaining Meena's respect.

"Noreen, you sound lovely," Inder said. "I would love for Kabir to inspire his elders. Instead, he spends all his time smoking joints in ruins."

"Poppa, please," Kabir said.

"Inder, stop embarassing your son and go speak to your editor," Meena said.

"May I have another whiskey first?"

"No."

"The wife has spoken. Jo hukum mere aaka," Inder said. "Nice meeting you, ladies."

"What does jo hukum mera aaka mean?" Noreen asked after his parents had left.

"Your wish is my command," Kabir said.

"So, Kabir, you smoke joints?" Ruby asked.

Kabir glanced at Noreen. She'd told him her mother was a smoker, but he didn't know her well enough to read her intent. "Yes."

"You know marijuana has a detrimental effect on developing brains and your brain isn't fully developed until twenty-five? How old are you?" Ruby said.

Kabir cleared his throat. "Twenty-four. But I've cut back. I only smoke once a week or so."

"Good," Ruby said. "Everything in moderation. You know my daughter doesn't smoke. She also does not suffer fools gladly."

Noreen groaned. "Mom! Why do you always want to over-extend the joke? That's the last of that genre for tonight, okay?"

"You took away all of my 'here's a cute story from Noreen's childhood' material," Ruby said. "At least leave me my jokes."

"I'd like to hear a cute story from Noreen's childhood," Kabir said.

"Not happening," Noreen said.

Ruby planted a light kiss on the side of Noreen's head. "All right, kids, the bar calls. I'll catch up with you soon."

"Sorry about that," Noreen told Kabir. "My mom tells people I'm eighteen going on thirty but then she'll treat me like I'm five."

"She seems pretty cool to me."

"She is, most of the time. Your parents also seem nice."

"Please. My mother didn't ask either of you a single question about yourselves," he said. "And I'm sure you noticed how she was looking around the whole time."

"Well, I'm sure there are a lot of important people to talk to at this party."

"But you're important to me, and that should be enough. Hey, you hungry? Should we hit the kabobs?"

"You speak my language," she said.

They got a skewer of everything: chicken tikka kabob, seekh kabob, vegetable kabob, and paneer tikka kabob, and took over a white marble bench at the far end of the lawn, talking and eating from the plate balanced on Kabir's lap. Noreen spoke of pollution, how she had to force herself to stop reading about it and, for her own sanity, enter a state of semi-denial. Kabir talked about film school, how he dropped out because he hated delegation and oversight and half the work of making a film was managing other people, many of whom had bloated yet fragile egos. He preferred to work alone, which was why he was thinking of pursuing photography more seriously. He talked about his grandmother, who had rapid onset dementia, how yesterday, for the first time, his naani hadn't once recognized him. She told him about her loving but complicated relationship with her own naani. They went on, trading stories, through the distant Isha call to prayer and a second plate of kabobs. Only when they heard the dismantling of the kabob stand did they realize the bar had shut, the party down to two dozen. They joined Ruby on the patio, where she was laughing with two women she introduced as Pooja, a human rights lawyer, and Camille, a French designer. They all chatted a bit more before calling it a night. Pooja was taking Camille home, and Kabir said he could drop off Noreen and her mother.

Noreen and Ruby were waiting inside the entrance for Kabir to bring the car when they heard Akash approaching from behind, calling out "Ruby Sun!" They ran through the gate and Kabir pulled up right as they came out the other side, an aptly timed ending to a mostly excellent night.

So we board the Air India plane, and it's not very old, but it already has airplane arthritis. It's creaking and groaning, and it's not even moving yet. Then I see that my broken armrest is being held together by one measly little strip of masking tape—not even duct tape. Masking tape. Last Christmas, my nine-year-old cousins made a gingerbread house with some baked dough and frosting. Their gingerbread house was more structurally sound than this plane I'm on. I'm a pretty easy flyer, but between the weird noises and my broken seat, I'm freaking out a little, and my mom says, "Try not to think about it too much." Which bring me to Rule Number Three: A little denial goes a long way.

eleven

Air Quality Index: 216. Very Unhealthy.

AS A FORM OF transport, an auto rickshaw left you vulnerable, both to the elements and your fellow passengers. The auto's open sides meant no barrier of metal and glass to shield you from the thick January fog, the black exhaust spewing out of the tailpipes of trucks, the beggars' outstretched hands, the men weaving their way through stalled traffic hawking washcloths and light-up plastic toys, the stares of people on motorbikes, in cars. The auto's compact back seat required you to lean in close and speak loudly to be heard over the din of traffic; right now Kabir was shouting instructions about his naani's medicine into his phone, his hand cupped over the mouthpiece.

Noreen wore her dupatta on her head, holding one end over the lower half of her face as an impromptu (and ineffectual) pollution mask. Their autowallah had his own makeshift mask, a red plaid handkerchief tied over his nose and mouth. Ruby had sent Noreen a video from the *Guardian*, in which they tested the lungs of a Delhi autowallah who drove his auto an average of ten hours a day and found them to be functioning at 50 percent capacity. As the traffic slowed, the autowallah leaned out the side, lifted his bandana, and unleashed a stream of green mucus onto the asphalt. A photo of the goddess Lakshmi dangled from his rearview mirror. Another photo was taped on the back wall near Noreen's head, a cutout of a Bollywood actress wearing a tight blue lengha choli, stomach bare, hips thrust to one side, her bangled arms wide open.

"Sorry about that," Kabir said after he hung up. "Naani's nurse had to go back to her village for her daughter's shaadi, and the substitute messed up her meds yesterday."

Kabir had shaved and traded his usual uniform of soft, button-down shirt and lackadaisical pants for a traditional kurta pajama, delicate silver embroidery on the kurta's collar and cuffs. He'd combed his hair back, a hint of gel making it almost ruly.

A scooter idled next to them, carrying a family of six, three small kids sandwiched between the father in front and the mother seated sidesaddle at the back, the right half of her sari blouse hitched up to accommodate the baby nursing at her breast. Only the father was wearing a helmet.

"Have you taken a photo of your reflection in the auto's rear-view mirror?" Kabir asked. "Firangs seem to especially love those. That and posing with a group of children somewhere in Africa."

Firang was slang for a white person.

"No. I rarely take photos—not because I don't appreciate the medium, but I never think to."

It was disconcerting, to have the handsome boy you were crushing on mere inches from your face and to have to yell to be understood. He could surely see the inflamed zit near her right eye, an unwelcome place for a pimple, especially because she considered her eyes her best asset.

At the next red light, a gaunt rose seller tapped Kabir's shoulder with a red rosebud. "Le lo, Bhaiyya. Behen ya dost ya aashiq, sab ko phool pasand hai."

Take one, brother. Sister or friend or aashiq, everyone likes flowers.

"Would you like one?" Kabir asked her.

"No, thank you. I've never been that into roses, especially red ones."

"Really? Well, brace yourself, because the dargah's covered in them."

After Kabir's fourth polite refusal, the rose seller moved on.

"What does *aashiq* mean?" she asked.

"Lover," he said.

"Ah."

Noreen looked down at her hands, toying with the hem of her dupatta and trying to keep a straight face as the words ricocheted, singsong, inside her head. lover *aashiq* aashiq *lover* lover *aashiq* aashiq *lover*.

A beggar woman startled her out of her reverie by reaching into the auto and touching her side, calling her Didi in a gravelly voice and pleading for cash. In her arms was a toddler with a distended stomach and hungry black eyes. A thick white pus oozed from his tiny penis.

Noreen opened her purse, but she only had a five-hundred-rupee note and one of the four-crayon packs Tammy had given them. The kid had a genital infection; he needed medicine, not crayons. She took out the crayons anyway, and Kabir reached across to give the woman a twenty-rupee note. After tucking the note into her sari blouse, the woman accepted the crayons from Noreen, but did not thank her as she had Kabir. Noreen watched the woman's retreat in the side-view mirror, the child's head bobbing off her bony shoulder as she wove through the honking cars.

Her mother had told her begging here was largely run by organized crime, that the beggars had to turn over their money to their gang leader, who gave them enough to barely subsist on and kept the rest. Noreen wondered how much of those twenty rupees the woman would get to keep, if the baby's genital infection would ever receive proper treatment, if she'd get any money for the crayons.

The pull-yourself-up-by-your-bootstraps story was a nice narrative, her mother said, but the truth was that the course of most people's lives, all over the world, was determined by the circumstances into which they were born.

"What are you thinking?" Kabir said.

"How the main thing separating me from that woman is the luck of my birth."

"I should warn you there are a lot of beggars at Nizamuddin dargah," he said. "Dargahs have always been a refuge for the poor. The Sufi saints wouldn't turn people away based on religion or caste or class; all visitors were treated with respect and fed the same food. The disciples who performed qawwali in the evening performed for everyone, paupers and kings, God most of all, of course; sometimes they'd be so overcome by their love for the divine that they'd stop singing and enter a trance. I would love to have seen that. It's another place I'd go if I could time travel, visit while Hazrat Nizamuddin was still alive, hear Amir Khusro perform."

Amir Khusro was Hazrat Nizamuddin's most famous disciple, a musician and poet. Noreen knew him because one of his poems, "Chaap Tilak," was so popular she'd heard many versions. Two of Amir Khusro's poems were on Sonia Khala's favorite qawwali songs playlist.

"What are you thinking?" Kabir asked.

"How excited Sonia Khala would be if she knew where I was going."

"Maybe she does know."

From what Noreen had read, in Islamic tradition it was a given that the dead could communicate with the living. This happened primarily through dreams, as sleep was considered the time when the spirits of the dead and the sleeping could meet and communicate. When she'd read this, Noreen regretted not paying more attention to the few dreams she'd had about Sonia Khala after she died. She hadn't had one in a long time, at least not one she could remember. Kabir said the devotees who came to the dargah believed that Hazrat Nizamuddin was still "alive," and although there was a veil between him and mortals so they could not see him, people still felt his presence. She wondered if this could apply to non-saints as well, if she might feel Sonia Khala's presence at the dargah, and know that she was well, and at peace.

The auto dropped them off near the entrance of Nizamuddin basti, which, Kabir explained, was an urban village, a settlement that, after being engulfed by the city, had retained its tangled lanes but replaced its mud houses and open space with crowded concrete buildings. Food stalls lined the lane leading into the village: huge steel pots of biryani, stacks of fresh, fluffy tandoori naan, pakoras frying in vats of blistering oil, red tandoori chicken quarters sizzling on the grill, served with onions and drizzled with fresh lime.

As they continued deeper into the village, the lane narrowed. When Noreen and Kabir stepped aside so a cycle rickshaw could pass, she found herself sandwiched between the cycle rickshaw and a stall of pirated books. Across the back seat of the cycle rickshaw lay a dead, skinned goat, its eyes wide open, its head about to brush Noreen's hips. To prevent the carcass from touching her, she moved back as far as she could, her ass resting on the edge of the book table.

She looked to see what book her butt cheeks had defiled. *Chicken Soup for the Soul*. She was fine with that.

Kabir touched her sleeve. "You look a little pale."

"I wasn't expecting the passenger to be a dead goat," she said. "But if I can eat it, I should be able to look at it, right?"

"Fair point," he said. "Ready to keep going?"

"Ready."

They passed a neon-green sign advertising the services of Pir Sufi Kashan Baba, a holy man who offered "Spiritual Treatment for Any Kind of Problem. Business and Marriage, Bad Air, Success, Children, Love, Education, Black Magic, Journey, Court Case."

As she read it, Noreen thought, *Grief. Don't forget grief.*

The lane turned into a covered marble passageway. She knew they were close because now the stalls sold only spiritual goods, prayer rugs and prayer beads, green scarves emblazoned with Quranic verses, framed photos of the Kaaba in Mecca and red rose petals, available by the Styrofoam plate or small plastic bag.

They reached the official dargah entrance, marked by a marble archway inscribed with Quranic verses, left their shoes with the last of the shoe minders, and entered another covered passageway, this one lined with alms-seekers insteads of stalls. It felt Dickensian, except this was India, not England, with its own kind of suffering, and the fact she was even using Dickens as a reference was its own ripple of colonialism. Noreen had only the five-hundred-rupee note, and wished she'd known to make change. One woman, admonishing a young girl to stay still as she braided her hair, had repurposed a yogurt container as her begging bowl, and Kabir dropped a ten-rupee note into it, as he'd done for the blind man and the one missing both legs and the woman with burn scars along her arms and face.

It was a relief to step into the courtyard, where in spite of the crowd, there was sky overhead, a little space to breathe. Red rose petals, fallen from the bags and plates carried by the devotees and crushed underneath the crowd's bare feet, carpeted the courtyard's white-and-black marble floor.

Kabir pointed to a large red archway. "That leads into the masjid, which was built in the fourteenth century. And in front of us is Hazrat Nizamuddin's tomb—the beating heart of it all."

The marble tomb had a striped dome, its walls ornamented with gold and lit by the electric lamps that hung between its pillars. The tops of these pillars were bright gold, and the scalloped archways connecting them were painted in greens and golds and decorated with Quranic verses. Like the all the important tombs she'd seen in Delhi so far, this one sat on an elevated platform. Unlike the others, it was built on a modest scale, the tomb itself the size of their living room, the platform only one step off the ground.

"Why don't you wait here," Kabir said, "and I'll buy us some offerings."

Noreen stood like a statue among the sea of devotees, their competing currents forced to flow around her. Nearby, four women spanning three generations, two girls, their mother and grandmother, formed a circle on the ground. They were dressed in bright clothes, silver-fringed dupattas framing their narrow faces. The elder daughter held the younger, a scrawny infant, in her lap. The mother was young to have two kids and the grandmother was withered, not so much her skin but her bones, brittle and curving and caving in. All of them were underfed; a tableau of malnourished women, from birth to death.

Her view of the family was blocked by two young blond women dressed in flowy printed blouses and peasant-style skirts, colorful cotton scarves draped loosely over their heads. They were nodding intently as they listened to their guide, an Indian hipster with square black glasses and a chiseled goatee.

Kabir returned, holding a Styrofoam plate of rose petals with two red-and-yellow threads resting on top, and the guide happened to look their way.

"Kabir!" he said, and came over, the young women following.

"Hey, Lal," Kabir said. "Long time. Meet my friend Noreen."

Lal nodded at Noreen. "Hello. This is Hannah and Mila, from Hamburg."

Hannah and Mila said their hellos, then Hannah told Lal, "We'd like to take some photos of the entrance to the mosque."

"Yes, you must," Lal said. "I'll meet you there in one minute."

"The heritage walks are going well, then?" Kabir asked.

"Khoob. Moved out of my parents' flat and into my own place last month," Lal said. "And I charge double for private walks like this. Kam se kam I book three private tours a week, one hundred percent word of mouth."

"Your reputation precedes you."

Lal came closer, lowering his voice. "These firang girls, they love my walks. My Nizamuddin dargah and Agrasen ki Baoli walk, one hundred percent guaranteed to get me laid." He glanced at Noreen. "No offense, huh?"

"Uh-hunh," Noreen said.

"Chalo, I should go. Nice meeting you, Noreen."

"Isn't he charming," she said after he'd disappeared into the crowd.

"We call him Launda Lal. He's at Delhi University, getting a master's in medieval history and chasing skirt."

"What's the other place he said, Agras something?"

"Agrasen ki Baoli. It's a fourteenth-century step well. It's quite lovely, but never go on a weekend because it's chockablock with couples doing romantic photo shoots. Even though it's haunted. You ready to seek blessings from the saint?"

"Yes," she said. "But you have to explain to me what to do."

"Well, only men are allowed inside the tomb—"

"Shocking," she said.

"It is, actually. Hazrat Nizamuddin used to meet directly with both his male and female followers and held them to the same standards of piety. One of his famous quotes is, 'When a lion comes out of its den no one stops to ask, Is it male or female?'"

He sounded quite cool, Hazrat Nizamuddin. Noreen knew little about Sufism, or Sufi saints. In the one year she'd attended Sunday school at the masjid, they'd mentioned masturbation but never mysticism.

"So if I can't go inside his tomb, what do I do?"

"Take one of these red-and-yellow threads, go up on the platform to one of the tomb's jalis, say a prayer for your khala, and tie the thread onto the jali."

"What's a jali?"

"See those big marble lattice screens on all sides of the tomb? Those are called jalis. Notice how on each one people have tied threads to the lattice."

It sounded simple enough.

Kabir left to join the line of men and Noreen made her way to the tomb and stepped onto the platform. Devotees clung to every jali, and no one seemed in a rush to leave. To even approach one of the jalis required weaving your way through the bodies occupying the platform, women reading Quran, praying, daydreaming, chatting, one woman swaying in a trance.

Tying this thread would require some stealth and aggression. When a devotee who'd been clinging to the closest jali turned to leave, Noreen moved as nimbly and quickly as possible and was almost there when her foot brushed a woman's shoulder. The woman yelped in annoyance, then began to berate her. She looked old and frail, but her voice was strident and sharp.

Noreen, holding on to the jali, said, "Maaf kijiye, I'm really sorry."

Hoping this would solve it, she pressed herself to the jali to secure her spot. Through the carved gaps she could see inside the tomb, where the male devotees circled the cloth-draped sarcophagus, setting their offerings of gold-fringed green scarves and platefuls of rose petals on top. She touched her forehead to the lattice.

Bismillah ar-rahman ar'rahim. Dear Hazrat Nizamuddin, I ask for blessings for Sonia—

A hand smacked her leg. "Oy!"

The woman she'd brushed with her foot resumed her rant at Noreen. Noreen tried to understand—something about how Noreen's foot had touched the woman's shoulder and now Noreen was standing between her and the jali, which wasn't exactly fair because one, the woman had chosen to situate herself right in front of the jali, making it difficult for others to reach it without disturbing her, and two, unlike the other two women at this jali standing with arms wide, Noreen was trying to take up as little space as possible.

"I'm so sorry. Main ek minute mein jaoge," Noreen said, realizing too late she'd referred to herself in both the wrong person and gender.

Her apology, and perhaps her grammar, incensed the woman further, and also riled the woman's two companions. Together, they formed an angry chorus. She wished she knew what they found so offensive about her so she could try to fix it. Was it her clothing, the fact she couldn't keep her dupatta on her head? Or something more intangible? Privilege? Skepticism? Foreignness?

She needed to block out these women until she'd tied the thread for Sonia Khala. Focus, Noreen told herself as she looped the thread around one edge of a six-pointed star.

The woman hit her leg once more. Noreen jumped, rubbed her stinging calf. The thread was gone, but she didn't dare get down to look for it. The women raised their voices again, and this time she ran until their voices faded. She imagined the old woman finding her thread and thinking, *That chickenshit, overnourished Amreeki girl, she couldn't manage to tie a simple thread.*

She managed to cross the platform only to discover she'd gone in the wrong direction. In front of her was another tomb, a four-walled marble enclosure open to the sky. Here, the people at the jalis were not praying, but watching. She'd meant to leave the dargah, message Kabir where she was, but then she heard moaning from inside the tomb, a feral and guttural lament. She walked to the jali and looked through it into the tomb, where three women, spread out amid the three marble sarcophagi, were engaged in a form of synchronized madness. Along the wall opposite, a moaning woman clawed at her face and chest as if trying to dig her way inside. As her moaning intensified, the woman lying lengthwise along the middle sarcophagus rose to kneeling, arched her back, and began slapping the ground with such force she shattered her bangles. As she lay back down on top of red shards of glass, the third woman, who'd been slumped like a rag doll in the corner, stood up and started to swing her long, dark hair, back and forth, back and forth, then in circles. As the woman spun her hair faster and faster, round and round and round, Noreen felt compelled to watch, even though it was making her dizzy, even as she silently pleaded with the woman to *please stop please stop please stop*.

The woman went limp, arms dangling, hair sweeping still. Show over, the onlookers began to drift away from the jalis, but Noreen kept watching the woman. *What happened to you*, she thought.

The woman lifted her head. Her hair parted, and Noreen saw her own face looking back at her.

Noreen blinked. No. It was a momentary lapse, a trick of the eye. This woman was nothing like her; a good ten years older, at least, with a small forehead, deep widow's peak, gaunt cheeks, pointed chin.

Someone nearby was speaking in accented English, and Noreen moved toward the comforting sound of her mother tongue. It was Lal, the tour guide, talking to the Germans—what were their names? Meeting them seemed like a lifetime ago.

"Though born a few centuries later, the Mughal princess Jahanara was a devoted follower of Hazrat Nizamuddin Auliya. This devotion is reflected in how close she's buried to his tomb. It is a longstanding tradition that women who believe themselves to be possessed by jinn come to her tomb to seek blessings and solace."

"But these women seem mentally ill," one of the German girls said. "Shouldn't they be receiving psychiatric treatment?"

Lal smiled. "You have to understand that, if you take India as a whole, there is approximately one psychiatrist for every thirteen thousand people. For many women, the blessings of Princess Jahanara and Hazrat Nizamuddin are their only hope."

Someone touched Noreen's shoulder and she cried out, not recognizing her own voice.

"Hey, hey," Kabir said, pressing one hand to his chest in apology. "It's me."

Kabir had found her.

Thank Allah, Thank Hazrat Nizamuddin, Thank Ganesh, Thank Mother Earth, thank them all.

"Are you all right?" he asked.

"Better, now that you're here."

"What happened?"

She knew she would not be able to answer his question properly as long as they remained in the dargah. "Can we get out of here?"

"Of course. Do you want to go home?"

She shook her head.

"I have to pick up my car. How about we do that, get kati rolls from Khan Market, and go eat them someplace quiet?"

She loved that he always knew what to do. "That sounds perfect."

Kabir opened his fist to reveal the two bright red rose petals lying side by side on his palm. "First, let's each have one of these. Blessings from the saint."

twelve

Air Quality Index: 221. Very Unhealthy.

THEY STOPPED AT KHAN Market for kati rolls, which were like handheld Indian burritos, and Kabir ran into three different people he knew. Noreen lived in a New Jersey suburb of 25,000 and didn't run into people with the frequency that Kabir did in this city of twenty million. Kabir said Delhi contained many different worlds, and the privileged ones were their own kind of provincial.

It was the tail end of rush hour, which meant incessant horns and stalled traffic and nearly an hour's drive to get to Kabir's friends' graphic design office. In the car, Noreen listened to Goan jazz, grateful that Kabir was letting her be. Her mother would have been peppering her with questions. What happened? What went wrong? But it felt less like *doing* something wrong than *being* something wrong. And why should that surprise her? Here, she was people she'd never been. A girl who looked Indian but clearly wasn't. A girl who wished she could make herself less apparent, a girl so very conscious of *being* a girl but who still couldn't get her goddamn genders right. A girl who'd failed at fulfilling her aunt's dream.

After the album ended, Kabir asked if she had any requests, and she turned down the volume and told him what had happened, beat by beat, beginning, middle, ending with the fleeting, climactic moment when the woman bore her own face. "Isn't that crazy?"

"Unusual, but not crazy," he said. "Do you know how many strange, ajeeb o gharib things have happened at that dargah, from when Hazrat Nizamuddin was alive until now? Maybe it was some kind of message."

"From who? The Mughal princess or the saint?"

"Either one? Both?" he said.

"And what's the message?"

"Maybe . . . maybe that we all have something we need to release or express. Whipping her hair was that woman's way."

"So I need to find my own version of whipping my hair?" Noreen said.

"Perhaps. But it could also be simple as a trick of the eye. Not everything has to mean something."

"Even at the dargah?"

"Even at the dargah. We're here. I'll park and then it's a ten-minute walk."

They entered another urban village. Sixty years ago, Kabir

told her, this area had been mainly grazing land. Now it had been absorbed into the city, paved over with cement. Along the narrow lanes, multistory concrete buildings stood shoulder to shoulder. A tangled canopy of electrical wires stretched across opposing balconies, some dipping so low Noreen could almost touch them. It was evening, but there were more stray dogs out than people. The street was lit with harsh fluorescent lamps. She hated this light; it reminded her of visiting Sonia Khala in the hospital.

In the midst of concrete, they came upon an old banyan tree, a lonely remnant of the neighborhood's rural past. At its base was a makeshift altar with a few small statues of gods, clay diyas, the stubs of burned incense sticks. A few feet away, dozens of empty incense boxes littered the ground.

"If trees get depression, then that tree is probably depressed," Noreen said.

"Look at our sky," he said. "Every tree in Delhi must be depressed."

They went deeper into the village, passing a group of young women chatting in front of an ornate iron gate with a sign that said *Ladies PG Housing* and a burger joint called Bunderful Burger, an extended family taking up the one long table inside. A few doors down, a saddled white donkey was tied to a post, its head hung low.

As Noreen regarded the woeful donkey, a scooter came gunning from behind, almost scraping Kabir's side. On it were four young men, two of whom were holding liquor bottles in paper bags. As Kabir moved closer to her, she thought of the lipstick pepper spray in her desk drawer, its utter futility in two against four. The guys whooped as they turned the corner, and she was glad when Kabir stopped in front of a squat, unmarked building and pushed open the door.

They entered a small lobby, the walls streaked red from people spitting betel, and took a rickety elevator to the fourth floor. It opened directly into a modern, loftlike office. A large sign featuring a winking purple cat in a turban welcomed them to Purple Cat Productions. The office had a start-up vibe, an open layout, a stocked kitchen, a foosball table. Near the entrance, candid Polaroids of hipster young people covered an entire wall.

In the lounge area, two girls and a guy were hanging out, drinking beers. They waved, calling Kabir's name in unison.

"Everyone, meet my friend Noreen," Kabir said. "Noreen, this is Yasmeen, Tara, and Varun, cofounders of Purple Cat Productions, the coolest new design firm in India."

"This is why we keep him around," Varun told Noreen, his voice projecting across the room. Noreen guessed he was one of those people you first heard coming. He sat with his legs splayed on a red stuffed chair shaped like a hand. Yasmeen was slouched at one end of the purple velvet sofa. She still had her backpack on and was using it as a kind of cushion, her long legs resting on Tara's lap. Abby would have appreciated Tara's style: knee-high combat boots, a black lace dress with a high collar, dramatic eyeliner, a short, sharply angled haircut.

"Nice to meet you all," Noreen said.

"I'll grab a beer," Kabir said, walking over to the kitchen. "Noreen? Anything?"

"Water, please."

"Sit," Tara told Noreen, gesturing at the cane love seat piled with Bollywood pop art cushions.

"Are you from the States?" Yasmeen asked.

"I am." Noreen always sounded semi-apologetic when saying this. "Are you all from Delhi?"

Tara stuck her thumb out at Yasmeen and Varun. "These two are. I'm from Manipur. Heard of it?"

When Noreen had first moved here, she'd been surprised by how many people from East and Southeast Asia lived in Delhi. After googling Nagaland and talking to Kabir, she learned that many of them were not expats from Asia but rather Indians from the Northeast of India, an area of once independent tribal confederacies that were colonized by the British and became part of India, and where a lot of people had East Asian features. Before coming here, Noreen's imagination of India consisted of North and South. None of the Indian novels she'd read or the Bollywood movies she'd seen featured people or settings from the Northeast.

"I know Manipur is a state in the Northeast," Noreen said, grateful that earlier this week she'd reviewed a map of India with Kabir.

"Just the other day, Noreen and I were discussing racism against people from the Northeast," Kabir said. "It doesn't get much airtime in America."

"It gets no airtime here, either," Varun said. The right third of his head was shaved, the rest spilling over with curls.

"You may think this what I look like," Tara said, "but I'm actually the spitting image of Priyanka Chopra."

The others snickered, and Noreen looked to Kabir for translation.

"They made a Bollywood movie about Mary Kom, the legendary Olympic boxer from Manipur, but instead of casting an actual Northeastern actor to play her, they cast Priyanka Chopra," he explained.

"They do that in Hollywood too, cast white actors to play minorities—whitewashing, they call it," Noreen said.

"This is so-called Indian washing," Yasmeen said. "Because most people from the Northeast look 'Chinese,' they aren't 'Indian' enough to be Indian."

"Do you know they put prosthetics on Priyanka's eyes to try to make her look like Mary Kom, but then they were scared the prosthetics would fall out in the boxing match scenes," Tara said.

Varun pretended to throw punches, then slapped his hands over his eyes. "Help, help, my eyelids have fallen!"

"Oh God, Varun, I need to smoke a joint before I hear another one of your jokes. Tere bal mein kuchh maal hai?" Yasmeen said.

"Mere bal mein kya nahin hai?" Varun reached into his hair

and pulled out a joint from behind his left ear. "Let's have some happy talk, yaar. We've been talking about depressing stuff all eve."

"Like what?" Kabir asked.

"Like I was talking to my brother this morning, and he was telling me when he takes the train, he doesn't dare to even eat chicken," Yasmeen said.

Noreen remembered the first time she heard about a train attack. After some passengers had gotten into an argument with two Muslim boys about seat assignments on a train, a mob formed, accused the boys of eating beef, and butchered them with knives. The younger boy, aged fifteen, bled to death in his elder brother's lap. The lynching was covered by the Western media, and they'd talked about it over dinner at her grandparents', Azra clucking her tongue as she did when something was too tragic for words. Only after living here did Noreen realize the regularity of such lynchings.

"My mother again told me the other day to take down the Ayat al-Kursi hanging in my car," Kabir said.

"I know a mob is a mob, but you're only a quarter Muslim, and your name can pass for either," Yasmeen said. "My brother's name is Hassan Ibrahim."

"But Kabir's circumcised," Varun said. "If they pull his pants down, he's done for."

Noreen didn't know where to look.

"Varun!" Tara said.

"He's right," Kabir said.

Varun handed the lit joint to Yasmeen. "Hell, I won't eat meat on a train and my name is Varun Sharma."

"I have nightmares about it," Yasmeen said. "If lynchings are becoming normalized, what next?"

"It's not so much better in America," Noreen said. "We've normalized school shootings."

"Don't worry," Tara said. "We've never looked to America for moral high ground."

"The lesson is to enjoy life while you can." Varun lifted his lighter, pressed it thrice before it lit. "The right spark, and India, the whole world will go up in flames."

Tara shook her head. "Ths is your version of happy talk?"

"By the way, Tara," Kabir said, "I hear congratulations are in order."

"Why—because I came out to my family?"

"Did it go well?" he said.

Tara rolled her eyes. "It went okay, except I have to *keep* coming out to them, like every week."

"I told her she should set up an automated monthly message to her parents. Hello, Mama, Papa. Yes, I am still gay, love you, bye," Varun said.

They laughed. Yasmeen blew out a smoke ring. It hung in the air for a moment, dissipating as she spoke. "Oh, Kabir, I read a nice interview with your father the other day. How are your parents doing?"

"Good," Kabir said. "Listen, I was hoping to show Noreen the view of the Qutub from the terrace."

Varun waved them off. "Please. Our casa es su casa."

The terrace had tall screens on either side for privacy. There was space for a few plants, a small cane table, and two wood recliners—the kind you'd find at a fancy swimming pool. It boasted a clear view across to the Qutub Minar, a thirteenth-century tower that was once the heart of Delhi. Noreen had visited the monument with her mother. The minar had five narrowing stories, decorated with carved bands of red sand-stone and dark red, honeycombed balconies. Up close, Noreen had been awed by the intricacy of the carvings, the beautiful flowers and scrolling vines, calligraphic Quranic verses and arabesques.

Seeing it from a distance, at night, was its own magic, the minar illuminated and ethereal, the top of it almost kissing the sliver of moon.

"Now that's a phallus I can get on board with," Noreen said.

Kabir laughed. "I really love it here, at night. I think about the medieval travelers to Delhi, how they would see the minar from afar and know they were close, like a beacon for home."

"That is lovely."

She watched as he lit the candle on the table. It was in a glass jar, a mini Christmas-style wreath around its neck. He untied the black plastic food bag, handed her a napkin and one of four kati rolls. It had become cold but was still delicious, the mutton tikka succulent and juicy and nicely spiced, the paratha fresh and flaky.

She cleaned some chutney from her chin with a napkin, which felt rough and waxy against her skin. "Your friends seem nice."

"Yeah, they're cool."

"My mom has a close-knit group of friends, mostly from college and grad school. She worries that I don't have enough friends. She was hoping it would change in college."

"And then you didn't even go."

"It's good I deferred. I wasn't in the right space to make friends. What would I have led with? Hi, I'm Noreen; my heart is a hole."

He smiled. "That's kind of how you led with me."

"You led with writing a letter to the jinn!"

"I did open the door to heavy."

"But it felt good to write that letter. Thank you."

"Welcome. Are you feeling better now, about what happened at the dargah?"

"Yeah."

"It's also my fault," he said. "Thursday is supposed to be the most blessed day at the dargah, but that makes it the most crowded. The dargah may be a sacred space but it's not always a generous one. If you'd like, we can go back, early on a Monday morning or something, when it's more peaceful, and you can tie the thread for your khala. And I should also take you to Chirag Delhi."

"What's Chirag Delhi?" she asked.

"It's a much more chill dargah, of a Sufi saint known as Chirag Delhi, the lamp of Delhi. The light is a symbol of the divine, and the Sufis believe that the path to God is lit by the lamp of your heart; the light within."

This reminded Noreen of a Rumi quote she'd heard at a wedding of one of her mother's work friends, something like, *If there is light in your heart, you will find your way home*. Funny, how white people loved Rumi but conviently forgot he was Muslim.

"I'd like that," she said, "to go back to Nizamuddin when it's quiet, and Chirag Delhi, too. Also, what happened at the dargah isn't your fault. If anyone's, it's mine. I think it triggered something in me."

"Like what?"

A scooter barreled down the lane below, the riders' hollers ripping through the quiet.

"Well, for starters, I have some daddy issues," she said.

"Don't we all?" he said. "You've met mine."

"But your dad is present, physically, at least."

"Ah." Kabir sat up to face her. "Is yours—"

"No, he's alive. My parents split before I was born. He lives close by, in New York, but we don't have a relationship. I saw him a few years ago, and he basically told me I'm better off without him, and though it's probably true, it still stings. When those women were yelling at me, deep down, I was like, you can't speak Hindi, you can't move through this space properly, who do you think you are, you're not that funny, you'll never write again, isn't it obvious why your dad doesn't give two shits about you?"

For one brief but glorious moment, Kabir rested his hand on her knee. "That woman was initially upset because she took it as an insult that you touched her shoulder with your foot. But you apologized, and the reasons they kept yelling, it had to do with them, not you. You see the lives most women have here, how they're treated by men; even money doesn't save you from it, and imagine if you have none. You were their scapegoat for something beyond your control. Are you okay? Here, have this."

She took the extra napkin from him, used it to dab her eyes, blinked away the last of her tears. A star, or maybe a planet, shone through the smoky haze.

"Wow," she said. "I can't remember the last time I cried. Usually I swallow my tears."

"Maybe that's why you're having a hard time writing," he said. "Your jokes are drowning inside all your swallowed tears."

"Yes. I need to aim for the right salt water to jokes ratio. Gotta at least keep the jokes floating on top."

"Like lotuses."

Noreen laughed. "Exactly. You know, as upsetting as it was, I'm glad I went to the dargah. I think what happened happened for a reason. Which is ironic, because I used to be more of a deadpan cynic. But after Sonia Khala died, I felt more of a desire to believe in something, you know, but I didn't know what. And

I still don't know what, except that I do believe there's more to the world than what we can see."

As she unwrapped her second kati roll, she became conscious of Kabir looking at her. She swallowed, licked the chutney from her front teeth.

"I hope you're liking Delhi, then," he said.

"Very much. Don't you?"

"Of course. It's my home. But I need to get out of my parents' shadow. If it weren't for my naani, I would have left. I thought as long as she can remember me, I should stay. Now the doctor says in six months, we won't recognize her, either."

She could hear herself breathe; even the dogs had gone quiet. If they kept talking about depressing stuff, they'd never kiss. She felt his eyes on her, this time turning to meet his gaze. He was smiling.

"What?" she said.

"You're so beautiful, Noreen," he said.

He put his hand on her cheek and pressed his forehead to hers, their eyelashes almost meeting. She set her roll aside, glad she'd requested no raw onion.

"I've wanted to kiss you since the day we met," he said.

After weeks of pent-up longing, of dreaming of the first and thousandth kiss, she rejoiced in this confirmation that she had not been alone, that in his own dreams, he'd been kissing her back. Emboldened, she gently pushed him against his seat, but as she went to straddle him, she misjudged the width of the recliner, and Kabir had to hold her hips to prevent her from toppling off one side.

"You okay?" he said.

She rubbed her right thigh. "I'm fine, though I'll have a nasty bruise tomorrow. What can I say? It's hard to be bold *and* smooth."

He laughed. "I wish I could take a photo of this," he said, lifting his hand from her hip to brush the hair off her face. "You, the minar, and the moon."

She leaned forward to kiss him. There they were, together at last, from the dream world to this one, two lovers interwined, framed by a poisoned indigo sky, lit by a solitary candle and the benevolent glow of the crescent moon.

thirteen

Air Quality Index: 182.

Unhealthy.

Adi Uncle: *What are you doing?*

Noreen: *Eating the delicious breakfast Sarita made.*

Adi Uncle: *What.*

Noreen: *Aloo puri.*

Adi Uncle: *Another day at Downton.*

Noreen: *Ha yes.*

Adi Uncle: *How goes it with your new boyfriend?*

Noreen: *He's not officially my boyfriend, but great. When are you coming to visit?*

Adi Uncle: *Let's see. Might try to finagle something. Have to make sure I approve of Kabir.*

Noreen: *Haha. You will!*

Adi Uncle: *(typing . . .)*

Noreen: *Dude.*

Adi Uncle: *What.*

Noreen: *Mom's getting ready and I heard her singing.*

Noreen looked up to thank Sarita, who'd come out of the kitchen with two freshly fried puris and stood with her head cocked toward the direction of Ruby's singing.

"Aaj subah Ruby kaafi good mood mein hain," Sarita said as she set down the plate.

Her mother, who'd amped up the chorus, was indeed in a very good mood this morning. Noreen thanked Sarita and dabbed two napkins' worth of excess oil from the bread, not that it mattered; she'd still be paying her dues on the toilet later.

Adi Uncle: *What song?*

Noreen: *I think I know but let me get closer. Hold on.*

As she crossed the living room toward her mother's door, Ruby went quiet. Noreen raised an eyebrow at the painted marble statue of Ganesh. The elephant-headed god regarded her with his ever-placid expression, a faint aroma of coconut wafting from his feet. He was the centerpiece of the slender rosewood table along the living room's back wall, halfway between either bedroom door. In the mornings, Sarita attended to him first, applying a fresh red tika to his forehead and replacing the offerings on the small silver tray at the base of his feet: betel nuts and leaves, shredded coconut, the occasional marigold.

Ruby resumed her singing.

Noreen: *She's singing "Friday I'm in Love."*

Adi Uncle: *The Cure before coffee?*

Noreen: *Yup. Gotta go, she's coming. Will report soon.*

149

Adi Uncle: *Okay.*

Her mother had had a few boyfriends over the years, but only one important enough to warrant an introduction. "You and I have a good thing going," Ruby had said to her once, "and I'm not going mess with it for just any Tariq, Diego, or Hari." But Miles was not just any guy, he was her first boyfriend, first kiss, first love. They'd dated for a few impassioned months in high school, writing each other long letters and exchanging mixtapes. Given how strict Azra and Jameel were, the time they actually spent together was precious and all too brief. One day, a suspicious Azra tore apart Ruby's room, found the mixtapes Miles made her (all except the latest one, which was still inside her school backpack), tied them in a plastic bag, then left the house and threw the bag in an undisclosed public trash can because she didn't trust Ruby not to dig them out of their garbage. Miles left for Stanford, then Ruby for Penn, and they lost touch. When, a few years ago, Miles, now an astrophysics professor in New England, had reached out on Facebook and asked her to dinner, Ruby bought a tape recorder and listened to the last surviving mixtape on repeat. He was recently separated, had two tow-headed kids, was teaching at Columbia for the year. They had one dinner, then another, and Ruby said it felt like a combination of curling up with an old, cozy blanket and soaring through space. Convinced it was fate, her mother fell fast, sang "Pictures of You" and "A Forest" while spooning coffee into the stove pot espresso. Noreen had liked him—he was nice and geeky and fond of bad puns—but most importantly, when Ruby looked at him her eyes shone. Her mother's eyes kept shining, until six months later, when, as she was walking out of Barnes & Noble with a book on blended families, Miles called to tell her he was going to try to make it work with his wife.

And now here she was, singing The Cure once more.

Ruby came out humming the jazz riff from "The Lovecats," spun around once, took the plate of aloo fried with cumin from Sarita's hands and bumped her hip against hers.

"Good morning, Sarita! Good morning, my darling daughter!" she said.

Noreen and Sarita looked at each other.

Ruby sat down opposite Noreen, asked Sarita for some plain toast, and poured herself coffee. "That aloo puri looks good."

Noreen slid the puri across. "Have some."

"I can't; it'll put me on the toilet later."

"If that's your criteria, you might as well starve."

"I'm out in the field today visiting a slum and a landfill with an NGO that works with garbage pickers. Can't mess with the long intess."

"Garbage pickers? You should take some photos for Tammy to share with her church," Noreen said.

"#thanksforthecrayons?"

They laughed. Noreen leaned back, arms folded, and jutted her chin toward her mother. "So?"

"So?"

"You tell me, jolly Punjabi," Noreen said.

"Hey. It's always a Punjabi wedding somewhere in the world."

"Mom. Spill it. Adi Uncle and I need to know."

Ruby grinned, cupping her mug with both hands. "Ask me what a poop deck is."

"What's a poop deck?"

"A poop deck is a deck over the cabin at the stern of the ship, from where the captain can see most of the ship and bark out orders."

Noreen wrinkled her forehead. "Does this mean you—"

"Met a sailor? Yes!" Ruby said with a clap of the hands. "You know I went to a dinner party with Pooja and Camille last night?"

Since meeting at the art opening, Camille and Pooja had become her mother's besties. They drank on Fridays and took a yoga class every Wednesday, taught by a brusque Russian they'd nicknamed Lady Stalin.

"The one hosted by that gay designer?"

"Yes. There's this guy at the party, he looks like a model, hot body, chiseled face, but he has this long, shining hair, almost to the small of his back. Think male Indian Rapunzel, which would not normally be my thing, but we both reached for beers at the same time and boom! Electric. We started talking, and the next thing we know, it's after midnight. His name is Hari—"

"Tariq, Diego, and Hari!" Noreen said.

"A sign?"

"You tell me."

"Well, not sure about sign, but turns out this Hari's a sailor—a captain, actually. Hence, poop deck! He spends six months at sea, six months on land."

Noreen picked up a third puri but thought better of it. "Didn't you swear off men after Miles?"

"I know, but this is different. I like Hari, but there's definitely no long-term potential. He's a wanderer, adamant about never wanting to settle down, no wife, no house, no kids. He's back on ship around the first week of March, and we only have a few weeks left after that anyway."

"The first week of March! It's not even February yet. Plenty of time to get attached," Noreen said.

"Like you?" Ruby said with a wink.

Sarita returned with two pieces of toast. Ruby protested at the amount of butter and Sarita insisted she needed it because she was too thin.

"Man, I'm going to miss her," Ruby said.

Noreen's phone buzzed.

"Hey," she said. "Kabir sent me a link. Listen to this—Curator and Philanthropist Akash Chakraborty Accused of Repeated Sexual Misconduct."

"You don't say. Go on."

"Akash Chakraborty, the high-profile founder of the Mangata Arts Festival, has been accused of repeated sexual misconduct.

The Instagram account IndiaArtTimesUp has posted anonymous accounts from three women accusing Chakraborty of inappropriate advances, unwanted touching, and forcible groping and kissing. Several well-known artists, including video artist Rashid Abbas and sculptor Meena Bakshi—that's Kabir's mom—have announced they will withdraw from the Mangata Arts Festival unless Chakraborty steps down as director."

"How do you like them apples?" Ruby said.

"Chakraborty is the latest in a string of prominent artists, intellectuals, politicians, and Bollywood celebrities who have been called out by India's burgeoning MeToo movement. Chakraborty did not respond to requests for comments."

"What a piece of shit," Ruby said. She'd scraped off the extra butter into a pile at the side of her plate. "Good on those women for speaking out. I hope it prompts some actual change."

"At least people are talking about it," Noreen said.

"Yes." Ruby lifted her mug to her lips, making a face when she saw it was empty. "At the very least, I hope ass-thete Akash gets his due."

fourteen

Air Quality Index: 223. Very Unhealthy.

NOREEN WAS NAVIGATING THE uneven uphill footpath of the busy GK 1 market when she almost tripped over a step, to the mild amusement of a shop doorman whose tall navy turban was pinned with a teardrop costume brooch, the tips of his shoes and mustache curling emphatically upward. As she dusted herself off, a flyer taped to the wall caught her eye.

HEY, YOU!
YES, YOU!
GOT JOKES?
ANNOUNCING OPEN MIC COMEDY NIGHT
EVERY FRIDAY AT DEPOT!
SIGN UP AT WWW.DEPOTDELHI.IN

A few shops later, the footpath inexplicably ended, forcing her to step onto the road, three successive cars honking at her as if she had any choice in the matter. By the time she reached the café, she was simmering with outrage on behalf of all the city's pedestrians.

Kabir was already seated. He waved at her, folding the corner of the page before putting his book aside.

"That sidewalk!" she said. "It's built like a game of Tetris, up and down and up and down, and then suddenly it ends, and then it's up and down again—it's like they want to make walking as unpleasant and stressful as possible. Though I suppose it's my fault, for leaving my palanquin and manservants at home."

Kabir laughed. "Will a kiss help?"

They shared a quick peck across the table, and she showed him her calf. "I also tripped on the footpath. Thankfully, it was more embarrassing than painful."

He reached down to massage her leg. "You'll have a big bruise tomorrow."

"Huge." The sweet fact of him remembering this made her want to kiss him again, tamping any residual anger.

"Should I kiss it for you?"

She blushed. "Maybe later. Whatcha reading?"

He showed her. *A Guide to Understanding Dementia.* "I thought it might help me with Naani."

"How's she doing?"

"Lately she's been quite agitated, but today she had a good morning. I played her some Mehdi Hassan ghazals, which really seemed to calm her, and then we went for a leisurely walk and sat on a bench and watched butterflies for nearly half an hour. First one came, and then it summoned all its friends, and it was like they were putting on a show for her. One was a stunning iridescent blue, with wings that looked like they were made of lace. I really wanted to take a photo, but Naani's been getting upset when I bring out my camera."

"How many portraits have you taken of her?"

"In the past few months? Maybe a hundred. I should start developing them, but I've been putting it off." He rested his hand over hers. "I missed you."

"It's only been two days, silly," she said, though she'd missed him too. She noticed the music: "Vivir Mi Vida," one of Sonia Khala's favorites. Underneath the table, Kabir traced the jut of her ankle bone with his toe, and she played it cool by perusing the menu. The floor of the café was white subway tile. It reminded her of home. She wondered if they would ever play footsie in a café in New York, if their love story could sustain a change of location, a season two.

As she perused the café's selection of ethically sourced, house-roasted, single estate indigenous coffee drinks, someone said in peppy American English, "I love you too, Mom. Can't wait to see you!"

The girl seated two tables down got off the phone with her mother and returned to journaling, a set of three pens, red, purple, and green, laid out like silverware next to her leather-bound diary. Her blond hair was tied in a loose bun, a white Om-printed scarf wrapped around her neck. She wore a long cotton skirt and chunky silver bracelets, the blue-and-gold bindi on her forehead slightly off-center.

Marc Anthony gave way to Ed Sheeran's "Shape of You." "What is it with this song?" Noreen said. "I swear I've heard it like twenty times since I've come to Delhi."

In response to her derision, Kabir began lip-synching, channeling his inner boy band. He certainly had the right hair for it.

God, even his mock sexy was sexy.

She laughed, threw her cloth napkin at him. It hit his shoulder, but he was looking past her and didn't notice.

"Ankita?" he said.

The aforementioned Ankita was standing at a table catty-corner to them, her beet salad barely touched. She was lithe and beautiful and teary-eyed and seemed vaguely familiar, though Noreen couldn't place why.

"Kabu!" she said, clasping her phone to her chest. "You won't believe what's happened."

Kabir rose from his seat. "Kya hua?"

Ankita's neck was lovely and long, her cotton sari pleated in a manner that bared most of her stomach. There was no item of woman's clothing more flattering or sexy than a sari, and Ankita carried hers with effortless grace. As she made her way toward them, Noreen's own body began to feel leaden and awkward.

Kabir and Ankita hugged tight, and even after they separated, the way they continued to hold each other, Kabir's hands on her svelte waist, hers low on his back, implied a former intimacy. But why did she assume it was former? What made her think that Kabir and she were exclusive, that she was the only girl he was romancing in ruins? Had Kabir and Ankita also kissed first on the terrace, the minar as their witness? Had she made a mistake in trusting him—in trusting her own instinct to trust him?

"Tell me what happened," Kabir said to Ankita.

Ankita let go of Kabir, used her pallu to dab her tears. "It's Dara Khan."

Noreen had read about Dara Khan in the newspaper. He was an extremely popular student activist who spoke out openly against the government on behalf of the rights of minorities: Dalits, Muslims, Christians, Adivasis.

"What?" Kabir said. "What happened?"

"He was walking to participate in an event at Oxford Bookstore and two men on scooters rode by and shot him."

"Shit! Is he all right?"

Noreen was eye level with the flawless brown valley that was Ankita's stomach, no hair or bumps, nary a whisper of dirt in the belly button. Kabir was rubbing Ankita's silky arm.

They made a handsome couple.

"He's in the hospital, but they're saying he should be okay. One bullet hit his leg; the other missed, thank God. It's gone too far!" Ankita flung her hands, her eyes flashing with indignation. "Journalists and activists are being murdered outside their own houses, and now they've shot Dara in broad daylight near

CP. That's how empowered they're feeling. And we are all complicit!" The bells of Ankita's anklet chimed as she stomped her foot against the tile. "We must speak out or we will lose everything precious about this country!"

"Ankita, you are speaking out! Every article you write—"

"It's not *enough*—"

"Paige! I've been *dying* to talk to you!"

The girl two tables down had accepted a video call. She slipped her earphones in, and, not noticing the look Ankita shot her, so withering that Noreen shrunk from simply being in its periphery, continued to speak in loud American.

"Oh my God, Paige, it's been *so* awesome, words can't even describe it. No joke, this trip has changed my life. We painted an entire orphanage. Poor people here have like literally nothing, but they're happier than so many people in America who have, like, everything. They've been such an inspiration. I'm so grateful I came here; India has been such a blessing."

Ankita inhaled sharply. She walked up to the girl, her lustrous black hair sweeping to one side as she braced her palms against the edge of the table. It took a moment for the girl to notice her.

"Can I help you?" she said, taking out an earphone.

"You come here and it's all yoga retreat and paint a few walls for the less fortunate and isn't India amazing," Ankita said, her voice excoriatingly polite. "We don't need you to save us. India does not exist to bless you, or so you can post photos of you and all the happy poor brown orphans on social media. Do you even have a clue what the fuck is going on in this country? But why should you bother? Anyway, you've already done the greatest thing you'll ever do, which is be born a white American."

The girl's mouth hung open, her blue eyes damp and bulging.

It was harsh, but Noreen had to admire Ankita's mastery of the extemporaneous tirade.

Kabir touched Ankita's shoulder. "Chalo, Ankita, let's go."

Ankita looked as though she'd say something more, then brushed Kabir off and headed for the door.

"Sorry about that," Kabir said to the girl. "A friend of hers was shot today; she's quite upset." He turned to Noreen. "Come on, let's catch her before someone else gets scorched."

"Have a nice day," Noreen told the girl.

The girl watched them go, her phone poised to start filming in case Ankita returned for a takedown redux.

"You apologized to her, didn't you?" Ankita said to Kabir when they caught up with her. "Of course you did, you're Kabir. You know nothing I said was wrong."

"You frightened her," he said. "I know you're upset, but you'll get an ulcer if you keep this up. Thoda chill karna bhi seekho, take a break for a while. Remember that place we liked in Goa? Why don't you plan a trip there for a week, decompress?"

Noreen pictured Kabir and Ankita in a beach hut, their exquisite, naked bodies writhing underneath a mosquito net.

"My mom's in the middle of chemo; I can't leave her." Ankita had been losing steam, her body caving, conveniently, toward

Kabir. He gripped her shoulders, massaging them with his thumbs. She closed her eyes for a moment, then said, "I'm okay, really. I need to go make some calls. My piece on Dara is due tonight."

"Noreen and I can drop you," he said. "Arre—have I introduced you two? Sorry! Ankita, Noreen, Noreen, Ankita."

"Hi," Ankita said. "I don't usually make such a big scene, I promise."

"That's okay," Noreen said.

"I have Mum's driver with me, so I'll make a move. I'll call you later." Ankita kissed Kabir's cheek. "Bye. Bye, Noreen."

Kabir watched her walk away, his hands cradled behind his head. "She really is going to get an ulcer one of these days. She carries too much on her shoulders. Her idea of relaxing is having a glass of wine and making a list of her remaining goals for the year."

"Are you hooking up with her?" Noreen said. It came out nastier than she'd intended, and Kabir recoiled.

"What?"

"We haven't had the talk, you know, about if we're still hooking up with other people."

"I'm not hooking up with her, or anyone but you."

This should have made her happy; it was the answer she wanted, but instead it opened the door to more doubts.

"Noreen, what's the matter?"

"Have you ever hooked up with her?"

"Yes. We used to date."

She knew it. "How long ago?"

"We broke up last year."

Now she remembered where she'd seen her: on Kabir's Instagram. His feed was mostly landscapes and portraits, some shots with friends, but she'd been in some of the photos he was tagged in, though never the two of them alone.

"How long were you together?"

"Almost two years."

"Two *years*?" All the things she did not know about him, all the ways she could get hurt, stretched before her like a dark void. "Why didn't you tell me?"

Kabir ran his fingers through his hair. Noreen loved doing this to him, because it made his hair ever more fluffy and adorable, but now she understood that Ankita had also done so, a thousand times, more than she ever would, and probably better.

"It hadn't come up yet—we haven't talked about our exes."

"That's because I don't have any exes." Liam, but he didn't count, not like Ankita.

"I wasn't hiding anything, if that's what you're implying. Noreen." He reached for her, but she sidestepped him. "Why are you so upset? Is this only about Ankita? Is there something else I've done wrong? Come, let's go back in and talk about it."

"Sir."

It was a waiter from the café, his white uniform shirt too loose for his slim frame. "Sir, please, ma'am ka bill."

Kabir accepted Ankita's unpaid bill, and Noreen read it. One fresh lime soda, one beet salad plus tax, rupees 745.

He took out a credit card, but the waiter shook his head. "Sir, to pay by card you must come inside only."

"I'll be right back," he said to Noreen.

"I'm going to go."

"What? Why?"

Because I'm scared you're going to hurt me. Because right now I can't get the image of you and Ankita in Goa out of my head. Because she's way more beautiful than me and even though she was kind of a bitch to that girl she was an eloquent bitch with a point.

"I'm not feeling well," she said.

"This will only take one minute," Kabir said.

"Sir, bill, please," the waiter said.

"I'll call you later," she said. As will Ankita, she thought. Maybe we'll call you at the same time and then who will you choose?

She walked away, gave the finger to the auntie in sparkling sunglasses who honked at her as she crossed the road, climbed into the first in the line of autos waiting at the market entrance, did not attempt to bargain, though the auto driver quoted more than double the cost of her Uber here. She already felt cheated by the world—what was a hundred rupees more?

fifteen

Air Quality Index: 226. Very

Unhealthy.

IT DIDN'T TAKE LONG for Noreen to regret everything. Neither she nor her mother were ones for drama or raised
voices; Azra delivered enough of this for three generations. Her
usual response in the face of conflict was cold, polite retreat; she
may not sleep much that night, but she would not have yelled.
Replaying the scene, she cringed at the echoes of her grandmother in her accusatory tone, her dramatic departure. All Kabir
had been doing was comforting a distraught ex, an action that
exemplified the very things she cherished about him: empathy
and kindness and concern.

Her mother was home, thank God, smoking a joint on her
bedroom balcony, her feet up on the cane table, windshield wiping her legs to "Age of Consent" by New Order.

"Mom. I fucked up."

Ruby turned down the music, stubbed her joint in the

ashtray. "What happened?"

She began with Kabir noticing Ankita, backtracked to introduce the girl talking to her mom, returned to Kabir and Ankita. She tried to remember verbatim what Ankita said to the girl, had to paraphrase it except for the last line.

"Harsh indeed," Ruby said. "Also possibly true. Go on."

In the retelling, Noreen realized it wasn't quite as bad as she thought; she hadn't actually raised her voice, or stomped her feet, or said something terribly mean. What she had done was behave like a naive, inexperienced eighteen-year-old who'd never had a boyfriend and couldn't handle the fact that her boyfriend had an ex. Exes. "He's twenty-four; of course he had a life before me," she said. "I think maybe the real reason I was upset was because Ankita was a big, beautiful reminder that I've fallen for a guy I can never have."

"You have him now. What was it that Adi Uncle's mom used to say?"

"Remember the past, look to the future, but live in the moment."

"Has he messaged you?" Ruby asked.

"I turned my phone off to prevent me from texting in anger."

"How wise. Are you angry now?"

"Nope."

"So check."

Three WhatsApps from Kabir. **Did you reach home safely? Are you okay? I'm sorry. Can we talk about it? Call me.**

Her sweet Kabir. She wasn't sure how he'd survived his parents, who were so generous with criticism and spare with praise. She wanted to hug him, and comfort him, go down on him.

She wrote back. **I'm sorry! I'm not upset. Can you talk now?**

In a talk at IHC. Will call as soon as I can sneak out.

Okay!

It was going to be okay. She relaxed, put her feet up on the cane table. Because it faced the back, her mother's balcony was more private than their front terrace. On the roof of the house across, a stooped maid stood on a three-legged stool, hanging sheets to dry on a clothing line. In the alley below, one of their colony's well-fed stray dogs met her eyes as it squatted to take a shit.

You're in love with him, the dog said. *Admit it.*

Noreen thought of the woman at Princess Jahanara's tomb, of how Kabir had told her that many of the letters at Firoz Shah Kotla were written by young women desperate to marry the person they loved but whose family would not allow it because of differences in caste or class or religion. Maybe the derailing of love was what had led that woman to the dargah; better to be possessed by a jinn than exist in a world that will continually crush your heart.

"I think I'm in love with him," she told her mother.

"Duh."

"But also, I'm leaving. If it already hurts to even think about leaving him, how will it feel when it actually happens?"

"Gut-wrenching. But show me a person who hasn't known any sorrow and I'll show you a superficial," Ruby said in a thick Southern accent.

"What?"

"It's from *Streetcar.*"

"Ah." Her mother had played the role of Mexican Woman in her high school production of *A Streetcar Named Desire*. She'd had one line, singing out *Flores, flores para los muertos.*

"My point is, I wish I could tell you it won't hurt when you leave; it will. But that's part of it. So let yourself love, even if it'll hurt later. Don't try to be a superficial. Text him and tell him you're sorry. Invite him to spend the night this weekend."

"Really?"

"Well, you're not about to spend the night at his parents', are you?"

"No."

"And I'd worry about you hooking up in some dark corner somewhere. I prefer you here, where it's safe. Our bedrooms are conveniently located on opposite ends of the apartment. Speaking of safe . . ."

Ruby went inside. Noreen closed the balcony door to prevent the bad air from entering her mother's room.

A female servant turned into the alley, walking a golden Labrador in a mint-green sweater vest and silver collar. It stopped to sniff the stray dog's freshly laid shit pile, the servant crying "*Chee!*" and pulling at its leash.

Noreen closed her eyes, tilted her face upward. It was early February, and though the sky was still polluted and the nights remained chilly, the afternoons were beautiful, light breezes and warm, gentle sunshine. Here, she'd noticed, a lot of the trees lost their leaves in January and February. It reminded her of how foreign she was, not knowing the trees, when they shed and when they bloomed.

Ruby returned to the balcony holding a strip of three condoms. "Before we left, Divya told me to pack some condoms because Indian ones aren't as good. I have some lube too, if you want."

"Mom!"

"What? It's unopened."

Noreen squealed and covered her face.

"Hey," Ruby said, tossing the condoms into her lap, "you should be grateful you can talk to me about this stuff. I wasn't even supposed to *talk* to boys unless absolutely necessary. You know how I learned about the birds and the bees? Reading *The Thorn Birds* and *Flowers in the Attic* with a flashlight under the covers in middle school. Pale siblings committing incest in an attic is a pretty fucked-up way to learn about sex. And porn, forget it. You guys have the internet. You want to know what my porn was?"

"What?" Noreen said.

"My porn was this scene in the movie *A Room with a View* where George and Freddy and Mr. What's His Name bathe and run around a pond naked, and you can see their butts and glimpses of penis. This scene lasts for at least two whole wonderful minutes. I must have rewound and played it fifty times when my parents weren't around. That and *The Name of the*

Rose. A young Christian Slater plays this apprentice monk, and in one scene he has sex with this woman, and if you paused it at the exact right moment you could see his penis, full frontal. My friend Joanna and I used to pause it and put our hand on the TV screen and yell, 'We're touching Christian Slater's penis!'"

Noreen laughed. "Now that you mention it, I do remember that scene from *A Room with a View*."

"See? Memorable."

Her phone buzzed. A message from Kabir.

Hey call you in 5.

No worries, she wrote.

He responded by sending her "Shape of You."

Omg. Any song but that.

He sent her "(Everything I Do) I Do It for You" by Bryan Adams.

Bryan Adams?

Don't u know? Indians LOVE Bryan Adams. Then, now, forever.

Please tell me you're joking.

Nope. Google it.

She made a note to google *do Indians love Bryan Adams*.

You want to come over this weekend? As in spend the night?

It's cool with your mom?

Yup.

It's a date.

He sent a fire emoji, followed by two hearts.

With this much pollution, to live in Delhi, you need to operate on some level of denial, but the level of denial can be quite shocking. If it's AQI 170 in Delhi, people are like, what a beautiful day, let's eat outside, smoke some cigarettes. AQI 170 is shit air. If it's AQI 170 in Beijing, people wear masks. But AQI 170 in Delhi? Cigarette picnic! An auntie told me foreigners exaggerate and the pollution isn't that bad. I was like, so you can't see the entire sky is choking, but from twenty feet away you can see the zit on my nose and the fact I'd gained one inch on my hips.

sixteen

Air Quality Index: 114.

Unhealthy for Sensitive Groups.

LYING DOWN WITH HER legs splayed, Noreen learned the hard way that you should never get a Brazilian wax after eating a big bowl of rajma chawal for lunch. It took great bodily fortitude to control her kidney bean flatulence on behalf of the women waxing her, because of course there was not one, but two women waxing her crotch. One of the consequences of labor being so cheap in India was that tasks that could be completed by one person were often done by two or three or four, and not necessarily any more efficiently, which meant she was now half-naked underneath two women, one short and plump, a thick, oiled braid sitting over her shoulder, the other tall, with vitiligo patches across her face and neck. Braid would stir the wax, then Tall would apply it with a stick, then Braid would hold her skin taut while Tall ripped off the wax, then Braid would blow on her freshly waxed skin.

They were almost done with her labia. This time, when Braid blew, Noreen could feel her breath on her clitoris, which might have been vaguely erotic if it hadn't also been painful as fuck.

"Peeche bhi karna hai?" Tall asked when they'd finished with her lips.

Peeche meant back, which, in this case, referred to her backside.

"Yes, please," Noreen said.

Tall gestured for her to bring her knees to her chest, and Braid held her butt cheeks apart as Tall ripped off the wax. Her mother had warned this was the most humiliating but least painful part of getting a Brazilian. Noreen closed her eyes, praying that she would not release a lethal rajma fart, that it was all as clean as she thought back there, and that there was nothing untoward about her anus.

After it was over and she was mercifully alone, she sat in cobbler pose and took a closer look. She'd asked them to leave a sizable strip in front because a hairless pussy seemed about as attractive as a literal hairless pussy. She spread apart her labia, wrinkled, brownish-pink, and examined herself in the unforgiving fluorescent light. On the left side, between her labia majora and minora, she discovered a tiny birthmark.

She needed to tell Abby. When discussing matter of bodies and sex, they delighted in the details. Noreen had first realized they were going to be close when, at the Thai diner on their first friend date, Abby said, "Do you ever sniff your own underwear after a long day and think, man, I smell goooood?" and Noreen had laughed so hard she sprayed Thai iced coffee out her nose.

Noreen: *Survived my first Brazilian. TWO women waxed me. My life will never be the same. Also I discovered a birthmark on my labia—pretty cute.*

Abby: *Know thy vulva, know thyself. Though haven't you heard—a full bush is the new black. Wait—you had 2 women up your butt?*

Noreen: *Yup.*

Abby: *Wow. Nervous about tonight?*

Noreen: *Yes and no.*

Abby, being an expert in the totally random but apropos video response, sent her a bizarre music video of a song called "What What (In the Butt)." Noreen watched it in the Uber, laughing, forwarded it to Adi Uncle, then leaned her head against the window with a sigh. She wished Abby could visit her; whenever she tried to describe her life here, she felt she wasn't doing it justice.

As she shut the gate to their house, the gas she'd been holding back broke through in great, voluminous glory. Thankfully, no one was within striking distance. Geeta Auntie was relaxing on the patio. Ila, Raju's school-age daughter, was singing multiplication tables while pressing Geeta Auntie's calves.

"Two twos are four," Ila sang. "Two threes are six. Two fours are seven."

"Eight," Geeta Auntie corrected her. "Ila, you need to learn this if you want to be class topper this year. Noreen! Come have some chai."

"No chai for me, Auntie," Noreen said. "Really. I have to go make a phone call."

"Achcha suno, they are starting a laughing club in our colony. Every Wednesday evening in the park. You and your mother should come. Laughter is the soul's best medicine."

"Sounds good. Bye, Auntie!"

"Bye! Aage sunao," Geeta directed Ila.

"Two fives are ten," Ila sang. "Two sixes are twelve . . ."

Noreen dashed up the stairs straight to the pot, determined to clear out her system before the arrival of her beloved.

seventeen

Air Quality Index: 69. Moderate.

SHE'D NEVER HOSTED A boy in her bedroom
before. Liam and she used to meet at his place, a three-room
suite attached to his parents' McMansion that featured a private
entrance, a kitchenette, an entertainment system with surround
sound, and a pool table they'd only used for sex.

Her Delhi bedroom felt impersonal. She'd never have chosen
the drab brown curtains or clinical tube lighting. The furniture
was sparse: a wooden bed with a slim, hard mattress, a white
desk and chair. Almost an entire wall consisted of built-in almirah cabinets, with ample hanging space and multiple shelves and
drawers. Each drawer had a lock, as did all the almirah doors.
One of these doors had a mirror facing the bed, which was useful in figuring out which positions flattened her stomach while
flattering her breasts.

She adopted one of these now, cross-legged on the mattress
edges, leaning back with a slight arch, watching Kabir exam-
ine the three photos she'd taped above her desk. In the center,

Abby and Noreen made silly faces, their four zines splayed like a deck of cards in their hands. To the left, Sonia Khala, Amir, Sohail, and Noreen posed with cherry blossoms at the Japanese Tea Garden. To the right, a group photo from Ruby's birthday last year, when her mother's friends had thrown her a surprise EDP, Adi Uncle flying in from LA. EDP stood for Early Dance Party, a tradition Ruby had started when Noreen was around a year old and she finally had the energy to dance but still needed to be in bed by 10:00 p.m.

"You and your khala have the same chin," Kabir said.

"Did you know that we are the only animals with chins?" Noreen said.

"Really?"

"Sonia Khala told me that, the first time she took me to the San Francisco Zoo. That was also my first trip to San Francisco. I was so excited about it I kept everything—every ticket stub, my Muni pass, the fortune from my fortune cookie."

"What was the fortune?"

"'Learn to laugh at yourself. You'll always be amused.'"

Kabir chuckled. He picked up her Moleskine notebook that Abby had gotten her for graduation. She'd hoped to fill it with notes and ideas during her time in India, but every page except the first remained blank.

"You kept this too," he said.

He was holding the ticket from Firoz Shah Kotla that had been sticking out from the top of the notebook, though she could have sworn she'd tucked it in back.

The ticket read, *Visitor Type: Indian.*

A complicated story, in three words.

"Guilty," she said.

He smiled. "I kept mine as well."

This set off a heartmelt-lust synergy so powerful she thought *I'll die if I don't touch him right this second*, but he was on his way to her; he was on top of her. She hooked her legs around his hips, ran her hand through his hair. He told her a story about how he'd cried on his first trip to the Delhi Zoo because he'd found it so depressing, but she was only half paying attention, tracing the whorl in his stubble, observing the blackheads sprinkled across his nose, the cilia-like hairs on his ear cartilage, how the tips of his lashes nearly reached his eyebrows.

"Are you listening?" he said.

"Not really. I'm too distracted by your beauty."

She loved the way his Adam's apple asserted itself when he laughed. She loved all of it, his eyes most of all.

"So you're definitely not still upset?" he said.

"No! That was me second-guessing myself, paranoid about getting hurt. I'm not upset, I promise. And now you promise to stop apologizing."

Though it was Noreen who'd lashed out at him, he was the one still saying sorry. Kabir cared, to an unhealthy degree, about being likable. He'd told her how if a friend became upset at something he'd done, he'd become so upset that they were upset that the friend would end up feeling bad for him. It was a frequent bone of contention between his mother and him. To survive in the art world, Kabir, she'd tell him, you need a thicker skin.

"I promise," he said. "And you know I only want to be with you."

"I know."

He tapped the hollow between her collarbones. "You haven't written anything in that notebook yet?"

"Only the letter to the jinn. And a few sentences on my laptop that I promptly deleted. I was thinking maybe I should try to finish something old—I have so many half-finished pieces."

"I'm like that, too. I begin my projects very enthu, but—"

"Enthu?"

"Enthusiastic."

Indians and their love for abbreviations: senti for sentimental, enthu for enthusiastic, funda for fundamentals. "So you start out enthu, and then?"

"And then I start second-guessing myself: I think this is terrible, this is derivative, this will never work, no one will ever like it, and I stop."

"What about your photos of the sadhus in the mountains on your Instagram? Some of those images are really arresting." There were twenty or so, a few years back in his feed, stark black-and-white portraits of wandering holy men with ash-covered flesh and knotted hair and weathered faces, staring into the camera with ferocious intensity.

"You think so? Thanks. That project ended when I realized there were a dozen other stoner chaps in their twenties wandering around the Himalayas snapping black and whites of sadhus, that I was a walking cliché."

Noreen laughed. "Well, I still like them. And not everyone is going to like what you do, no matter what. You can't make art to please everyone."

"But what if it pleases no one?"

"I doubt that would ever happen. And I know your situation is complicated by your parents, though leaving Delhi will help that. All any of us can do is put our heart into it and give it our best. Nothing important in life comes with a guarantee."

"You're very wise."

She smiled. "Remember that the next time you see me trip and fall flat on my face."

Kabir excused himself to pee, returning with the half-empty box of nose strips from her bathroom counter. Since coming to Delhi, where the dust and pollution blackened everything from your snot to the soles of your feet, she'd become more diligent about exfoliation. "These get rid of blackheads? How does it work?"

"You stick it on your nose, then rip it off, and the blackheads are supposed to come off with it."

"Will you put one on me?" he asked.

"Sure. But you have to wet your nose first."

"Now what?" he said after she'd stuck the strip to his damp nose.

"Now you wait a few minutes for it to dry completely."

"Like the length of a song?"

"Sure."

"Dance?"

"Now?"

"Why not?"

He had a point.

"What song?" she asked.

"Do you know Fareed Ayaz?"

"The qawwali singer? One of his songs is on Sonia Khala's playlist."

"He's one of my favorites. I recently heard a good techno song with him and Hamza Akram as vocalists. You have a speaker? I'll play it."

Sonia Khala had been a traditionalist when it came to qawwali and used to trash the remixes, but Noreen thought the techno beat in this one worked well with the qawwali vocals. She could even make out a few words: *destiny, I drank from your eyes.* Kabir's dancing was endearingly enthu, and he was camping it up for her benefit, accenting his slightly maniacal, rhythmic movements with a comical Bollywood flair. *At least one of us isn't dancing with a limp*, she thought, and cheered as he jumped onto the bed. The sight of him, nose strip and all, performing exaggerated hip thrusts toward all four corners of the room, had her laughing too hard to dance.

When the song ended, she said, "Come down now. Your strip is dry."

"Is it going to hurt?"

"Nah. Now stay still."

Straddling his lap, she tore off the strip in one quick movement, keeping close to the skin.

"Ow!" he said.

"Do you seriously think that hurt?" She was about to add, do you have any idea what I got ripped off me today, but held back. He'd see it for himself soon enough.

"A little." He touched his nose. "Are they gone?"

"Mostly."

"Are you more attracted to me now?"

She kissed his nose. "If I was any more attracted to you, I might implode. I liked that song, by the way. What's the name of it?"

"'Mohe Pi Ki Najariya.'"

"What does that mean?"

"My beloved's gaze," he said.

"And what was that other word for beloved, the one the rose seller used?"

"Aashiq."

"Aashiq," she repeated carefully. "Will you speak to me more in Urdu? And Hindi?"

"You know they're pretty much the same, conversationally. And yes, I will speak it to you, if you speak it back."

"Maybe, if you promise not to laugh."

"I promise I won't—unless it's very funny."

She swiped at him playfully. He caught her hand, kissed it, placed it over his heart.

"Teach me another word for beloved," she said.

"Sajnaa. For a guy, you'd call him Sajan."

"Sajan," she repeated, and began to undo the top button of her kurta. "What else?"

He cleared his throat. "There are so many. You know Urdu is the language of love. Sayonee means soul mate. For beloved you can also say janam."

"Janam." She undid her second button. "What else?"

"Dilruba."

"Dilruba."

"Mehbooba."

"Mehbooba."

"Sanam."

"Sanam." She undid the fifth and final button, nestling her hips further against his. "What else?"

Kabir swallowed. "If you want to get very poetic, rashk-e-qamar."

"Rashk-e-qamar. What does it mean?"

"Envy of the moon."

"Envy of the moon," she said.

"I feel like we're in an Urdu soft porn video."

"Is it hot?" she asked.

"Hell yeah."

Noreen grinned and took off her top. He reached for her, and they fell back onto the bed, entangled, laughing.

eighteen

Air Quality Index: 107.
Unhealthy for Sensitive Groups.

NOREEN WOKE UP AT 7:30 a.m., naked and smelling
a lot like sex and a little like Kabir, sweat and semen and earth.
She checked to make sure Kabir was asleep, lifted her side of the
blanket, found the outline of the wet spot caused by her ejaculat-
ing during orgasm, and took a quick sniff. Inoffensive, with a
slight tang. Definitely not urine.

She went to the bathroom, switched on the geyser, and peed.
While waiting for the geyser to heat the water, she stood naked in
front of the mirror and recalled scenes from last night, watched
her nipples grow hard under the fluorescence. In the shower,
she lathered up, the smells of sex replaced with honey and apri-
cot, and sang "Thank U." Kabir had never heard the song, and
she'd played it for him last night in between their two rounds of
sex. The chorus had confused him. Why, after India, did Alanis
Morissette thank terror, disillusionment? According to Wikipe-
dia, the song documented Ms. Morrisette's spiritual awakening
while on a trip here. White woman found her guru, Kabir had

said, but pretty soon he was singing it too.

Thank you, India . . .

She wondered if she should wake Kabir with kisses, but they'd been up so late it seemed cruel. Instead, she closed the gap in the curtains, googled female ejaculation (the forceful expulsion of fluid through the urethra due to sexual arousal, containing similar enzymes to those found in male prostate fluid), got dressed, continued googling, and tiptoed out of the bedroom. She read that the clitoris had eight thousand nerve endings, something Abby had also told her, and was reading about how, in 2014, the UK banned female ejaculation from its porn, along with caning, when a deep voice said, "Good morning."

Noreen dropped her phone.

A man sat reading *The Indian Express* on the most uncomfortable sofa in the world, his feet up on the coffee table. He was wearing the white bathroom slippers her mother had filched when she'd visited the spa at the Claridge's hotel. He lifted his hand in apology. "Didn't mean to startle you."

She took in his long, dark hair, parted in the middle and tucked behind both ears, reaching past his chest.

Hari.

"Your mother's still asleep; I didn't want to wake her," Hari said. "You must be Noreen."

"And you must be Hari."

"Yes." He folded the paper with impressive efficiency and set his feet on the floor. Her mother's slippers almost fit him; she had large appendages.

Only now did she see her mother's WhatsApp message from last night. **Heads-up—Hari's staying over too.**

"Is your phone okay?" he asked.

"This phone case is indestructible. There's a video of someone driving a tractor over a phone with this case on it and the phone hardly has a mark."

"Was the tractor all right?"

Noreen laughed. "Would you like coffee? I was going to make some."

He gestured at the mug on the table. "Already did. There's more in the kitchen."

"Oh, cool. Thanks. I'll go help myself."

Noreen went to the kitchen and poured herself a cup. The man made good coffee. He also seemed very laid-back, which she appreciated, not least because it made this whole situation a little less awkward. She warmed up the coffee in the microwave, had the first sips on the little plastic stool, then returned to the living room to chat with her mother's lover.

"Good coffee," she told him. "Is there cardamom in it?"

"Yes. I crushed a cardamom pod into the coffee grounds."

Hari had traded the newspaper for a novel: *Wolf Hall* by Hilary Mantel.

She took the no less ugly but much more comfortable armchair across from the sofa. "How are you liking the book?"

"It's great so far," he said. "I've never read historical fiction written in the present tense."

"It's one of Sonia Khala's favorite books. She loved historical fiction. She said it gave her all the pleasures of fiction while expanding her knowledge of history. Sonia Khala is—was—my mom's sister."

"Yes," Hari said. "Your mom told me about her. Yesterday, she was telling me how she washed her body."

In Islam, female relatives were supposed to prepare a female corpse for burial. There were women at Sonia Khala's masjid trained to do it, but the deceased's female relatives were expected to assist, so Ruby and Imran Khalu's sister had helped wash and shroud Sonia Khala's body.

"What did she say?" Noreen said.

"That it was the most beautiful and difficult thing she'd ever done."

"I offered to help as well," Noreen said, not sure why she felt compelled to tell Hari this, "but everyone said I was too young." Instead, she'd sat on top of the car hood in the parking lot, listening to the extended version of "Purple Rain" on repeat. Later, her mother told her though she'd been nervous beforehand she was glad she'd done it, that it had given her a sense of closure. At the time, Noreen thought this ironic; how much more closure could you get than death itself? But now she understood; wasn't that what she was seeking, why she hoped to "see" Sonia Khala at the dargah, in her dreams?

Hari folded the edge of the newspaper with his long, elegant fingers, tore off a slender, even strip, and used it as a bookmark.

"I've never washed a dead body," he said. "But I did crack open my father's skull." Seeing her alarm, he added, "In the cremation fire. Cracking the skull open releases the body's soul."

"Ah." She recalled seeing this in a Bollywood movie, and decided it was probably wise to shift the conversation in a less macabre direction. "Mom says you're a captain?"

"Yes, for the merchant marines." He lifted a section of his hair and fanned it with his fingers. "That's why I'm allowed these tresses."

It had not occurred to her until then that sailors might have a regulation haircut. Her view of the seafaring life was a romantic one, mostly based on *Pirates of the Caribbean* and *The Witch of Blackbird Pond*. Almost every time she'd actually been on a boat, except for commuter ferries, she'd gotten seasick. She wondered if, knowing this, Hari would think less of her.

"When did you know you wanted to go to sea?" she asked.

"Oh, since I was a kid. My father took me to Bombay, and we visited the docks. I remember looking at all those ships and thinking, each of them is coming from somewhere and going somewhere. From that moment, I knew that I wanted to be on one. I joined the merchant marines right after college and have been with them ever since."

"No regrets?"

"Never. I love it. And now that I'm captain, I get so much time to myself. I can spend hours on monkey island. The times when the sea is gently rolling, you can convince yourself that the sky is moving instead of you, and lie back and watch millions of stars swim."

"Wow," she said. "What's monkey island?"

"The compass deck. The highest deck on the ship."

"It must be nice," she said, "to know what you want to do, and then know you made the right choice when you do it."

"What do you want to do?" he said.

"I've long dreamed of becoming an actuary," she said. "But apparently you have to be good at math."

His eyes narrowed. "Why do I think you're kidding?"

"I am kidding."

"You and your mother really enjoy taking the piss."

"But we do it with love," she said.

"Good morning!" Ruby said as she came out of the bedroom. "Nor-bear! You're awake?"

"The sun woke me up. Kabir's still asleep."

Ruby mussed Noreen's hair, walked over to Hari, and did the same to him. "What have you two been talking about?"

Hari smoothed his hair down and raised his eyebrows at Noreen. She smiled back.

"We were talking about the sea," Noreen said.

"Did he tell you the one about drinking cobra blood with vodka in Borneo?"

"Thought I'd save that for breakfast," Hari said.

"Ha. Speaking of, any coffee left?"

"I finished it," Noreen said.

"I'll make more," Hari said, but Ruby set her hand on his shoulder.

"You relax, I'll do it. I'll make some eggs, too." It was Sunday, Sarita's day off, the only day they cooked. Sarita had taught them her egg bhurji recipe and they'd started a tradition of EBS, Egg Bhurji Sundays.

"Need help?" Hari asked.

"I'll help," Noreen said, jumping up and following her mother into the kitchen. She removed the plastic doorstop, let the door swing shut.

"Did you have a good night?" Ruby said.

"Amazing. You?"

"Same."

They nodded at each other, a tacit agreement to leave the rest unsaid.

"I'll chop the tomato and the green chili *and* the cilantro if you'll do the onion," Noreen said.

"Deal."

Noreen was beating the eggs, which had lighter yolks and tasted better than the eggs back home, when the door swung open and Kabir walked in.

"Good morning, ladies," he said.

"Good morning." Ruby wiped a tear from her eye. "I hope you like egg bhurji and coffee."

"Love them. Tell me what I can do," he said. "Should I chop that other onion?"

"Go chat with Hari," Ruby said.

"Pukka? Sure I can't do something to help?"

"Go," Noreen said. "I'll call you if we need you. Mom—do you know where Sarita kept the lal mirch?"

"I think it's in the drawer to the left of the stove."

Noreen added a teaspoon of red chili powder to the eggs.

"What do you think they're talking about?" her mother said.

"I don't know, but they're both so easygoing I'm sure it's fine."

"This is a little weird, isn't it?"

"Kind of," Noreen said. "But, and I don't know if this is because we're in Delhi, it also feels weirdly normal."

"This is also true."

Hari poured mimosas for everyone but Noreen, and they gathered at the table. Kabir buttered the toast, and her mother ladled generous portions of egg bhurji on everyone's plates. The Morning After, Noreen thought. That would be the title of the episode. It would begin last night and end at breakfast. Or maybe it could begin at breakfast, completely normal, and work backward, becoming weirder as the night grew young. But it couldn't be all amazing. There would have to be some comic mishaps. Like maybe one of the guys walks into the wrong room.

Jesus, that was *terrible*, on multiple levels.

"This egg bhurji is delicious," Kabir said.

"It's even better than my mother's," Hari said. "She would die if she heard me say that. Sorry, Ma."

"Thanks," Ruby said. "Our maid, Sarita, taught us how to make it. It's pretty much the only thing we cook here. Speaking of being cooked—Kabir, we saw that Akash got MeTooed."

"Yeah," Kabir said. "I ran into Dee yesterday; you met her at the opening. She was really upset."

"That he got MeTooed?" Noreen said.

"No, no! She thought he was a creep, like everyone else. I may have mentioned she was supposed to have this big mural in the festival. She's been working on it all year, so she was hoping that after he stepped down, the board would take over and keep the festival going, but it's been canceled. It was mostly his money, so there wasn't enough funding to move forward. Plus it was basically his baby, and no one seems interested in trying to save it."

"Hopefully it's replaced with some new, feminist-run festival that Dee can show her work in," Ruby said.

"That would be great," Kabir said.

Hari dabbed the corners of his lips with his napkin. He was particular with his table manners, had moved the fork and spoon and cup to their proper places upon sitting down. "I was talking to some friends about MeToo the other night. One guy said he won't even approach women at a party anymore, that his new policy with women he doesn't know is to only speak when spoken to."

"Hmm," Ruby said. "I don't know your friend, but I'm gonna guess it's probably better that way."

"Maybe with him. But a lot of guys, nice guys included, are confused about how to flirt now. I'm only reporting what I hear."

"All a guy needs to do is be nice and pay attention," Ruby said. "But so many of you do neither. You know how many times men have ignored me and talked to each other as if my role is to stand there and nod admiringly? And you'd think the NGO world would be better, but I've met many an insufferable man there, too. Like the head of our foundation."

"The twenty-eight-year-old tech billionaire?" Kabir said.

"Twenty-seven. And not a billionaire but close enough. Every time he sits in one of our meetings, he'll nod like he's listening but obviously hasn't been. We'll be discussing the on-the-ground challenges of programs addressing female malnutrition and he'll interrupt with, 'I think what you need to do is find a way to gamify it.'"

"In any case," Hari said, resting his knife and spoon diagonally across his plate, "I've never been very good at approaching women."

Ruby laughed. "You? Come on!"

"Seriously. I never had any practice because they always approach me."

"Oh, here we go." Ruby tossed her napkin at him.

"It's true!"

"Really, because I remember that at the party, you started talking to me."

"There was no way I was leaving that party without talking to you."

The sappy meeting of the eyes between Hari and her mother was worthy of a rom-com moment, some song like "Eternal Flame" by The Bangles playing in the background. Or "(Everything I Do) I Do It for You" by Bryan Adams, in a nod to the Indian setting.

She glanced at Kabir, and he winked. Noreen's phone buzzed.

Kabir had sent a link to the video for "(Everything I Do) I Do It for You."

She didn't need Geeta Auntie to interpret that sign.

They could have a beautiful life together.

"Someone eat the last of the eggs," Ruby said.

"I can't, I have to run," Kabir said.

"Where are you off to?" Ruby said.

"He has a date to play squash at Siri Fort," Noreen said.

"And have my ass handed to me," Kabir added. "I haven't played squash in years."

Noreen kissed Kabir goodbye in a protected part of the stairwell, then kept her distance as they continued downstairs. Raju, who was cleaning Geeta Auntie's car with a rag and bucket, greeted them with a namaste as a pigtailed Ila peeked at them from around the hood. After Noreen said goodbye to Kabir at the gate, Geeta Auntie, now standing on the patio with a cup of chai, called her over.

Indian walk of shame, she thought.

"Good morning, Auntie."

"Was that him?" Geeta Auntie said, gesturing toward the gate.

"That was Kabir."

Geeta Auntie arched one eyebrow. "Good-looking chap. Is your mother home?"

"Yes." Noreen understood this as code for does your mother know you had a boy over? Wait until she saw Hari leaving.

Geeta Auntie beckoned her closer with the crook of her finger. "You are practicing the safe sex?" she said in a low voice.

Noreen almost choked. "Yes," she squeaked.

"Make sure you do. My friend Jyoti's daughter is a gyne and once each month she's giving the abortion pill to a well-educated young woman from a good family. Some expat girls, too."

"You don't have to worry about me, Auntie."

Geeta Auntie smiled and pinched Noreen's cheek. "I know you are a responsible girl. And when you go home, tell your mother the same. Kaun jaane what diseases these sailor boys carry?"

nineteen

Air Quality Index: 101.
Unhealthy for Sensitive Groups.

WHEN NOREEN RETURNED, RUBY was on a video call, and there was no sign of Hari.

"Hold on, Ma, Noreen's home," Ruby said. She tilted the phone down and gestured for Noreen to hide the prosecco bottle. Noreen moved it from the dining room table to a dining chair, taking the overzealous but reassuring step of covering it with a cloth napkin.

Even after so many years of FaceTiming, Azra rarely fit her entire face inside the screen. Right now they could see her forehead, and the glittery teardrops of the family room chandelier.

"Assalaam alaikum, Naani," Noreen said.

"Kya ka rahe ho?" Azra asked.

"Oh, nothing much," Ruby said. "Sunday morning chilling."

"Everything good?"

"Great. You?"

"I am not great." Azra shifted the frame, the chandelier replaced by sniffling nose, red eyes.

"What's the matter?" Noreen said.

"I went to Five Guys," Azra said.

"You went to Five Guys?" Ruby said.

"I like their fries. Anyhow, I ran into Rani there."

Noreen and Ruby exchanged a glance. No story that opened with Rani ended well.

Rani Auntie was an old friend of Azra's, and her daughter Hina had been born one week after Sonia Khala. Both Hina and Sonia were super-nerds who aspired to Harvard Medical School, and Rani Auntie and Azra had always been competitive about their daughters. Once, Rani Auntie had hosted a joint birthday party for the two girls, and Azra was annoyed for days because she thought Hina had the nicer cake. The girls' lives had followed a similar trajectory: Ivy League educations, not Harvard Medical School but Columbia and Johns Hopkins, followed by prestigious medical fellowships, marriages to Pakistani American doctors (Sonia first, Hina a few years later) and two children each (Hina quickly, Sonia after years of miscarriages and failed IVFs), except that Hina settled down a few miles from her mother and Sonia moved coasts, which meant Rani Auntie had effectively won. Once, observing a conversation between Rani Auntie and Azra as they shared photos of their grandchildren would have been an excellent exercise in the art of subtext. But now, Rani Auntie viewed Azra with pity, which Azra couldn't abide, and it was all too painful to watch.

"And then Rani asked me," Azra continued, "how is Ruby?

I haven't seen her in so long. I was too ashamed to tell her you were in India. But Rani's very tez, she kept asking questions about you, and finally I had to admit my only living daughter has abandoned me."

"I haven't abandoned you, Ma."

"We'll be back before you know it, Naani," Noreen said.

"It's not fair." Azra was crying again. "Why can she have Hina but I can't have my Sonia? Ya Allah, I miss her so much."

"I know, Ma," Ruby said. "We miss her, too. Every moment of every day."

As Noreen added her own words of comfort, Azra squinted and frowned, like she was trying to see past them. "Woh kya hai?"

"What?" Ruby said.

"Peeche. Is that an idol?"

They looked over their shoulders. The beatific elephant god Ganesh looked back.

"Why is there a buth in your flat?" Azra said.

"What's buth mean?" Noreen whispered to Ruby off-screen.

"Idol," Ruby whispered back. "It's not ours, Ma. It was here when we moved in."

"And those offerings?"

"Our maid leaves them," Ruby explained.

"So every day there is a puja in your house?"

"It's not a big deal."

"Is there a Quran in your house?"

Lie, Noreen mentally signaled to her mother.

"No," Ruby said.

"So every day there is puja in your house but no Quran. Do you even have Allah's name written anywhere? Or now you rely on Ganesh to protect you?"

"Sonia had Allah's name in every room of her house, but it didn't protect her, did it?" Ruby said.

Azra gasped, and her eyes grew wide and hard like she was about to yell. But her lip only quivered, and she didn't speak.

"Don't be upset, Naani," Noreen said. "We miss you and we love you. And we'll get a Quran."

"Promise?"

"Promise."

This seemed to placate her, and they got another view of the chandelier's crystalline tiers as Azra blew her nose. "I miss both of you so much. Come home."

"Miss you, too," Ruby said. "Listen, we have to go. We'll call you later. Khuda hafiz."

"Allah hafiz."

Ruby tossed her phone aside. "Goddamn Rani Auntie."

"I'm sure she was only being nice."

"That's the problem."

"You shouldn't have said that about Sonia Khala," Noreen said.

"I know. And you know what's funny?" Ruby said. "I actually brought a pocket Quran, and a janamaz, and have been praying some."

"I didn't know you were still praying," Noreen said. Ruby had started after Sonia Khala died, because Sonia Khala was devout, and they said the prayers of your family were heard first. "Why wouldn't you tell Naani?"

"Because I'll never be the kind of Muslim she wants, so I'd be setting her up for disappointment."

"Yeah, I can see that. By the way, where did Hari go?"

"Shit!" Ruby ran into the kitchen and returned with a solemn-faced Hari.

"How much did you hear?" Ruby asked him.

"Most of it," Hari said. "What's Five Guys?"

"A place I can't imagine my mother running into Rani Auntie," Ruby said.

"They do have good fries," Noreen said.

"I'm going to roll a joint," Ruby said.

Hari rubbed her arm. "You chill. I'll do it."

If she were Azra, Noreen thought, she'd find it painful to see Rani, though she'd never have a friendship like theirs. Azra didn't have any real friends, not in the sense of people you can confide in and trust to hold your secrets safe.

She checked her own phone. While they'd been talking to Azra, Kabir had sent a message.

"Holy shit!" Noreen said.

Hari and Ruby rushed over. She looked up at them. A limp cigarette, emptied of tobacco, stuck out between Hari's fingers.

"What is it?" Ruby asked.

"Kabir's dad has been MeTooed."

twenty

Air Quality Index: 254. Very

Unhealthy.

FROM THE INSTAGRAM ACCOUNT of IndiaArt-TimesUp:

Many years ago, I worked as a research assistant to Inder Chaudhury. He would often make remarks about my clothing or how pretty I was looking. One evening, I stayed late to finish my work, and he suggested we break for a drink. Halfway through the drink, he put his hand on my leg and said, "Tell me, did you stay for this?" I tried to laugh it off, but I was very uncomfortable. I was relieved when he asked me to refill his glass, because it gave me an excuse to get up and say I didn't feel well and leave. The next day, he offered to get my book manuscript into the "right hands."

At a book launch of a young female writer, I overheard Inder Chaudhury say to a male colleague, "If only her work moved me as much as her breasts." Later that night, he looked at my cleavage, told me I looked good, and asked, "Why don't you dress like this more often?"

Built in 1321, the third of Delhi's eight cities, Tughluqabad was so large it once had fifty-two gates. Now it lay in ruins, and rhesus monkeys, pink-faced, red-butted, and unafraid, roamed the ramparts. As her Uber pulled into the small parking lot, Noreen watched a monkey swoop down, snatch a naan from a food cart, then scramble up a tree as the irate proprietor brandished a yellow-and-red-striped umbrella. Another monkey was chilling on top of a parked auto rickshaw, hugging his knees to his chest. Monkeys stalked the entire winding, uphill path from the parking lot to the ticket booth. Noreen wondered if they could be the descendants of the monkeys her great-grandmother had once watched leap from roof to roof.

Near the ticket booth, a baby monkey with wise eyes was humping another baby monkey. After paying the foreigner's price, she passed through the entry gate and stood astonished. She'd entered another world, a vast wild expanse scattered with crumbling ruins. For all the complaints, all the gaalis you could hurl at Delhi, the city was never boring.

Kabir called to her. He was leaning against the remains of a wall, dressed in his squash outfit. She ran to him, took both his hands.

"Hey," she said.

"Hey." He rested his head on her shoulder, and she stroked his back.

In the distance was a series of tall arches reminiscent of a Roman aqueduct. They were being overtaken by jungle, plants growing on top and all around, green leafy tentacles bursting through the arches' cracks. Another hundred years and they'd be swallowed whole. A village girl led two goats along a narrow upward path that led deeper into the jungle. As the two goats, then the girl, disappeared into the high grass, Noreen wondered where she was going, and if it was safe for her to be alone.

Kabir lifted his head. "You want a tour?"

"Sure," she said.

They began walking down the brick path that led into the ruins. He told her how Sultan Ghiyasuddin Tughluq had a vision of building a vast city with a grand palace, its fortifications strong enough to withstand the fiercest Mongol army. He wanted this dream realized fast, so he commanded every laborer in Delhi to cease their work in order to build his dream city. The trouble was, a few of these laborers were building a new well for Hazrat Nizamuddin so that there would be enough water for all those who lived in and visited his khanqah.

"Wait—the sultan messed with Hazrat Nizamuddin?" Noreen said.

"Yes. When, by orders of the sultan, the work stopped on Hazrat Nizamuddin's well, the saint cursed the sultan, saying either your city will be inhabited by goat herders, or no one."

"So did the city get built?"

"Yes, and in four years at that, but the sultan died before it was done. His son, who they call the Mad King, oversaw the city's completion. There were many neighborhoods, houses and markets and masjids, a citadel, a grand palace, and some of the thickest ramparts you'll find in any fort in India. But it was never fully populated, and within fifteen years the city was abandoned."

"There's a lesson in hubris," Noreen said.

"Yes."

They had the ruins nearly to themselves, aside from the black-and-white cow nibbling at the straw-like grass, a couple sitting on a boulder, and three young men posing for pensive portraits underneath a fully intact archway. The brick path they'd been following became dirt, and they stopped at a shallow lake, both bucolic (elegant white egrets dipping their beaks into the water, yellow butterflies flitting above the grass) and depressingly human (the small field bordering the lake littered with plastic bags, small packets of Haldiram's snack mix, discarded Cadbury chocolate and condom wrappers, quarter bottles of the local hooch, and, in the shade of a thorny bush, a used sanitary napkin).

The "goat herders" of Tughluqabad were up to no good.

They watched a kite circle overhead.

"You ready to talk about it?" she asked, and was relieved when he nodded.

"Yes, but let me show you the view from the citadel first."

They walked through an underground passage that stank of guano, climbed up a scrubby hill strewn with rubble. At the top of the citadel, they found a rock flat and wide enough to fit them both and admired the panoramic view, the striking and confounding juxtapositions of past and present. Inside the thick rubble ramparts were ruins and miles of jungle and desolation and human detritus, just outside, crowded, concrete rooftops, an arterial city road choked with traffic. And, on the other side of the road, the grand marble dome of the tomb of the cursed sultan, who didn't live to see his dream fulfilled.

Noreen was going to miss Delhi, its domes, its dissonance.

"How are you feeling?" she asked Kabir.

"I do want to talk," he said. "But do you mind if we sit quietly for a little while? Once we leave, there's no coming back."

She took his hand and kissed it. "We can stay as long as you want."

twenty-one

Air Quality Index: 303.

Hazardous.

TOO DISTRAUGHT TO DRIVE, Kabir had left his car near Siri Fort, so they took an auto to his house. His parents lived in a peaceful, leafy, planned neighborhood set far back from the main road, clusters of monochromatic, low-rise residential buildings set among walkways and courtyards. According to Kabir, it was hailed as an architectural feat when built but had since been poorly maintained, some of the buildings streaked with grime and starting to crack. They pulled up in front of a three-story townhouse that had been stylishly renovated, with twice as many windows as its neighbors and a glass solarium on the roof. The interior of the house was decorated with art and beautiful objects and flooded with natural light from above. She followed Kabir up a narrow industrial staircase and down the hallway. From the other side of the last door, they could hear Kabir's parents arguing.

Kabir shook his head. "Noreen, I shouldn't drag you into this. Maybe you should—"

Meena opened the door. "Here you are! You could have at least answered my messages. Have you said anything to your friends?"

"What do you mean, anything?" Kabir said.

"I mean confirmation, denial, anything."

"I haven't said anything."

Meena looked at Noreen. "Except to her."

"She's my girlfriend."

Girlfriend.

Beautiful word, shitty context.

Meena looked at Noreen for a moment, then waved them into Inder's office. Inder was lying on the leather sofa like a patient in psychoanalysis, framed by an entire wall of books.

"Your son is here," Meena announced.

Inder kept his gaze on the ceiling. "Left the ruins to grace us with your presence?"

"Listen to me, Poppa," Kabir said. "You need to apologize."

"Apologize?" Inder got up and Noreen took a step back, her spine pressed into a bookcase. He paced the length of the sofa as he spoke, tipped forward as though fighting a heavy wind, two fists clenched behind his back. "Why should I apologize? For what? Her accusation is conveniently devoid of context, such as the fact that she had been flirting with me for weeks."

Kabir turned to his mother, who was leaning against her

husband's enormous rosewood desk, a portrait of calm, her hands clasped loosely over her perfectly pleated pants. "Ma?"

"It's complicated," she said.

"I didn't ask her to stay late," Inder said. He'd gone back to sulking on the sofa. "She asked me if I wanted a drink. I said, sure, if you're having. She poured the drinks. We had a pleasant conversation. I offered to put in a good word with an editor because I do that with all my assistants. That's why they work for me, hai na, for the connections? She worked for me for another month, then left for grad school in the UK. Khatam kahani. The end."

"That's not her story," Kabir said.

"So you will believe her over your own father?"

"Did you proposition her?"

"She was flirting with me, so yes, I probably flirted back. But this unwanted touching nonsense—I have class. Or do you not believe that about me either? Are you so willing to pronounce me a scoundrel?" Inder reached for the glass tumbler on the end table, but Meena got to the decanter before he could, moving it to the second-highest bookshelf.

"You need to stay sober," she said.

"Even if you did think she was flirting, you were her *boss*," Kabir said. "Consider the power dynamic."

"And what about this? Do I have any power now? The truth doesn't matter. I am screwed. If I even utter one word in my defense, those young, rabid feminists will eat me alive. Woh sab mujhko kha jaingi. What kind of generation is yours, that casts such a wide net and leaves no room for nuance? Tell me, who is vetting these anonymous posts? Don't they understand that what they are doing can destroy a person's life, his life's work?"

"They are trying to change the world, Poppa," Kabir said. "And it's not going to change from a whimper."

A vein in Inder's forehead had started throbbing. Noreen noticed Meena check the time on her watch.

"Do you think, if I am the man they claim, I would be married to your mother? She has more balls than the Indian cricket team combined! Do you know how much the right wing is enjoying watching this, the leftys' heads all rolling, one by one? Tell your young feminist friends to have fun dating those right-wing chuddis because they're all that will be left after we're gone!"

Inder began to circle the sofa, upright and fuming, his forehead and armpits damp with sweat. Meena stayed by the bookshelf, her focused expression reminding Noreen of Ila's as she sang her multiplication tables. Noreen wondered what she was calculating.

"And the old feminists too," Inder continued. "Mujhe bilkul yakeen hai ki Madhu is the one who made the second allegation. I'm certain it was her! She's been wanting to get back at me ever since I wrote a poor review of her novel for *LRB* ten years ago. Madhu didn't even look good in that dress! I said it to be nice. And you want to know what that high and mighty moral Madhu was doing every night of the Jaipur Lit Festival? Fucking her best friend's husband. Shall I write an anonymous post about that? What I should do is sue for defamation!"

Meena clapped her hands.

"Shut up," she said. "Yeh badle ki baat chhoro. Any more talk of revenge, and I will walk out the front door and leave you to deal with this alone."

Inder sat with one leg crossed over the other and turned his face away from Meena.

A phone vibrated on the end table.

"See who it is," Meena told Inder.

When Inder ignored her, she walked over and picked up the phone, holding it at arm's length to read it. "It's Deborah."

"Not now."

"She's your agent. It's the middle of the night in New York and this is the second time she's called. You want to listen to her and make sure they don't pull your book, or you want to keep running your mouth and digging yourself a bigger hole?"

She handed Inder the phone, stood over him while he called back.

"Hello, Deborah! So good to hear from you. How are things in New York? Better weather than London, I'm sure?"

He crossed the room, his jovial voice an unsettling contrast to his glowering eyes and angry gait. Noreen, who'd been standing near the office door, moved quickly to get out of his way.

Inder left the office and Kabir looked across at Meena.

"So you're sticking by him?" he asked.

"For God's sake, Kabir, don't be so dramatic. I'm not Hillary," Meena said.

Noreen's nose tickled and she sucked in her stomach to hold back the sneeze. Kabir's mother seemed to have forgotten her and she preferred it that way.

"I don't understand. When the Akash thing broke, you were up in arms, talking about how we must believe women," Kabir said.

"I do believe women! I am a feminist! I have been in the trenches, fighting this fight since I was a girl! How many young female artists have I mentored?" Meena retrieved the decanter from the bookshelf and poured a shot of whiskey into Inder's glass, swirling it a few times before drinking it down. "You're still a child, Kabir. You don't know anything about the world."

AH-CHOO!

Noreen removed her elbow from her face, uncurled her toes, attempted a benign smile.

"I'm sorry," Meena said, "what is your name again?"

Noreen cleared her throat. "Noreen."

"Noreen, how do we know you won't return to America and write all about us in your blog?"

Ah, the irony. For someone who was having issues writing three sentences, blogging was like the third circle of hell.

"I hate blogging," Noreen said. "And also I would never do that."

"You can trust Noreen," Kabir said. "This affects my life, too. I'm not going to hide it from her."

"You know, if you focused half as much on your work as you do on your girlfriends, you'd be doing a show in Berlin and would be far away from all this," Meena said. "I need a cigarette. Does anyone have a cigarette?"

Noreen shook her head.

"I don't think I can be with you or Poppa right now," Kabir said. "You're both behaving like children."

"You're not going anywhere. I was supposed to leave for Vipassana tomorrow, but I've canceled it. I need to be here, and so do you."

"In this house? Around him? I can't."

"Your father needs you."

"You mean you need me. He doesn't give a shit."

Meena laughed. "And you accuse us of behaving like children?"

Once again, that accursed tickle in her nose. She didn't dare sneeze again and risk more of Meena's snarky wrath. She motioned to Kabir that she was stepping out.

"I'm coming with you," he said.

"Fine," Meena said. "Go. But if you care about this family and its future and the future of our careers, including yours, you will not say a word to anyone until we decide upon a strategy."

"Fine," Kabir said.

When they reached the bottom of the stairs, he told Noreen,

"One sec—I'll quickly check on Naani."

Noreen waited for him in the living room, where their maid Charu was cleaning a series of small stone statues, picking up each one and brushing it with a feather duster. The statues were abstract, headless female bodies in various positions. In between each body was a female head, so you could presumably mix and match. In AP Art History, they'd learned that the Romans made their statues with detachable heads. That way, if a hero or ruler lost honor or popularity, you could easily replace their head with someone in the public favor.

Noreen heard the thump-thump of Inder's footsteps upstairs as he walked back to the office, could make out Meena's voice but not her words, prayed neither of them would decide to come down.

Charu dusted the last statue, stepped back, frowned, shifted the bodies and heads a degree to the left or right. When she was satisfied, she nodded at Noreen and disappeared to the back of the house. The smell of cumin seeds frying in hot oil wafted from the kitchen. Noreen walked over to the bar cart, repurposed from a vintage red-and-black magician's coffin. There were a half dozen bottles of whiskey, mostly aged scotches like her mother drank, a bottle of Old Monk rum, a small-batch gin, a bottle of mescal. Noreen decided she wanted a drink and that she'd have mescal, which her mother and Adi Uncle had gotten into after a trip to Mexico City. She poured a small shot into a heavy glass tumbler and drank it, taking perverse pleasure in the slow throat burn that followed. The best-case scenario was that she'd feel better for an hour and crappy for the next five, but she was determined to enjoy the hour.

Kabir's dad.

Noreen understood both selfish behavior and the inclination toward self-preservation, but not once had Inder expressed remorse or any empathy for the assistant, not even an *I'm sorry she feels that way*. It had been all about him.

Inder was a dick. And Meena didn't even remember her name. On the bright side, *girlfriend*.

Where was Kabir?

She wondered if she'd ever meet Kabir's naani. What did Naani think of Inder? And had Kabir told Naani about her? They were so close. But even if he had, she'd probably forgotten. Kabir said a few days ago she'd become very anxious and withdrawn. Maybe she'd sensed the impending storm.

She looked up at the large, framed photograph over the bar, a black-and-white print of two women. Her grandparents would call them hijras, but after moving to India she'd learned some preferred the term kinnar. The photo was of the reflection of the two in a dressing table mirror. The closer one sat at the dressing table, darkening the inside of her lower lid with kohl. The table was covered with compacts and nail polishes, lipsticks and little pots, stacks of bangles loosely wrapped in paper. Behind her, on a wooden cot, the farther one, dressed in a blouse and petticoat, was shooting up. Her drug addiction had laid waste to her body, ribs slicing through her flesh. The needle she was using to inject herself bulged underneath her skin like a metal vein.

"You ready?"

Noreen jumped at Kabir's voice.

"I had a shot of mescal," she confessed.

"That's not a bad idea. Pass your glass?"

She handed him her empty tumbler. He chose scotch, drank twice as much as she had.

"Let's bounce," he said. "We can grab an auto from the main road."

The ten-minute walk through the neighborhood to the main road was, on a purely aesthetic measure, one of the most pleasant she'd had in Delhi; a sidewalk unbroken and spacious enough for two, no beggars, no sleeping or urinating men, no tree roots to trip over or random holes to circumvent.

They'd almost reached the main road when Kabir sank into a crouch. He slid his hands through his hair, breathed "Fuuuuck."

"It's going to be okay," she said. "Maybe not in the short term, but life is about the long game."

Was that the best she could do? She blamed the mescal.

"I knew my parents were flawed, but I honestly thought they were better than this. Why am I so surprised? I owe my moral compass to Naani, and she's all but gone."

He'd hidden his face with his hands, and when he let them drop, Noreen was sure he'd be crying. No tears, only a sad, wretched face. Noreen hugged him. That, at least, she couldn't mess up.

She would have kept on holding him, but a brush wallah was riding toward them, all varieties of brushes and mops and household clothes secured to his bicycle. He slowed down to assess their customer potential, sped up when he determined there was none.

They held hands and walked to the main road. An auto stopped for them right away, but when she climbed into the back seat Kabir didn't follow.

"Listen," he said, leaning into the auto, "my friend Sunny's gone to Ladakh for a shoot, and I have the key to his barsati."

"His what?"

"Barsati—it's a type of flat. I'm going to head there for the night."

"I'll come with you," she said.

Kabir shook his head. "I'm a mess right now, babe. I need to be alone for a bit."

"Are you sure?"

The auto was idling, and the autowallah turned his head. "Chalna hai ki nahin?"

You want to go or not?

"I'll call you tomorrow, pukka promise," Kabir said.

Kabir knocked on the roof of the auto and the autowallah started driving. He kept glancing at her in the rearview, curious probably, as to what had transpired between sad girl and even sadder boy. She ignored him, focusing her attention outside the auto, her thoughts vacillating between rationalizing Kabir's desire for solitude and feeling hurt and insecure. Wouldn't most people want to be alone right now? She'd spent a lot of time alone when grieving. But she hadn't had a boyfriend. Did this mean she was not a comfort to him? Wasn't this whole situation also a test of her worth as a partner? If she helped him through this, he'd have another good, solid reason to love her, and the more reasons someone had to love, the more inclined they were to stay. But if she fucked it up, if she made it worse, then she risked losing him.

At the next red light, they idled in front of a mural spanning the entire wall of a four-story building. The mural was of a young woman, painted from the waist up, her right hand raised in a fist, the other gripping a book. She wore a denim jacket over her red sari, a thin gold hoop in her nose. On the hand with the book, gold brass knuckles spelled out HOPE. Written in a cursive arch above her head were the words: *The Future Is Female*.

As they drove on, Noreen watched in the side-view mirror as a man paused in front of the mural, gazed upward, unzipped his trousers, and started to take a piss.

twenty-two

Air Quality Index: 154.

Unhealthy.

RUBY WAS READY WITH some of Noreen's favorite snacks: Khatta Meetha snack mix, fancy salt and vinegar potato chips. As her mother hugged her, Noreen thought about what Kabir said, how growing up he'd found acceptance and comfort in his naani's arms, how, with her illness, he was trying to give the same to her, as best he could.

"Don't ever get dementia," she said.

"What?" Ruby said.

"Everything was going so well, and now it's all falling apart." She lolled her head on Ruby's shoulder.

Ruby rubbed her back. "My sweet Nor-bear jaan. It's going to be okay."

"He didn't even want to be with me tonight. And on top of that I'm a terrible person, because I'm focusing on myself when I should be focusing on the women who came forward and what they're going through."

"You are not a terrible person. Yes, you should be concerned about the women, but you still have to take care of yourself, and process how this is affecting you and those you love."

"I don't know what to do; I don't know how best to help him. I couldn't even tie a thread at Hazrat Nizamuddin's tomb."

Noreen glanced around the living room but, unlike home, there was no cozy, yielding couch to throw herself upon. Everything was stiff and formal and bathed in hard fluorescence. The water was poisoned the air was poisoned the men were poison. She grabbed a cushion from the sofa and lay down on the carpet. In the miniature on the wall, the great Mughal Emperor, Akbar, looked kindly upon the falcon on his wrist, his head framed by a golden halo. Kabir said Delhi may never have been a comely city but it always had breathtakingly beautiful elements. She could not imagine Emperor Akbar's Delhi, sun-sparkled streams and fresh air and colorful, unbroken tombs. Were the people happier back then too?

She wished she could go for a run but then her lungs might implode.

"Fruit and Nut?" Ruby said, carrying the tray of assorted snacks to the coffee table.

"Yes, please." The Mirza girls ate their way through crisis. Noreen was not one who'd subsist on bowls of thin soup after having her heart broken. She'd tried this approach when Liam ghosted. It worked for about two hours, and then she got hungry.

Ruby opened the family-sized Cadbury, broke off a row of chocolate for Noreen and a row for herself. "By the way, did I smell booze on your breath?"

Noreen cupped her hand over her mouth. "I had a little mescal."

"You?"

"Delhi has made an occasional drinker out of me."

"Well, if any city will do it, it's this one," Ruby said. "Eat."

The Cadbury was satisfying; sometimes you opened ones here to find the chocolate had melted and re-hardened, both the taste and texture off.

"You only started dating him, you know," Ruby said. "No one would fault you a graceful exit."

"How can you say that?"

"Listen, you've got six weeks left."

"Six weeks is a long time!" Noreen said.

"We'll be in Rajasthan for ten days of it."

Jaipur, Jodhpur, Udaipur. Pink City, Blue City, City of Lakes. She'd completely forgotten about their big March trip, strategically planned for shortly after Hari left.

"I can't go to Rajasthan."

"Oh." Ruby unfolded a napkin and rested her remaining square of chocolate in the center. "It's still a month away."

"Yes, and maybe things will change, but as of now I can't leave him. He didn't do anything wrong."

"I know that. My suggestion was not a reflection on him but

on the situation. I don't want you to get hurt. His parents seem pretty self-absorbed."

"And what kind of person would I be if I abandoned the nice, kind guy I love because things got complicated through no fault of his own?"

"Well, I suppose you wouldn't be Noreen Mirza. Loyal to a fault."

"Only to a select few."

"And you're sure he deserves it?"

"Yes."

"All right, then." Ruby opened a bag of potato chips, offered her first dibs. Noreen didn't like savory after sweet but ate one anyway.

"I'm sorry about Rajasthan," she said. "I mean, me not going is based on the assumption he still wants to be with me, because he doesn't right now."

"It's been an insane day and he needs some time alone to think things through. Stop reading more into it or you'll drive yourself crazy. Why don't we order food and do a triple feature movie night—ooh, we still have some of that chocolate and tender coconut ice cream; we can make those hot fudge Bounty sundaes again?"

"Fine. But no rom-coms."

"Hell no. I was thinking horror. And maybe a taut psychological thriller? Or a poignant Pixar? Legal drama?"

"I think there's enough drama happening right now."

"True. And I do want to help you process all the drama, but first let's get some real food in that belly."

Noreen checked her phone. No messages. She set the volume to the highest bar.

Ruby returned with the stack of non-Indian restaurant menus the German had left behind and fanned them on the coffee table. "What do you think—Italian? The burger place? You love their sweet potato fries."

"Didn't you have plans with Hari this evening?"

"I have lots of time to see him. Tonight, it's me and you. And in the morning, it'll be you and Kabir again. You'll see."

"Can you say that with one hundred percent confidence?" Noreen said.

"I'd place highs odds."

"Like seventy-five percent?"

"Oh, I'd go ninety, easy."

During the opening scene of *Up*, Kabir messaged.

At Sunny's. Thank you for being there for me today. I was thinking, maybe in a day or two you could come stay. We'd have the place to ourselves. Only if you'd like.

Her heart at ease, she responded, **I'd like that very much.**

I read about how the Sri Lankan cricket team stopped a match in Delhi because it was so polluted, they started throwing up. I looked up the AQI that day, and it was 331. Hazardous! But people in Delhi called the Sri Lankan players wimps, accused them of doing drama, pointed out with pride that the Indian cricket players were playing without masks and they were fine. I mean, of all the stupid machismos, pollution machismo? You think that's a wheeze, listen to this! Oh, you think your lungs are bad? You see this cigarette pack warning? They used my lungs as the model! And people told me I couldn't be a model. Hey, you call that a deformed sperm? Mine can't even swim. They can only move in circles, chasing their own tails. Pollution machismo. You know what the grand prize is for winning that contest? Idiot sperm and early death.

twenty-three

Air Quality Index: 236. Very

Unhealthy.

SUNNY'S BARSATI CONSISTED OF three basic, stand-alone concrete rooms built on top of a roof terrace: a bedroom with a door, a bathroom with a door, and a narrow kitchen with an open doorway. It was indoor/outdoor living; to go from one room to the other you had to cross part of the terrace. The bathroom was so small you took your bucket bath practically on top of the toilet. The kitchen was stocked with beer and chips and little else. The bedroom had a mattress on the floor, two floor cushions for seating, two squat stools that doubled as tables, an old, broken record player and a few crates of records, a modern bi-level desk with a swivel office chair, a Mac desktop with a fancy ergonomic keyboard and huge flat screen, and an ancient, crusty window AC unit. A poster of the dreadlocked god Shiva against a Rastafarian background and a framed, black-and-white film still of the actress Shabana Azmi faced each other from opposite walls.

When Noreen was young, she'd watched a film starring Shabana Azmi with her grandparents. They called it an art film, as opposed to Bollywood. She remembered finding Shabana Azmi as luminous as she was in this photo, and that the film had no songs and a tragic end.

Not only did the barsati necessitate having to go outside to use the kitchen or bathroom, the bedroom had no air purifier. Noreen had become accustomed to sleeping with one, taking comfort in the blue light indicator, this (possibly false) visual reassurance that the toxic particulate matter in the air had been reduced to safe levels. The first night in the barsati she kept imagining microscopic particles of smoke, soot, sulfate, dust, and tire rubber entering her nostrils, settling in her lungs, the tiniest particles coursing through her heart, contaminating her blood. "Gives a whole new meaning to meditating on your breath," she joked with Kabir.

On day two, Ruby brought over the air purifier from Noreen's bedroom. On day three, Inder released a statement.

I unequivocally deny the allegations leveled against me on the IndiaArtTimesUp Instagram account. I have never behaved in an inappropriate manner with anyone who has worked for me or otherwise. The allegations in their entirety are fabricated and false.

After reading his father's statement, Kabir went to the kitchen and returned with a bottle of Kingfisher. He'd been subsisting on a diet of hash joints, beer, Haldiram's snack mix, and guava sprinkled with a little salt and chaat masala. The guava came from the fruit seller who pushed her cart down the block around eleven o'clock every morning.

"I knew he wouldn't apologize," he said. "My father can barely apologize to my mother. He's always had this chip on his shoulder, wasn't loved enough by his father. He thinks the world owes him something, that he deserves more: more publicity, more prizes, more money. His next book was finally going to give him the fame he's due. I hope they cancel it."

When his phone vibrated, he turned it off and threw it aside. It disappeared in the sliver of space between the mattress and the wall.

"Kabir," Noreen said. "You must have like a hundred unread messages on your phone."

"I'll look at them tonight," he said. "Maybe tomorrow."

Though deeply empathetic to Kabir's struggles, Noreen couldn't say she approved of all of his decisions. After Sonia Khala died, she'd spent a significant amount of time idle in her room, dealing with grief and layers of guilt, including guilt over lying around doing nothing. Her therapist told her that, after entering the cocoon, caterpillars slowly digest themselves. Noreen was not "wasting her time," she was digesting her grief. But she was also working at the ice cream parlor, running nearly every day, and volunteering at a food pantry. Kabir wouldn't even go to the local park.

She could understand the desire to sequester oneself, but he ought to check his phone, respond to his friends and family who were worried and loved him.

"Do you want me to reach out to your friends?" she said. "Tara, Yasmeen, Varun? I can get their numbers off your phone."

Kabir finished his beer and lay down on the mattress. "Any time someone sees me, they'll think of what my father has done."

It was true that for someone who placed great importance on being liked, this was a nightmare.

He ought to get out for a bit, she thought, he should move.

"Hey, you want to go for a walk?" she said. She was about to say, some fresh air might be good, except here there was no such thing.

"Maybe later."

She lay down next to Kabir, curled her arm around his waist. "It's going to be okay."

"And those women, who have to read my dad's statement calling them liars? Is it going to be okay for them?"

"Eventually," she said. "They can't let your father's actions define their life, prevent them from achieving happiness. And neither can you. You are not your dad, Kabir, like I'm not mine."

"Yes, but your dad's not all over the fucking papers."

Fair point; Inder may be a minor headline, but he was a headline.

"Hey." Kabir turned his head toward her, touched her cheek. "I'm sorry for dragging you into this. You shouldn't be spending your time in Delhi shut up in here with me."

"I want to be with you." It was true; there was nowhere else she'd rather be.

They kissed and Noreen got a little turned on but knew sex was out of the question. The day passed; Kabir talked some and stared at the ceiling a lot, Noreen went to the market and jotted down some notes for a scene where Noor, suffering from academic anxiety and recurring nightmares that she's fallen behind in school, has her first appointment with a therapist who peppers her speech with analogies. After spending an hour trying to think of one that was seemingly inapposite but would, by the end of the episode, make sense, she gave up. Anyway, it was time for bed.

When she woke, it was the middle of the night and Kabir was gone. He'd been thrashing so much in his sleep that the sheet had come untucked on his side, exposing the mattress. In the gauzy moonlight filtering through the red curtains, she could make out the mattress stains, dried beer and the dank fluids of strangers. She'd have to go out and find a fitted sheet tomorrow.

Kabir's shawl was on the chair. It had been his grandfather's, woven from a soft, fine wool that was incredibly warm. She wrapped it around herself and went outside. The sky was a murky purple, the moon low and pale. On the front part of the terrace, Sunny had put together a pleasant hangout area: cane love seat and table, a cane chair, two woven bamboo stools, a reed floor mat, a money plant. Kabir was on the love seat, smoking a joint.

Half-naked, with his necklace of wooden beads and mop of hair, he reminded her of those iconic photos of Jim Morrison that Ruby had shown her after they'd visited his grave in Paris, except Kabir was darker and hairier, with a solid layer of muscle over his ribs.

"You're up?" he said, and moved over to give her room.

"You'll catch cold," she said, drawing him into the shawl. "Can I have a hit of that?"

"I thought you didn't smoke."

"I don't." She inhaled and started coughing smoke.

Kabir rubbed her back. "You okay?"

"Forget it. I can't do the tobacco. Do you have to put it in there?"

"Without the tobacco, the hash won't burn."

Noreen rested her head on his shoulder, enjoying the peaceful lull of this time of night. Here, the houses were only a few feet apart, and anyway a barsati made you more attuned to a neighborhood's rhythms since you spent so much time outside. So far, the evenings had followed a similar pattern; as darkness fell, the lights came on in the houses, the smell of sizzling cumin and green chilies and garlic floated through open windows, the tempering of the dal right before the meal. People ate dinner late, 8:00, 9:00, 10:00 p.m., and played their TVs loud, Indian news shows, sometimes with four people yelling at once, Indian soap operas with their over-the-top sound effects, the laugh tracks and familiar voices from *Friends* and *The Big Bang Theory*.

Then the lights would shut off, the TVs would go silent, and the neighborhood would become hushed, though not entirely peaceful, the quiet periodically broken by a shrill guard whistle, an angry car horn, the rev of a bike engine, a feud between strays.

It was quiet now, and there were no eyes on them, at least that Noreen could see.

"I realized I forgot Valentine's Day," Kabir said. "I'm sorry. I know it's a big deal in America."

"It's totally okay. My mom and I are both firmly in the Valentine's Day is a lame, capitalist holiday camp. By the way, it's a big holiday here, too. The ruins of Hauz Khas must have been hopping."

They laughed, and then he said, "You have the best laugh."

"So do you."

"I love it when you smile like that."

"Like what?" she said.

"Like I've done something to make you truly happy."

"I'm always happy with you."

It was true. When she was with him, her heart shone, though when he gave her a compliment, it shone a little extra.

Is this burning an eternal flame?

Kabir had lit the lamp of her heart.

If you have light in your heart, you will find your way home.

So that was love. A way home.

"What are you thinking?" Kabir said.

That I love you.

"I was thinking how I used to think romantic love songs were so cheesy," she said.

"And then you came here and gave Bryan Adams a chance?"

Noreen laughed. "Thank you, India."

They cuddled closer, adjusting the shawl so it covered them both. Noreen drew her fingers along his chest hair. She would have kissed him if she wasn't certain that someone, somewhere was watching. If you were outside in Delhi, you were never alone.

She looked up at the sky. Waxing crescent moon. One star that was possibly a satellite.

"What's the first time you remember seeing stars?" she said.

"When I was five. My parents and I went camping in Desert National Park in Rajasthan. I'd seen stars, but never so many, and I cried out, 'Poppa! The sky looks like Nehru Planetarium!'"

Noreen laughed. "Cute little city boy."

A door squeaked open on a nearby roof. Some of the houses had open roof terraces; a few, like theirs, had rooms built on top. The building to their right had servants' quarters, a row of concrete single rooms with corrugated tin roofs and no AC units, chilly in winter, suffocating in summer.

Noreen noticed Kabir's phone was switched on. "Did you answer any messages yet?"

"A few. Not any of my mother's. And my father hasn't called or messaged. I didn't expect him to, and I don't want to talk to him, but I still want him to care that I'm not talking to him. Does that sound stupid?"

"No, it makes perfect sense. He's your dad. Everyone wants to feel like their dads love them. And he does love you—"

"He's never taken the time to know me. Why would now be any different? You know, I went through this period of depression in high school, and neither of my parents had a clue. Naani knew. She'd take me to dargahs, tell me to leave it at the feet of the saint."

"But I'm sure you and your dad have had some nice times together," Noreen said. "Some bonding moments?"

"When he was teaching me how to drive. He used to have this old Ambassador with a cassette tape player. After every lesson we'd stop at this kulfi faluda place and eat in the car listening to old Bollywood songs, Begum Akhtar, John Coltrane. I picked up driving quickly, but I'd mess up on purpose because I didn't want our lessons to end. One night, he told me how his father used to thrash him if he received bad marks. For my dad's generation, that was pretty normal, but my dad said that his father, forever bitter about not having been allowed to marry the woman he loved, seemed to get some sick pleasure out of beating him."

"That's awful," Noreen said.

"We never talked about it again. Anyway, look at our families. They've suffered the traumas of colonization and Partition *and* they don't like to talk about their feelings. It's no wonder we're all so messed up. At least with colonization, we have an idea of what happened. My naani liked to tell stories about her life, but when it came to Partition, she was always vague. 'Many tragic things happened.' 'Many people died.'"

Noting how he'd referred to his naani in the past tense, she reached for his hand. On the street below, dogs barked and growled. Most of the colony's strays roamed in pairs or packs. Every night around 2:00 a.m., they got into aggressive fights, like the one happening now.

"I don't get it," Noreen said. "They all know each other, they know each other's territory—why still fight every night?"

"In my parents' circle, people have known each other for a long time. You could leave and come back ten years later, and they'd still having the same old scuffles over the same old things. This one sold his piece for so much money, this one got a prize and I wasn't even nominated, this one had an affair with so and so."

"So much intrigue," Noreen said.

"Who knows?" Kabir said. "Maybe it's far more simple. Maybe the dogs brawl because they're bored."

The strays ratcheted up their volume, signaling the climax of their performance. A brief crescendo of angry howls ended with a solitary whimper, then silence, as the dogs agreed to let it be for now, take it up again tomorrow.

twenty-four

Air Quality Index: 148.
Unhealthy for Sensitive Groups.

"GAAAH," SAID NOREEN WHEN she walked into the bathroom and saw that

Kabir

had left

the Toilet Seat

Up

AGAIN.

To be fair, she'd never brought it up with him, except for one throwaway comment she wasn't sure he heard. But she also felt like she shouldn't have to, that it was something he should know; if one is living with a woman, one must put the toilet seat down.

She wiped the drop of urine from toilet rim, put the plastic seat down, and marched back to the bedroom. It wasn't only the toilet. She and her mother had a high tolerance for clutter, as long as things were clean. Though Kabir rinsed the sink after he shaved, there were always some thick stubbly hairs clinging to the faucet and strewn across the cracked porcelain. If you had a little money in India, you could hire someone else to clean up after you, but Sunny's maid had not made an appearance since they'd moved in. In Delhi, each day brought a fresh layer of dust. It had been a week and the floors were so dirty you didn't dare walk barefoot, the terrace coated in grime. She'd have to ask Sarita if she'd come clean for some extra cash.

She messaged Adi Uncle, who'd been with his husband, Ryan, for ten years.

Noreen: *Is it normal to totally love someone but also want to kill them?*

Adi Uncle: *YES.*

That was comforting.

Kabir was licking a joint shut. Noreen took his headphones off.

"Hey," she said. "You have to put the toilet seat down."

"Have I not been putting it down?" he said.

For a moment she thought she might explode. "Um, no. Every time you do susu, you've been leaving it up."

Kabir laughed.

Noreen fixed her hands on her hips. "What?"

"Sorry. It was very cute, the way you said susu."

She bit her lip. "Did I mispronounce it?"

"No." Kabir reached for her, pulled her onto his lap. "Hey, I'm really sorry. This is the first time I've lived with a girl, and I've been distracted—but that's not an excuse. Maaf karo? I won't do it again, promise."

Adi Uncle had told her once that at least half of relationship issues stemmed from the negotiation of three things: family, money, and housekeeping. If there was a future Kabir and Noreen, future Kabir would need to be more concerned with cleanliness, future Noreen a little less.

"It's okay, I'm not mad anymore. But this barsati is getting gross. Didn't Sunny tell you his maid comes every day?"

"He did. He's in the middle of Ladakh with no service; otherwise I'd ask."

"Not that I don't love being here with you," she said. They were lucky, to have this space rent-free, no roommates or parents. Once they shut the bedroom door and drew the curtains and turned off all lights but the corner lamp, it was their own precious, private world. "I just need it a little cleaner. I'm sorry I blew up. The last thing you need is someone yelling at you. I've never really lived with anyone but my mother. Except for eighth grade summer camp, but that's a period of my life I prefer to forget."

"Kyun?"

"Because when you're a thirteen-year-old desi girl going through puberty and sprouting hair literally everywhere, the last thing you need is to share a cabin with two Korean Americans."

"Would they say stuff to you?"

"One was super sweet. The other never said anything to my face, but she didn't have to; it was the way she looked at me, my hairy arms, at my body when I was changing, like I was the human equivalent of leaving the toilet seat up."

"Oh, my beautiful Noreen. What can I do to make it up to you, on behalf of the mean girls and myself?"

"No worries," she said. "You've got enough to deal with."

"I'll think of something," he said.

They heard the sound of a fist against metal. To get to the barsati, you entered the house on the ground floor and walked four flights to the very top of the stairs, where a metal door led onto the roof terrace. Someone was banging on this door now, demanding to be let in.

"I'll get it," Noreen said.

On the other side of the door was a slight, older woman, her sari hitched past the ankles, the pallu wound around her waist. Her lower left leg was scarred, the pale skin pulled tight. She moved past Noreen onto the terrace, retrieved the reed broom called a jharu from between two potted plants.

"Urvashi?" Noreen said.

"Haan," Urvashi said.

At last, the maid had come.

"Bhaiyya waapas aaye?" Urvashi asked.

Noreen realized she was asking about Sunny. "No, Sunny's not back yet," she answered in Hindi. "But we are staying here while he's away."

Urvashi grunted her disapproval, likely because guests meant she would have to start reporting daily. She took the jharu from the kitchen and began to sweep the terrace, and Noreen went back inside to tidy the bedroom.

"The maid is here," she told Kabir. They stacked the record crates against the wall, picked up the bottles and cans, stuffed their bags inside the metal almirah, none of whose doors closed properly. Sarita used a broom and a spray microfiber mop, but Urvashi cleaned crouched on her haunches, first sweeping the floor, then wiping it down with wet rags. She worked quickly, the entire terrace done in thirty minutes.

A little while later, Urvashi came to tell her she was leaving and to buy more Lizol. Noreen thanked her, went to pee, saw that Urvashi hadn't cleaned the bathroom, called out, "Excuse me! El baño?"

"Kya?" Urvashi said.

Noreen shook her head. This was not first time she meant to speak Hindi-Urdu and Spanish emerged instead.

"Sorry—the bathroom. Ek second."

Noreen went and got Kabir. When he asked Urvashi why she hadn't cleaned the bathroom, she frowned and responded with a stream of animated sentences and dismissive gestures.

"What is it?" Noreen said.

"She doesn't clean bathrooms. She said there's a low-caste woman who works two houses down who comes to clean the bathroom."

"Seriously?"

"Yeah, it's a thing," Kabir said.

Urvashi's phone went off, her ringtone a tinny version of the Bollywood song "Aaye Ho Meri Zindagi Mein." She picked up, turning away from them and speaking rapid-fire into the phone.

"Fine," Noreen said, "but to have a woman come to clean only our bathroom because she's from a low caste . . . isn't that humiliating?"

"That's kind of the point," Kabir said.

"I did Amnesty International in high school," she said. "Junior year, I was chosen to attend a one-week social justice workshop in New York City. I know that in order to function here you have to live in a state of denial—which, by the way, could be a big reason why this city is so insane—but I need to draw the line somewhere."

Urvashi had finished her call and was listening. Noreen wondered how much she'd understood. When Noreen told her in Hindi that they would clean the bathroom themselves, Urvashi looked at her like she was nuts.

"You'll leave me a good tip?" she said. "You're two people, usually I clean for one."

Kabir assured her they would. By the time the front door closed, Noreen was having second thoughts. Noreen Mirza taking a moral stance to wash her own toilet wasn't going to get the low-caste woman who normally cleaned the bathroom equal treatment or better work. Maybe it would have been better to hire her and pay her well.

But now she'd decided, and the bathroom was filthy, and Kabir was holding the plastic bucket the maid had left by the kitchen door, rags ripped from old clothes hanging off the side.

"I'm really sorry," he said. "I want to be one of the good ones, but I can't even put the toilet seat up. I wish I had more role models, you know? But I promise I'll work at it, and I'll go clean the bathroom myself. It's the least I can do."

She walked over and hugged him. "Work at it without beating yourself up, okay? And you are one of the good ones. Now come on, we'll clean the bathroom together."

twenty-five

Air Quality Index: 98.

Moderate.

THEIR SECOND WEEK IN the barsati, loved ones arrived, with food. First her mother came with two bags of Thai takeout, then Tara, Yasmeen, and Varun showed up with chole, a rich chickpea curry. Noreen was happy to see them, to accept their hugs and hear Yasmeen say, "We're so glad you've been with him."

"Kabir's taking a bath," she told them. "He'll be out soon."

They waited for him in the lounge area on the terrace, Yasmeen and Tara on the love seat, Varun on the chair, Noreen on one of the squat but surprisingly comfortable woven bamboo stools.

"I haven't been to Sunny's in ages," Yasmeen said. "Do you remember when we used to sit out here and drink Old Monk until two, three a.m.? Where is he anyway?"

"Shooting in middle-of-nowhere Ladakh," Varun said.

"Some new BBC Earth-type doc."

"In winter! That Sunny. The more remote, the better," Tara said. "If it doesn't take a flight, a train, a bus, a motorcycle, and a pulley bridge to get there he's not interested. And how he lasts the summer in this barsati I have never understood."

"Don't you remember when he had that party one June, how much we were all out here sweating?" Yasmeen said. "And then we piled into his bedroom and the AC broke down."

"Oh yes," Varun said. "But at the end of the night, we had the first monsoon rain. That was quite spectacular."

"That's right!" Yasmeen said. "Wow, Varun, it feels like ages since you and I have danced in the rain like that."

"We used to be so young and carefree," he said. "Yaar, when did we get so old?"

"When we started a company," Tara said. "Achcha, tell us, Noreen, how is Kabir? What's he been doing?"

"I'll tell you," Varun said. "He's been holed up inside, feeling sorry for himself. Correct?"

"Somewhat." Noreen was all for ribbing friends and thought Varun was funny, but she'd noticed his Kabir jokes had an occasional edge.

"Do you know how many messages I sent him before he replied, and even then, he wouldn't say where he was?" Tara said.

"We all sent so many messages," Yasmeen said. "He must have gotten tons."

"He did," Noreen said. "I told him to reply sooner, but you know Kabir."

She heard the creak of the bathroom door. Moments later, Kabir appeared, grinning as he dried his hair with a towel.

"I was wondering when you'd show," he said.

"If Muhammed won't go to the mountain . . ." Tara opened her arms. "Come here."

She squeezed him tight, lifting him off his feet for a second. Tara was the most petite of the group but had a brown belt in Brazilian jujitsu and could kick all their butts. She'd told Noreen she'd taken up the martial art after moving to Delhi and experiencing one too many close calls with creepy men holding racist and misogynist views toward Northeastern women.

Yasmeen side-hugged Kabir, still wearing her backpack, then Varun hugged him straight on, Kabir dodging Varun's attempt to muss his hair.

Varun gestured at the three carryout bags on the table. "We have come with everything you need to get through a crisis— chole bhature, Old Monk, and Coke."

"Like old times," Yasmeen said.

"That's sweet of you, thanks."

"Please. We are beyond this thank you shmank you, okay?" Tara said.

"Fine, I take it back," Kabir said.

Noreen and Kabir went to the kitchen, wiped the dust off plates and cups and serving spoons, emptied the ice trays into a bowl. After they'd carried everything outside, Varun took out the aluminum foil containers of chole. Oil seeped through the top, dripped down the sides.

"We should put something on the table," Tara said.

"I have yesterday's paper in my backpack." Yasmeen twisted her body to unzip her backpack.

Noreen helped her layer pages from the *Hindustan Times* to create a makeshift tablecloth. They were about to set down the last one when Yasmeen said, "Let's put it other side down." As they flipped it, Noreen understood why; on the bottom half of the page, the headline:

Indian Literati Rocked by #MeToo: Art Philanthropist Akash Chakraborty, Curator Subash Iyer, and Writer Inder Chaudhury Join Growing List of Accused.

They spooned chole onto their plates. Varun passed around the bhatura, deep-fried bread made of white flour, the paper it had come wrapped in soaked through with oil. They were quiet for the first few minutes, hunched over their plates, licking their fingers, eating with their hands.

"Have you talked to your dad?" Varun asked Kabir.

"Not since the day it broke. I'm too disgusted by his attitude. He acts like he's the victim, like these women were out to get him."

"What uncle can admit he's wrong?" Tara said.

"He doesn't see anything wrong with a boss flirting with his much younger female assistant," Kabir said.

"Well," Tara said, "there was a pre-MeToo mentality of it's okay to have sex with your female assistant, as long you're not forcing her. And of course the whole trope of the artist and his young female muse."

"I'm not defending your dad," Varun said, "but we can all agree that what he did could be way worse. It's not like that newspaper editor who'd call the female journalists into his office and lock the door and forcibly kiss them."

"You know I almost interned with that editor in college?" Tara said. "Thank God I didn't."

"Varun has a point, Kabir," Yasmeen said. "If the standard is making misogynistic comments or a pass at someone, then practically our entire fathers' generation is guilty, including the liberals."

"Please," Tara said. "Some of the liberals are the worst offenders. In the beginning of MeToo, you remember these 'woke' old uncles were proclaiming their support for the movement, and I was like, I know for a fact you're a bloody harasser too. But Kabir, for what it's worth, your father was never creepy with me, and I can't say that to all of my Delhi friends."

"I get it," Kabir said. "He may not be the biggest jerk, but he is a jerk."

"The important thing is, nobody blames you for what your father did," Yasmeen said.

"I've been telling him the same thing," Noreen said.

A knock on the front door, too soft to be the maid, too brief to be her mother.

"Must be Ankita," Yasmeen said.

"Ankita?" Kabir said.

"Ankita?" Varun grabbed the remaining napkins to wipe his face and hands.

The last Noreen had checked her Instagram, Ankita was in Bombay, working on a piece about the city's drug-resistant TB epidemic, posting stark portraits of TB patients and the doctors who treated them, photos of crowded TB hospital wards and dilapidated tenements with poor ventilation where TB rates were surpassing 10 percent.

"I ran into her in Khan this morning," Yasmeen explained. "She said she'd been trying to reach you and I mentioned we were coming over. I hope it's okay?"

"Yeah, it's fine."

Kabir went to open the door and Noreen's heart twinged at their embrace. Ankita seemed much calmer than when Noreen saw her last. Her block print indigo dress clung to her curves as she walked toward them.

"Hi, everyone," she said.

Varun jumped up. "Here, take my seat."

"No, you stay. I'll sit with the girls." Ankita squeezed between Tara and Yasmeen on the love seat. "This place hasn't changed one bit."

"Do you want this cushion?" Varun asked, pulling out the barsati's sole sofa pillow from behind his back.

"No thanks, but I don't mind a drink."

Ankita filled a glass with ice, then Old Monk rum. Varun was ready with the Coke bottle, but Ankita told him she preferred it straight.

Noreen could tell this impressed him, but then it seemed like to Varun, even Ankita's farts would be jasmine.

Varun looked at Ankita, Ankita at Kabir, Kabir at the drink he was swirling, the ice clinking against the sides.

"Toh, Kabir, how are you?" Ankita asked.

"Well enough," he said.

"Have you spoken to anyone about this? I'm sure a few journos have tried to contact you."

"Only one, but I didn't respond," Kabir said. "Though I was thinking . . ."

"What?" Ankita said.

"I was thinking of reaching out to the assistant and apologizing on behalf of my father."

Varun smacked his forehead. "Why do you always want to default to the most senti move? You can't be so sentimental—the world will eat you alive."

"You sound like my mother," Kabir said.

"Do you know the assistant?" Ankita asked.

"Not personally, but it was easy enough to figure it out who she is. It's always five degrees of separation in Delhi."

"Two degrees," Varun said. "You've either fucked them or know someone they've fucked."

"Varun," Tara said. "Be serious."

"I am being serious!"

"I was twelve when she was his assistant," Kabir said. "I don't know her personally, or even remember her."

"You shouldn't reach out to her," Ankita said. "Anything you write to her could be posted on social media, made public. Your well-intentioned words could be used against your father. But you could make a public statement, if you'd like."

Yasmeen nodded. "Like Preeti Dixit."

"Who's that?" Noreen asked.

"She's an actress and comedian," Yasmeen said.

Noreen shook her head.

"She did a very funny bit about having sex during your period that went viral, and then she did a Netflix comedy special called *Auntie Flow*," Tara said. "She was always very outspoken about MeToo, and then her own father, who's a TV personality, got MeTooed. At first, she stayed silent, but when the accuser called her out for not saying anything, she issued a statement on Twitter."

Having pulled it up on her phone, Ankita read them Preeti Dixit's statement. "I wholeheartedly support the MeToo movement, and I resent the people trying to make the allegations against my father about me. They are NOT about me. This is not my responsibility or my fault or my shame. If my father is truly guilty, then he committed a despicable act. But this is his battle, not mine. I will continue to support the movement as well as stand by my father."

"How did people respond?" Noreen asked.

"You can't win," Ankita said. "Some people said, so what you're really saying is believe the woman and not the man, unless the man's your father. But others said, he's your father, if he denies it of course you'll believe him unless proven otherwise."

"But she had to make a statement because she's famous," Kabir said. "It's different for me."

"Kabu," Ankita said. "Have you checked your Twitter lately?"

Noreen wondered if she should have a nickname for Kabir. He didn't have one for her either. Did this mean they were more or less likely to last?

"You know I hardly check Twitter," he said. "And anyway, I've been avoiding social media."

"Kabir Chaudhury, heart on his sleeve, head in the sand," Varun said.

"Listen to this," Ankita said. "@susiefaluda tweeted: '@kabirwithalens, when are you going to speak up about the allegations against your father, Inder Chaudhury? Or does blood run deeper than MeToo?' So far, it has 192 likes, 53 retweets."

"Shit," Kabir said.

Noreen hadn't even known Kabir was on Twitter.

"But this isn't his fault," Noreen said. "How is that fair?"

Ankita shook her head. "You Americans love that word. Nothing in this world is fair."

"She's right, Kabir," Yasmeen said. "Some random right-wing troll is coming after you too. Listen to this—'@kabirwithalens u tweet against our great nation and say nothing when ur Marxist writer father is sex predator u are COWARD.'"

"But I haven't tweeted anything in months!" Kabir said. "Why would I start now?"

"You think trolls care about truth?" Ankita said.

Kabir turned to Noreen. "What do you think? Should I issue a statement?"

Everyone was looking at her now, including Ankita, but she was still a neophyte to India, hadn't even been to college yet. At the risk of emphasizing her naivete, it seemed wisest to defer to someone with more media savvy and understanding of local culture. "I think you should do what Ankita suggests," Noreen said.

"All right. Ankita, tell me."

"First off," she said, "delete your Twitter account, because you don't use it and anyway your presence is on Instagram. Then post your statement on Instagram, make sure you disable comments, and stop hiding out in this barsati like you've done something wrong."

"And what would I say in this statement?" Kabir asked.

"What do you want to say?" Ankita said.

Varun raised his hand. "I, Kabir Chaudhury, having only ever had consensual sex and being fully against capitalism's annexation of bodies—"

"Obviously not," Tara said.

"Everyone, let's give Kabir some space to think," Yasmeen said.

Noreen was beginning to grasp the friend dynamics. Yasmeen was the compassionate peacemaker, Tara enjoyed keeping Varun in line, and he enjoyed being chastened by her.

"I won't publicly denounce my father," Kabir said. "That I can't do."

"And you don't have to," Noreen said, glad to have something helpful to contribute. "Make your statement about you, not him."

"Well said," Ankita said.

Noreen flushed at the praise.

They went quiet so Kabir could concentrate. He'd stare up at the sky, say a sentence, they'd critique it. He'd modify, they'd again critique, and on it went. Nothing would be without flaws, they realized, eventually coming to an agreement to keep it short and simple.

I am a firm believer in and an ally of the MeToo movement. We must foster an environment where women and others feel safe to speak up, where their voices are heard and taken seriously. In regard to the allegations made against my father, I believe truth will prevail. This is all I have to say on the matter.

"Done," Kabir said.

"You disabled comments?" Tara said.

"I did."

"We're proud of you, Kabir," Yasmeen said.

"Yes," Varun said. "And we're here for you, one hundred per-cent."

Tara glanced at her large silver men's watch. "We have to go."

"Where are you off to?" Kabir said.

"Protest," Yasmeen said. "The two men who shot Dara Khan posted a video on WhatsApp bragging about it, saying they did it because he was an 'anti-national' and they're only sorry that their bullets failed to kill him. But of course the police still haven't arrested them, and a big protest has been called to demand their arrest."

"And Dara is out of the hospital and he's going to address the crowd," Ankita said. "He was only just now shot and he's already back on the streets, fighting against injustice. He's such an inspiration. It's going to be huge—you two should come. I flew in for it."

"You all carry on; I'm not quite up to it," Kabir said. "But Noreen, you should go. You've never been to a Delhi protest."

"And who knows how much longer the government will even allow them?" Yasmeen said.

"Yes, come with us," Tara said.

"Thanks, but I'll think I'll stay and keep this one company," Noreen said, nudging Kabir.

"Yaar, Kabir, how do you find these women who take such nice care of you?" Varun said.

"Varun, do you remember when you went to Jaipur with Dee for that shaadi and she broke up with you at the sangeet and you called Kabir from Jaipur crying at two a.m. and he drove through the night to be with you?" Tara said. "That's how."

"Varun, you, cry?" Ankita said. "I'm shocked."

It was the first time Noreen had seen Varun at a loss for words.

"Chalo, let's have a toast before we go." Yasmeen raised her glass. "To equality and justice for all."

"To equality and justice for all."

After everyone had left, Noreen decided to walk to the colony market. Ankita was still outside their gate, talking on the phone while smoking a cigarette. The creepy guard from the house across wasn't at his post, though there were plenty of other men to ogle her: other guards, drivers, lingering passersby, a few women, too.

As she debated whether to say something or keep going, Ankita hung up, saw her, and said, "Hey."

"I thought you were going to the protest," Noreen said.

"I had to take a work call. How are you doing?"

"I'm fine."

"This must be stressful for you, too. And Kabir has a tendency to wallow. It's good he's with someone who has time on her hands."

Noreen couldn't quite tell if this was meant sincerely, or as a burn, or a bit of both.

"Thank you, by the way," Noreen said. "For giving him all that advice. You really helped him out."

Ankita responded with a cryptic smile, and Noreen realized she'd yet to hear her laugh.

"Achcha, will you do something?" Ankita said. "Encourage Kabir to get out of Delhi. Living here, he'll be forever stuck."

"Yeah, we've talked about it some," Noreen said. "But I'll bring it up again. Maybe not this second, but I will." She spoke as if she was long on time, and wondered if Ankita would be saying something different if she knew Noreen was leaving in a little over a month.

"Hey, how's your mom?" Noreen said.

"She had her final round of chemo last week, and hasn't missed a single bridge club so far, so I guess she's good," Ankita said. "Thank you for asking. Are you sure you don't want to come to the protest? It might feel good to shout."

Noreen laughed. "No, thanks."

Ankita stubbed her cigarette against the boundary wall and walked away in the direction of the market. Noreen idled on her phone for a few minutes before following. En route, she crossed paths with the creepy guard reporting to work. He worked long shifts at the blue gate of the house directly opposite theirs and was always watching her come and go, alone and with Kabir. He knew the two of them were sleeping together in that one room, and the way he looked at her made her wish she could shrink inside herself, become *less*, less visible, less American, less curvy, less female. She turned her head as he passed but could feel him leering, his eyes piercing her skin, her chest, her tender chrysalis of a heart.

twenty-six

Air Quality Index: 177.

Unhealthy.

TALKING TO KABIR ABOUT Inder, the type of man he'd thought his father was and the one he was proving to be (not so dramatically different, perhaps, but still) had made Noreen consider her own father. She knew he was a prolific philanderer, that when Ruby was pregnant, her close friend Divya revealed Farhan had come on to her, which led to Ruby discovering he'd been lying and cheating since day one. Now Noreen recalled how, over the years, she'd overheard her mother's friends refer to him as a "smooth operator" and a "Pakistani Lothario." She googled Lothario—*a man who behaves selfishly and irresponsibly in his sexual relationships with women*—and wondered, just how selfish and irresponsible was he? Was Kabir's father a saint compared to hers?

She'd met her father once, a few years ago, when he'd remarried and his new wife, Leila, had messaged Ruby. Would it be okay if Noreen met her and Farhan for coffee some weekend afternoon? Ruby told Noreen it was her decision. Curious to see her father, and knowing she'd regret it if she didn't, Noreen agreed.

The three of them met at a café on the Upper East Side famous for its floral-herbal teas and homemade cookies, a place for well-heeled ladies to rest their shopping bags and gossip over macaroons. They were seated at a four-top, Noreen across from Leila, her father perpendicular to them. He was still very handsome, older, of course, graying temples, gray stubble across his square jaw. She'd inherited his coloring, light brown eyes, dark brown hair, caramel skin. With his black-frame glasses and low V-neck T-shirt under a tailored dark gray suede jacket, he looked like a cross between Bollywood star and hipster English professor. Noreen faced the door and so far, she'd observed three women doing double takes of her father upon entering. Two had then checked out Leila, with the critical eye women reserved for other women. The third also checked out Noreen, and Noreen wondered what she made of them. There was certainly no mistaking Leila for Noreen's mother. Leila was taller than Farhan in her stilettos and very skinny, all points and angles, a pointed chin and a thin, pointy nose and pointy breasts under her cashmere sweater and cheekbones that became even sharper when she smiled, which was often. Her teeth were almost as sparkly as the fat diamond studs in her ears, and her skin glowed. She had a successful dermatology practice nearby, so Noreen guessed this was part of the job description. Noreen had checked out her practice's Instagram account. *Life is short, look your best*, was the tagline.

Since their initial hellos, Leila had led the small talk—what subjects do you like at school, have you thought about where you want to go to college, what plans for the big 1-6. English, history, biology, minus lab, definitely a smaller liberal arts school but not sure where, birthday party at home. Her father barely spoke, choosing instead to check his phone, reread the menu, rearrange the stalks of dried lavender in the raindrop vase.

"That looks so much better," Leila said when he'd finished, though Noreen couldn't see much difference. "Your father has a very good eye; everywhere we go he's rearranging things. He could have his own HGTV show."

Her father responded with a small smile and the waitress came with their food. Leila had ordered for them, a French-press coffee for her father, a Moroccan mint pot of tea for her, a lemonade for Noreen, and a plate of assorted cookies. Her lemonade came in a mason jar and had a sprig of basil in it. The eighteen-dollar dollar cookie plate consisted of four cookies.

"Have one," Leila said.

Noreen selected the chocolate chip. It had Nutella inside. Delicious. No one else was eating, though, so she set the rest down on her china plate.

Farhan tried to serve Leila tea, but she stopped him.

"Thank you, azizam, but it needs to steep longer," she said, pouring the tea back into the pot. Then she reached across the table and touched Noreen's arm. A heart-shaped charm, studded with pavé diamonds and engraved with initials *L & F*, dangled from her rose-gold bracelet.

"Noreen," she said. "I'm sure you're wondering why we got in touch now, after so long."

Noreen looked at her father, who was holding on to the French-press knob, knitting his brow as though assessing the ideal moment to push it down. Noreen resumed eating her cookie; some things were too good to waste.

"When your father told me he hadn't seen you since you were a baby, it made me think of my cousin. Her parents were divorced, and her father died when she was two, and it kills her not to have her own memory of him, not to be able to picture him for herself. None of us knows the future. We could get hit by a bus tomorrow. That's what happened to my cousin's father."

"Oh. I'm sorry to hear that," Noreen said.

"That's all right," Leila said.

Her father had forgone the French press for the sugar packets, now lined up in a row in front of him. Noreen couldn't decide if his awkward third wheel act was better or worse than him at least pretending he wanted to be here.

"I didn't want something to happen to either of you without you two having met. It would have kept me awake at night."

Her father was putting the packets back in the container now, alternating real sugar, fake sugar, real sugar, fake sugar.

"Farhan," Leila said.

"I'm listening," her father said.

"Tell her."

"Yes." A stevia packet hadn't fit the pattern and he rubbed it between his fingers as he spoke. "If there's ever an emergency, know you can ask us for help."

"An emergency?" Noreen said.

"Emergencies, of course," Leila said, "but other things as well. If you ever need a recommendation for a good internist or gynecologist, I'm very well connected in the medical field. If you're interested in beauty care, our teen facials are very popular. Or if you ever want to go shoe shopping; I love a good purse, but my real weakness is shoes. I even have a special closet for them. I keep them in their original shoeboxes, and I tape a Polaroid of the shoes on the box, so I know what's inside. In other words, I'll always make time for shoes. Your father has a good eye for these things, too—his first gift to me was the most perfect pair of Manolos. I felt like Cinderella."

Half of her could not process what was happening, while the other half wished she could take notes.

Leila placed her hand through Farhan's elbow and leaned toward him. "The point is," she said, "we want you to know that, no matter what, blood is blood. Right, Farhan?"

"Yes," Farhan said, reaching for the French press.

They watched as her father slowly pushed down the plunger. As it hit bottom, he said, "They never brought my cream."

"I'll tell the waitress. I have to visit the ladies' room anyway."
Leila stood up and patted Farhan's shoulder. "It'll give you two
a chance to talk."

Her heels clicked against the tile as she left Noreen and her
father in silence. Noreen took a second cookie, coconut short-
bread dipped in dark chocolate. Also delicious.

As she ate her cookie, she noticed her father follow something
with his eyes and found the object of his attention: the young,
attractive, blond hostess, leading a mother and her pigtailed
daughter to their table. She wondered if he knew the hostess had
been checking him out a minute ago.

Her phone buzzed.

Adi Uncle. *How did it go?*

Noreen: *Still going.*

"Noreen. Listen." Her father folded his hands on the table.
He looked very serious, like a doctor with bad news. "I apologize if this is awkward for you. Once Leila's mind is made up, it's
easier to move the earth than change it. I know you must be very
upset with me, and understandably so, but I did what was best
for you and your mother. It would have been too . . . complicated
otherwise. I'm happy to see you're doing so well."

She wanted to say, Yeah, no thanks to you, but opted for a less
biting reply. "Does that mean I shouldn't call in an emergency?"

"No, no. If you ever need money or something . . ."

Hopefully she never got to the place where if there was something, she was desperate enough to contact him.

Farhan pulled out his slim leather wallet. "Do you need money to get home? Here, take some."

"I don't need money," she said.

The waitress returned, profusely apologetic about being late with his cream. Her father smiled and assured her it was no problem at all, and the waitress lingered, insisting he please let her know if there was anything else he needed, that she'd have it to him right away.

He poured a little cream into his cup, then coffee, then a little more cream. She would have taken him for someone who drank their coffee black. "How's the screenwriting going?" he said.

She raised her eyebrows. "How did you know about that?"

"Leila asked your mom what you might like for your sixteenth birthday, and she mentioned you've been working on some scripts."

"Oh."

"Maybe we'll get you a book about screenwriting. I know a few good ones."

"Do you write screenplays?" she said.

"I used to dabble, a bit. How's your mom? You look so much like her."

"She's great."

"Good." He opened the stevia, tapped a third of it into his coffee, and carefully folded the edge of the packet. She'd been watching to see if they shared any of the same tics or quirks, but so far nothing.

"There's still two cookies left," he said. "Have another."

How many cookies did he think she could eat? Well, three was a possibility, but not in front of Lamppost Leila, who was clicking her way back to them.

"The lotion in the women's bathroom has a lovely lavender scent," she said, placing one soft, manicured hand beneath Farhan's nose.

"Very nice," Farhan said.

If you were a dermatologist, Noreen thought, would it be the end of the world to wake up with a giant zit in the middle of your dewy forehead? In an alternate reality, she might have asked Leila this.

"Did you two enjoy catching up?" Leila asked.

Leila herself seemed to be in an alternate reality.

"We did," Farhan said.

Did we? Noreen felt a little sick from the two cookies plus the pint of lemonade, and was also tiring of whatever strange dance the three of them had been performing.

"I should be heading out," she said.

"So soon?" Leila said.

"She has to go all the way to New Jersey," Farhan said.

"Would you like to pack these two cookies for your mother?" Leila said.

"That's okay."

As she was putting her coat on, her father said, "Good luck with the writing."

"Thanks," she said.

Later, she wondered if Leila had really meant it, or if she'd made those offers assuming Noreen would never take her up on them, which she wouldn't, of course, though going shopping for shoes with her stepmother would make for an interesting scene. What was clear was that her father had not wanted to meet, that the real reason for it had been to soothe Leila's conscience. She may have been misguided and overly made-up, but she seemed nice enough. What did Leila see in her father, aside from his good looks and taste in shoes? And how could she not see the whole thing was farcical? No sooner had she left for the bathroom than her father had said himself Noreen was better off without him.

She probably was, but it still burned.

Noreen was hoping for the screenwriting book for her birthday, but it was the usual card, a fancy one this time, on heavy, velvety card stock, a gold-embossed *L & F* across the front. Inside was a check for $101 and a birthday salutation in Leila's overstated cursive, signed by her for both.

Dear Noreen, Wishing you all the best on your sweet sixteen!
With Love, Leila and Farhan

twenty-seven

Air Quality Index: 97. Moderate.

WITHIN FORTY-EIGHT HOURS OF his Instagram post, several things happened that were positive for Kabir, though not necessarily for the world.

His Instagram post received more than 1,000 likes, and he now had over 400 new followers. Silver lining, Noreen said. What is bad for you can be good for your social media.

A retired actress accused Rohit Chopra, a major Bollywood actor, of drugging and raping her five years ago, and this story took over the MeToo news cycle.

An older female journalist wrote an op-ed saying that these privileged female actors and journalists should stop "whining" about misogynistic microaggressions and instead use their privilege and platform to shed light upon the brutal physical violence inflicted upon poor and low-caste women who have no voice. The op-ed went viral, dominating the IRL and online MeToo conversations of the intellectual circles.

All this meant the Google news alert she'd set up for Inder

Chaudhury quieted down and Kabir left the barsati to visit his naani at home while his parents were out. He'd returned upset, because his naani had kept asking him when is Zohra coming back, when is Zohra coming back, and Kabir, who had no idea who Zohra was, had kept responding, soon, soon. She'd started wailing, and at one point when Kabir reached for her, she jumped back in terror, confusing him for somebody, or something, else.

As he wrung his hands and fretted over the brusqueness of the new nurse and how the recent tensions in the household were surely accelerating his naani's dementia, empathetic Noreen listened with concern, selfish Noreen was relieved that they'd had sex before he'd gone to see his grandmother.

After he calmed down some, she said, "Listen. When I saw my mom last night, she gave me the number of a therapist. Her friend Pooja goes to her and apparently she's amazing. She books up fast, though, so it's better to contact her soon."

She'd been nervous about bringing it up, worried he might get defensive, or be offended, but he said, "Sure. Message it to me."

"Really?"

"Why are you so surprised?"

"I mean, in my mom's circle back home it's weirder if you haven't done therapy, and it helped me a lot after my khala died, but I know there can still be a stigma about it here."

"It's becoming more acceptable, among certain groups of people," he said. "And ever since I watched *The Sopranos* as a teen, I've thought it would be cool to have a Dr. Melfi to talk to.

Now I have a good reason to do so, along with a phone number. Tell your mom thanks."

God, she loved him. She almost spilled it too, even said the "I" out loud, then made a gargling sound as she swallowed the rest.

"Are you okay?" Kabir said.

She coughed. "Tickle in my throat."

Someone knocked on the door.

"Are you expecting someone?"

"Nope."

For God's sake, Noreen thought, did no one in this country call before showing up?

"Kabir! I can hear you. Darwaza kholo. Open up."

Meena. Kabir had only exchanged a few messages with his mother since he'd moved out. He looked, pained, at Noreen.

"Guess I got you that therapist's number right in time," she whispered.

Kabir laughed, did the "fine, let's do this" shimmy-shrug that Noreen found so endearing, and answered the door. "Hi, Mom."

Meena pushed past Kabir, walked over to the lounge, sat down in the center of the love seat, crossed one leg over the other, looked around. The circles beneath her eyes were even darker than Noreen remembered.

"It has potential," Meena said. "Give me a cigarette, please."

"When did you start smoking again?"

She snapped her fingers and, with the same hand, caught the packet of Marlboro Lights Kabir tossed her in response.

"How did you know I was here?" he said.

"Ankita told me. One of your few friends who actually has sense." Meena frowned at the cigarette she'd removed from the pack, selected a different one. Before lighting it, she tucked her hair behind her ears.

"You want some chai with your smoke?" Kabir asked.

"That would be lovely," Meena said.

Kabir went to the kitchen, leaving Noreen alone with Meena. Meena exhaled toward Noreen. "How are things?"

"Fine." One of the challenges with Kabir's mom was that Noreen couldn't read her sense of humor; the things that would make her laugh would probably not be the ones Noreen intended. She decided that with Meena, it was safest to assert herself only if asked or in support of Kabir.

The few minutes they sat in silence felt like the longest of her life, then Meena said, "So you two have been shacking up? Have you ever stayed in a barsati?"

"First time."

"Did you see Kabir's Instagram post?"

"Yes."

"You think it was a good idea?"

"Yes," Noreen said.

"Because?"

"People would have judged him if he said nothing."

"He should call his father," Meena said.

"He says he's not ready yet," Noreen said.

"Kabir's similar to his father. He needs a woman who's strong, who can push him in the right direction."

She was glad Kabir was out of earshot. "I think he's waiting for his father to get in touch with him."

"Inder is as insecure as Kabir; he just hides it better. Will you please tell him he needs to call his father?"

She was saved by Kabir, holding a plastic tray printed with a photo of the Taj Mahal. He'd steeped the tea inside a teapot. Noreen hadn't realized Sunny had a proper teapot, or three tea-cups that matched.

"Before you say anything," he said to his mother, "please understand that I remain disturbed by Poppa's behavior, both past and present, and I'm not ready to speak to him."

"Do you know how exceedingly judgmental you're being? Do you know what other men do, have done? For his genera-tion, your father is one of the good ones."

Kabir poured an equal amount of chai into three cups. He served Meena first, then Noreen. "This is not about equivocation. This is about Poppa taking responsibility for hurting someone else."

"Kabir. Is this even about the accusation?" Meena said.

"You'll never understand."

Meena took a sip, added a second teaspoon of sugar. "Oh, I understand. Look, I am not asking you to sing his praises. But how do you think it makes him feel that you were willing to make a public declaration on Instagram but haven't called him once to check in?"

"He's not even on social media."

"People talk."

"I was careful not to incriminate him in any way."

"You say that like it's some kind of sacrifice! Your father has made mistakes, we all have, but he is not some rapist, not even close. You should be helping him through this. This isn't one of your art projects you abandon when it's not going your way. This is family. You stick by your family. He's been punished and he will continue to be punished. You'll google his name five years from now and MeToo will come up. We've lost friends over this. These days, close friends of twenty years will become turncoats on a single tweet. You broke his heart with your post—let me finish. He's been backed in a corner; no matter what he says, he'll be crucified on social media. You can direct your empathy toward complete strangers but not your own father in crisis? And your generation needs to understand it can't change the world simply by taking pangas at old people. If making a comment that objectifies women is a bar, then go. Go arrest ninety-nine out of a hundred men over fifty."

"That can't be the defense," Kabir said.

"It's not a defense, it's the reality. Do you know yesterday his UK publisher canceled the publication of another novel because the author was MeTooed?"

"He's only worried about his book," Kabir said. "Why does he even write if all his books end up making him miserable?"

"You'll understand one day, when you commit to the hard

work of being an artist." Meena moved to the edge of the terrace with her chai, shooing the crow perched on the waist-high wall. "Don't be a child. Your father loves you. Call him. He's gone up to the Shimla cottage, and I'm leaving for my meditation retreat tomorrow. Naani and the nurse will be staying at Bina's, but I still want you to check on her."

"You're disappearing for ten days?"

"Achcha, it's all right for you to disappear, but not me? This retreat is only three days. I need a break. I have been with your father twenty-four-seven, which you can imagine has not been easy. If you'd cared to ask, you'd also know that people have been hurling vitriol at me, from left-wing liberals to right-wing trolls. People are calling me complicit, a traitor, a self-hating woman."

"I know it hasn't been easy for you," he said.

"Then act like it. And check on Naani every day while I'm gone."

"Who's Zohra?" Kabir said.

Meena flinched. "Zohra?"

"Naani keeps asking when Zohra's coming back. Who is she?"

Meena dropped her cigarette butt, grinding it with the toe of her cobalt-blue sneaker. "Zohra was her sister. She was abducted by a gang of men during a Partition riot in Delhi when she was thirteen. She never came back. Presumably she was raped and left in some ditch to die."

A beat, as Kabir took this in. "*Zohra's Ascent*," he said.

"Yes."

Noreen recalled the miniature painting made by Kabir's mother, the young woman rising on the back of Buraq.

"Why didn't she tell me about her?"

"She didn't tell me, either," Meena said.

"What else do I not know?"

"Rahem karo, Kabir, it's a trying enough time as it is. Our family's tragic Partition stories will have to wait for another day. Will you make sure the new nurse dilutes the medications properly?"

"I will."

"Also, don't let Naani have meat more than once a day, even if she asks for it. Lately, she's been responding well to Bhimsen Joshi raagas. And please, no more posts on social media. And for God's sake call your father. At least tell him you love him. You can do that much."

"I'll think about it."

She pursed her lips, walked over, collected the pack of cigarettes and the lighter from the table, stroked Kabir's head once, and was on her way out when Kabir stood up, his palms pressed to his sides, and said, "Mom?"

"What is it?"

"You're correct when you say I shouldn't be so sensitive, that I can't please everyone. But my post was the right thing to do. For me."

Meena thought better of whatever she was about to say, shook her head, and left. Noreen and Kabir flinched as the metal door banged shut behind her.

"I'm proud of you," Noreen said. "You handled that really well."

"Thanks." Kabir returned to the stool, clasped his knees to his chest. "Noreen, thank you for being here. Please know that as difficult as this time has been, it's been amazing to be with you. And I'm sorry, I would have liked to take you other places, there's so much more to India than Delhi and Bombay, but because of all this . . . I've been such terrible company."

"Don't be sorry!" She moved her own stool in front of him, sandwiched his legs between hers. "Please know that every day with you is an adventure, no matter where we are. Hey, you want to walk and talk in Lodhi Gardens? Some ruins, some exercise, catch the sunset, eat some kabobs? Or kati rolls. I could go either way."

Kabir held her face and kissed her, their tongues still tasting of chai. "I'd love that."

And maybe, whispered the part of Noreen's heart that ran with such things, while we're in Lodhi Gardens, walking hand in hand past fifteenth-century tombs, you'll think, *Who will ever care for me like Noreen?* You'll tell me you love me and move to America for an MFA and we'll both find success and the world will have gotten a handle on climate change and human decency and we'll have a flat that's filled with light and photos and books and art, beautiful but not pretentious, and a rescue cat, and maybe even a baby, and we'll look back at this and say, yes, it was a dark time, but it was also the beginning of us, and look at how we bloomed.

One thing people are not in denial about in India are bodily functions. In America, when you first start dating a guy, you pretend like you never belch, never take a crap, never fart. I used to wait to pee until the guy I was dating had fallen asleep so he wouldn't hear. An hour ago, his head was between my thighs, but God forbid he hear me urinate—what did I think would happen? He'd say, "Holy shit! You urinate? I thought after sex your vulva disappeared like a Barbie doll's!" In India, you don't have to pretend so much. Here, if you date someone, you date them on chole, on rajma. And let me tell you, no one's a Barbie doll after two plates of rajma.

twenty-eight

Air Quality Index: 108.
Unhealthy for Sensitive Groups.

ADI UNCLE HAD FINAGLED a twenty-four-hour layover in Delhi en route to a conference in Bangkok, which made neither financial nor logistic sense but was the type of thing you did for love. It was a long-standing tradition that Adi Uncle's visits began with Catch Up and prosecco, and upon arrival he'd showered, shaved, and dressed in lounge attire: tapered sweatpants and a Kathy Griffin T-shirt, her red vinyl curls peeling at the edges. They were in the living room, the balcony doors open, pollution be damned, the room bathed in the silken late-day sun. Kabir had told her that this golden, liminal light between afternoon and evening was considered so flattering in Bangla it was known as the "light in which to view the bride."

"So six months of the year Hari is El Capitán, and the other six months, he chills?" Adi Uncle said.

"Well, he usually travels," Ruby said. "The reason he's stuck around Delhi is me."

"And he never wants to settle down?"

"Nope. He has the life he always wanted."

"And Kabir dropped out of film school and is trying to figure out his next steps?"

"Yes," Noreen said.

"Adi," Ruby said. "You're asking questions as though we're planning on marrying them."

"I know you aren't, but what about this one?" Adi waggled his finger at Noreen. "She's shaping up to be as much of a hopeless romantic as I am."

"I'm not allowed to get married until I'm at least thirty, remember?" Noreen said.

"Thirty-one," Ruby said.

"What?"

Adi Uncle nodded. "Thirty's still a threshold. Thirty-one's a better floor."

"The point is," Ruby said, "they have good hearts. They're two good men."

Adi Uncle raised his glass. "To good men."

When they'd finished their drinks, Ruby insisted they start getting ready for tonight's EDP. Party prep made her anxious, at least until the first guest arrived and she decided there was nothing more to be done. Adi Uncle followed Noreen to her room and lay across her bed. While her mother's response to getting older was to make breakfast smoothies with blueberries and hemp seeds and spirulina, exercise more and purchase pricey beauty products in tiny jars, Adi Uncle was allowing his body to soften and spread, prioritizing creature comforts over health. Ruby and Noreen worried about him, given the desi propensity for heart disease and high cholesterol, but if you pushed him on it, he'd crack a joke and change the topic, and if you kept on, he'd become defensive and leave the room. Almost every adult she knew was a baby about something.

"If you ever become a pirate, you can use this mattress as your plank," Adi Uncle said.

"You and Mom and the pirate jokes! Kabir and I sleep on a mattress even stiffer than this, if you can believe it. Listen, while we're alone, I want to tell you something."

"What's up, kiddo?"

"This whole thing with Kabir's dad has got me thinking about mine. I want to know more details, you know, about his cheating and stuff."

"I can't tell you that, that's your mom's purview."

"Obviously," Noreen said. "I'm giving you a heads-up that I'm going to ask her, after Hari leaves, of course. I feel like, whatever it is, I can handle it. It's not as though I'm under any illusions about the kind of man he is."

"What he is is a fool," he said, "for missing out on the most amazing daughter in the world. Come here."

Noreen went to sit next to him, and he patted her knee twice and put his arm around her. She noted how the hair on the back of his hands was starting to gray and prayed that he wouldn't die until he was very, very old.

"Adi Uncle?"

"Yes?"

"I think I'm in love with Kabir."

He smiled. "You think?"

"Am I going to have my heart broken?"

"Let's see what the Magic 8 Ball says." Adi Uncle shook an imaginary ball between his hands. "Cannot predict now, need more prosecco."

She elbowed him and he kissed the top of her head. "All right, Ms. In Love, gotta put on our party dress. You know how your mom gets when she's hosting."

twenty-nine

Air Quality Index: 141.
Unhealthy for Sensitive Groups.

KABIR SHOWED UP EARLY, with a bouquet of lilies for Ruby.

Her mother, having rearranged the furniture twice, was underneath the coffee table, wiping dust off Hathi Blingbling's golden toenails. She knocked her head on the glass as she rose to greet Kabir.

"You okay?" he said.

"Oh, sure. I prefer to begin all EDPs with a minor injury," she said. "Would you look at these beauties! How did you know I love lilies?"

"Noreen told me."

"I did?" Noreen said.

"Yeah, when we walked by that florist in Hauz Khas."

Ruby held the flowers to Noreen's nose. "They even have a lovely scent."

"They're the most fragrant ones I could find," Kabir said.

"That's so sweet of you," Ruby said. "I'll go improvise a vase."

Noreen kissed Kabir. "That's, like, ten brownies points right there."

"From you or your mom?"

"Both. Come, help me set up."

They laid the snacks out on the dining table: samosas, pakoras, salads, mini quiches, dhokla, small bowls of dried fruits, which was what they called nuts here. In the kitchen was biryani and chicken curry for later, a box of small pastries from the overpriced French bakery in Khan Market, where they'd also bought the quiches. After rearranging the appetizers, Ruby left to get ready and a bleary-eyed Adi Uncle emerged from his nap. Noreen made him coffee with cardamom and Kabir asked him what he liked best about LA (the weather, the Getty, the gay bar Roosterfish, concerts at the cemetery, his new couch, and the taco truck near his office), what trends he was seeing in his psychiatry practice (lately, two patients with an irrational fear of dying a particular way, like getting hit on the head with a hammer dropped by a construction worker several stories above). Ruby opened another bottle of prosecco. Hari arrived, then Camille, dressed in an emerald silk blouse and cigarette pants and high heels. Camille had lived in India for over twenty years and spoke fluent Hindi. She could swear like a Punjabi truck driver and was funny as hell—last time Noreen had hung out with her, she'd told a story about her first time using a squat toilet that had her rolling on the floor.

"Bonsoir!" she said, kicking off her heels and giving each of them a double cheek kiss. "Pooja said she'd be here soon."

"She sent a message," Ruby said. "*Had to pick up something—on my way. India is great but always late!*"

They sat around the coffee table, eating and drinking and talking with the ease of old friends. Hari asked Ruby and Adi Uncle how old they were when they met, and when they said seventeen ("younger than this was one is now," Ruby added, pinching Noreen's cheek), Hari wanted to know what it was like growing up desi in America when they were kids.

"Oh, I can tell you that," Noreen said. "Noreen, you're so lucky; when we were growing up we had no desi American role models, there were no desi shows, no desi comedians, no desi celebrities, no reference point; we were so confused."

Ruby laughed. "It's true! The first major wave of desi migration to America happened in the late sixties. So our generation was the first major generation of desi kids born in America. People didn't even know what to make of us, really."

"Yes, they did—weirdos," Adi Uncle said. "I remember people would ask me, why does your mom wear a dot on her forehead? Do they have toilets in India?"

"Oh, and don't forget, do you really eat monkey brains?" Ruby said. "Why does your food smell so bad? Is everyone over there as hairy as you? Once, I went to school with mehndi on my hands and the kids asked me if I had cancer. I was so embarrassed of being desi, I'd try to shed any vestige of it whenever I left the house. But one day, Madonna started wearing bindis."

"Yup, and she wore mehndi in the 'Frozen' video," Adi Uncle reminded her.

"Uh-hunh," Ruby said. "Now they'd call it cultural appropriation, but back then I was like, Thank fucking God Madonna has made us cool."

Adi Uncle nodded. "It's true. After Madonna I could be like, that dot on my mother's forehead is a bindi, bitch."

"Do you know I was inspired by Madonna to start voguing?" Camille said. "My last year of high school. I took it very seriously. I used to practice all the time in front of the mirror."

"Show!" Hari said.

Camille laughed. "Ask me again three drinks from now."

"Remember that song, 'Chhuti Hai,' Puppy Bilheri's cover of Madonna's 'Holiday'?" Hari said.

"Who's Puppy Bilheri?" Adi Uncle asked.

"He's an Indian singer who makes up Hindi versions of English pop songs," Camille said.

"He just got MeTooed," Hari said.

Everyone looked at Kabir, and, realizing this, looked away. Noreen reached for Kabir's hand.

"Let's talk about something else," Ruby said.

"It's okay," Kabir said. "I don't mind talking about it. It's important."

"He's right. These conversations need to happen," Camille said. "I'll tell you, being a white woman in India can be très difficile. Men here assume white girls are easy. I can't count the number of times I've been propositioned or touched. In order to make it happen less, I developed this expression, very hard, very cold, very tough—I call it my resting India face. Of course, it's not only India. I remember in Paris, I'd be coming back from high school on the Metro and almost every day some man would stand right in front of me and yell, '*T'es bonne toi!*'"

"It's everywhere," Noreen said.

"Eh, fuck men," Ruby said.

Yeah, Noreen thought, as she wrapped her fingers tighter around Kabir's. Fuck men.

"Hey," Hari said.

"If you say #notallmen, I will kill you," Ruby said. "Who's rolling?"

"I can," Kabir said, reaching into his pocket.

They were almost done with the first joint when Pooja made her grand entrance. Pooja had the most distinct laugh Noreen had ever heard. It began as a throaty rumble, bounded upward an octave, and culminated in a joyous trill that made everyone who heard it laugh along, no matter the joke. Her outfits were as bright as her laughter, today a combination of gold, peacock greens, and midnight blues. She was out of breath, having dragged a large, wheeled black trunk up the stairs.

"What is that?" they asked.

"Karaoke machine, doston!" Pooja said, bowing to the cheers that followed.

"Thanks, Pooja Auntie!" Noreen said.

"No Auntie," Pooja replied. "Only Pooja. Is that tequila blanco?"

Pooja poured shots of the tequila Adi Uncle had bought from duty free. As the adults tried to figure out how to set up the karaoke machine, Kabir stepped onto the balcony to take a call. When Noreen checked on him, he was off the phone, standing at the railing looking out. Across the park, someone was getting married, the marriage house festooned with alternating red and white Christmas lights, strung from roof to garden.

"Everything okay?" Noreen said.

"Yeah. It was my cousin Bina. She's planning my nieces' birthday party and her mother is insisting she invite my father. She wanted to know if I'd still come if he came."

"What did you say?"

"I said I'd have to think about it."

"You can't avoid him forever."

"I know."

The sliding door opened, and Adi Uncle stuck his head outside. "Hey. Everything good?"

"Yeah," Noreen said. "We were just talking."

"Mind if I join you? There are too many cooks in that kitchen."

Inside, Ruby and Hari were huddled over Ruby's laptop as Pooja read aloud from the karaoke machine instruction manual and Camille ate pakoras.

"Please," Noreen said.

Adi Uncle took a seat, setting his shot glass down on the floor because between her mother's party cleaning and now, a pigeon had shat all over the small bamboo table. "What were you two chatting about?"

"How family can be so complicated," Kabir said.

"Ah, I get that," Adi Uncle said. "Noreen can tell you stories about my family."

"Not as well as you can," Noreen said. "I grew up listening to Adi Uncle's stories."

"I'd love to hear one," Kabir said.

"Yes, tell us a story," Noreen said.

"What would you like to hear?"

"Tell Kabir about being the first in your community to come out," Noreen said.

"What about it?"

"I don't know. The hardest part?"

Adi Uncle laughed. "I could tell you the easiest part—coming out to your mom. The hardest part . . . so much of it was hard."

"Tell us anything, then," Kabir said.

Adi Uncle stroked the white stubble in the nub of his chin. "I was saving this for my TED Talk—"

"You're doing a TED Talk?" Kabir said.

"He's kidding," Noreen said. "Go on."

"Well," Adi Uncle said, "my parents weren't as strict as Ruby's parents, but I had similar expectations—get all As, become a doctor, marry an Indian girl, preferably also a doctor. And I knew I was gay ever since I was nine and watched a TV movie about Bruce Jenner and started dreaming about him every night. I thought it was abnormal, and I was ashamed, so I did what a lot of gay young men did back then, bury it deep and overcompensate. I dated Kavita, a smart, future doctor Indian girl from my community, I was part of the youth group at temple, I had a poster of Madhuri Dixit on my wall—"

"He also wore penny loafers," Noreen said.

"I was pretty buttoned up," Adi Uncle said.

"What are penny loafers?" Kabir said.

"I'll show you later. Sorry, Adi Uncle. In high school . . ."

"In high school, I got straight As, I founded a premed club. People in the community held me up as an example of the ideal son."

"That's a lot of pressure," Kabir said.

"Yes. When I went to college, there was an LGBT center of sorts—well, it didn't include the *T* back then. I was too scared to go, but I made my first out friend, a lesbian named Hannah. Junior year, I came out to Hannah and Ruby, but not to my family. I kept making excuses. Let my mom recover from surgery, let me study for the MCAT. Next thing you know, I was a junior, and one night, I had this dream that I was being strangled, and I woke up gasping for air, and I thought that's it, it's now or never."

"I had a dream like that the night before my SAT exam," Noreen said.

"Me too," Kabir said. "Before my boards. Except in mine I was chased off a cliff. So after the dream, you came out to your family?"

"I did, first to my sister, and a month or so later, to my parents. My dad was an early adaptor of cell phones, and when I called, they were in Dillard's, returning some ugly plate they'd received as a gift. I told them to go to the bedding department and find a mattress to sit on, and I told them I was gay, and after the shock wore off, they said, 'You'll always be our son.'"

"That's great," Kabir said.

"Oh yeah. It could have been so much worse."

One of the strings of light on the marriage house sparked and went dark, the neighborhood dogs barking in response. Adi Uncle waited for them to quiet down before continuing.

"But my parents didn't quite get it. My mom kept asking, what does this mean for your life now? How do you live as a gay? What about children? What if you get AIDS? Can't you still marry a girl? And my dad—I had so much admiration for him, he was a brilliant surgeon with a very generous heart. If anything happened to one of our relatives or someone in the community, he would be the first there to help, and he'd never expect anything back. But he had a very hard time talking about his feelings. After I came out to him, he never brought it up again, kept talking to me as if nothing had changed. Every time we had a conversation, I'd wonder if I should bring it up, but I'd decide to give him more time to process."

"And did the community find out you weren't the 'ideal' son?" Kabir said.

"Of course. Nowadays, you see queer desis in movies and TV, but back then, almost none of us were out. I was a scandal. Soon, even people in other Indian communities knew I was gay. As one of the first to come out, everyone's eyes were on me, and my family. When you're one of few, you feel that pressure, show everyone how you can be gay and desi and live a great life and be successful and a good son. You want to be an inspiration for the next kid who wants to come out but feels scared. But I was a mess, dealing with all the emotions of coming out, and I fell for an older guy I met at Woody's in Philly, who proceeded to mop the floor with my heart and then tell me a few months later he was HIV positive. I ended up being negative, thankfully, but meanwhile, I bombed physics, I fucked up the MCAT. I'd wanted to be a doctor even before I knew I was gay, and I got rejected from every med school I applied to. Then, four months later, my dad dropped dead of a heart attack."

"Oh no," Kabir said. "I'm so sorry."

"So much for ideal son," Noreen said.

"Exactly. There were people in the community who were supportive of me, or at least empathetic, but there were also a lot telling their kids—Adi is gay and see what happened? He didn't get into medical school and his dad died from all the stress. I'd hoped to be an example and now I was a warning. And I had to go to my dad's funeral, and face a community that thought my life 'choices' killed my father."

"Shit," Noreen said. She'd known about the dramatic timing of his father's death, but realized she'd only heard this story in snippets over the years, never as a whole.

"That must have been quite difficult," Kabir said.

"Oh, it was, and of course I was also grieving. I had my first panic attack a few days before the funeral, and I seriously considered not going. But I went, and I made a point to say hello to every single person, thank them for coming. I wanted them to see that I wasn't ashamed, that it wasn't my fault, even though deep down I wasn't one hundred percent sure myself. I held my head high, and gave a speech about what my father meant to me that brought everyone to tears. It was actually a turning point. I thought, if I can do this, I can pull my life together."

"And look at you now." Noreen raised her glass. "Aditya Lal, MD."

Adi Uncle bowed.

"Wow, Adi Uncle. That's so inspiring," Kabir said.

"He also gives great advice," Noreen said.

Adi Uncle raised his tequila shot. "Do as I say, not as I do."

"Any advice for us?" Kabir said.

"Advice for you two?" Adi Uncle took a sip of the tequila, winced a little. "Well, if you ever have to make a big, emotional decision, forget about the small stuff. Think to yourself, when I'm very old and look back upon my life, what would I have liked to have done? For me, I knew old Adi would have wanted young Adi to honor his father at his funeral. Of course, it's not always so simple, but you'll be surprised, too, at how often it is."

A car alarm sounded in the distance, setting off another canine chorus.

"Thank you for sharing that with us, Adi Uncle," Kabir said.

"You're welcome," he said. "That'll be three hundred and fifty dollars."

They laughed.

"How about I roll you a joint instead?" Kabir said.

"Done. Now shall we go in and do EDP right?"

They returned to the party, where the tequila had kicked in, the karaoke machine was working, and Ruby and Pooja were singing "Closer to Fine" by Indigo Girls. Then Adi Uncle sang "Vogue" as Camille demonstrated her high school moves across the living room and back. Noreen and Ruby went next, singing "1999" in honor of Sonia Khala as everyone else danced. Next, Kabir took the mic, solemnly announced, "This song is dedicated to Noreen Mirza," and proceeded to sing "(Everything I Do) I

Do It For You" by Bryan Adams, at some point getting down on his knees in front of Noreen to hoots and hollers, Noreen both utterly mortified and hopelessly charmed. This inspired Pooja, who'd seen Bryan Adams on all four of his India tours, to sing "Summer of '69" with Hari, the pair of them jumping up and down with such vigor Noreen was certain Geeta Auntie would send someone up to complain. Camille sang an old Bollywood song called "Jawani Janeman," Adi Uncle taking a break from his biryani to sing along because it was a desi gay anthem. Kabir and Noreen did a duet, half singing, half laughing, to "Shape of You" by Ed Sheeran. Then Adi Uncle passed out from jet lag on the most uncomfortable sofa in the world, and they decided to do one grand group finale before calling it a night. It took them fifteen minutes to decide which song, but it was a good one— "Brimful of Asha" by Cornershop brought the house down.

thirty

Air Quality Index: 238. Very Unhealthy.

THOUGH ADI UNCLE LEFT the next day, his wisdom did not; his story inspired Kabir to go out again, because old Kabir would want young Kabir to stop hiding out in the barsati as if he'd done something wrong. He eased into it; no social gatherings or art openings, but they had a date night at a Parsi café, dinner at a Manipuri restaurant with Tara and Varun, saw a Bollywood movie at the mall. He also decided that old Kabir would tell young Kabir to stop dicking around and start figuring out his next steps, and so after some research and deliberation, young Kabir announced he would apply to MFA photography programs this coming fall.

The evening of his announcement, Kabir stayed home to go through his old photos and Noreen went to the market to pick up a celebratory dinner from Burger Hut, where she'd become a regular. In the three weeks they'd been staying at Sunny's, which they now referred to as home base, they'd gotten takeout from here five or six times. It made her happy to walk into an establishment and know people, like at the Thai diner back home.

"Hello!" Swarna greeted Noreen as she walked in. Swarna usually worked the register and called Noreen "ma'am," even though she was older. "Two chicken jalapeño burgers and one sweet potato fries?"

"Hunh ji," Noreen said. "How was your weekend?"

"Weekend was good. My brother tried the paratha challenge."

"The paratha challenge? Tell me more."

"There is a dhaba in Gurgaon that makes world's largest parathas. If you eat three in fifty minutes, you receive free meals for life."

"Three in fifty minutes? How big are they?"

Swarna moved her hands nearly two feet apart. "This big each. And each weighing over one kilogram."

That was more than two pounds. "Wow. Two normal-sized parathas are my limit. I'll sometimes go another half beyond that, but I always regret it. Did your brother win?"

"No, he couldn't finish the second. In past ten years, only two people have managed to eat all three."

"Are you also working for them? Because I'm this close to signing up."

"No, ma'am, this is my only place of work."

Lost in translation.

A line had formed behind her, so Noreen stepped aside to wait for her order. She waved bye to Swarna and ate a fry from the bag, sustenance for the seven-minute walk from the market back to home base. Two mangy strays trotted over, side by side, to say hello. Only yesterday, Kabir and she had seen them circling each other, growling through bared teeth.

"Oh, so you two are buddies again?" Noreen lifted the takeout bag out of nose reach. "Don't fight anymore, okay? The world's shit enough as it is."

They accompanied her for a bit, falling back when she turned onto her street. The worst part about her walk home were these last five hundred feet, because of Creepy Guard. This morning, she'd left her house the same time as Sir, the guard's employer. Kabir and Noreen called him that because that's what the guard called him. Sir was standing next to the back door of his Mercedes SUV, his reflection visible in the black-tinted window: closely trimmed beard, red turban, gold chain. He tapped the window with his index finger as he waited for the guard to finish loading the trunk, his fat gold watch, worn over his shirtsleeve, glinting in the sun. When the guard saw him waiting, he said "Sorry, Sir," and rushed to open the car door. Sir responded with a harsh rebuke and slew of swear words, chutiya, behenchod. Later, Noreen saw Creepy Guard shouting at the kid who delivered newspapers on his bicycle for being late. She understood now that this was the way of Delhi; someone pissed on you and you pissed on someone smaller.

Now, Creepy Guard was hovering over a slight woman in a simple cotton sari, a straw basket piled with onions and potatoes balanced against her hip. The woman removed a rupee note from her sari blouse, and he made a show of looking around before pocketing it. He watched the woman walk away, and as Noreen approached the gate of her building, she felt his gaze shift toward her. He coughed, presumably so she would look up, which she did, for a moment. He gave her a half nod with a half smile, the look in his eyes hungry and hostile. She didn't need a translator for these thousand words.

I know you. I know what you're doing up there with him. I know that in that room you offer yourself to him every night like a whore.

Noreen flung open the bedroom door and announced, "I fucking hate men."

Kabir was lying on his stomach, ogranizing photos on his laptop. Seeing her distress, he jumped up, knocking over a bottle of Kingfisher, the piss-colored beer trailing him across the floor.

"What happened?" he said.

"Creepy guard."

"What did he do?"

"Nothing. It's the way he *looks* at me—it makes my skin crawl."

"I'll go talk to him," Kabir said, but Noreen blocked the door. "No."

"Why? He wouldn't dare hurt me."

"I know there's a big class difference between you two, but

he's still super shady; he's running some kind of racket right under Sir's nose. I don't want either of us to engage with him unless absolutely necessary."

"I'll talk to Sir, then."

"Forget it," Noreen said. "That guy's a dick."

"But things aren't going to change if we don't speak up. Isn't that the point of the MeToo movement?"

"I don't want to talk about it anymore."

"Noreen."

"I don't! Not right now, at least."

Kabir cupped her chin, searched her eyes. "You sure?"

"I'm sure." She picked up the paper towel roll lying in the corner and ripped off a sheet. He gently wrested it from her, tore off more sheets, wiped up the beer spill.

"It's your decision," he said, still on his knees. "But if you change your mind—"

"Then I'll tell you." She held up the bag. "Let's eat."

EXT. DELHI STREET - DUSK

GUARD, age 34, is standing outside his guard post. Young lovers SAMEER, 24, and NOOR, 18, walk hand in hand toward their barsati, talking and laughing. Guard watches them approach. As Sameer searches for the keys, Noor notices Guard leering at her. She whispers something to Sameer but stops him when he makes a move toward Guard. Instead, she gestures for him to stay back and walks over to Guard alone.

                    NOOR
          (in fluent Hindi)
     I am not, and never will be, ashamed
     of who I am, and you trying to shame
     me with that look of yours is only
     proof of your own weakness. I'm not
     an object, I'm a human being, with as
     much right to stand on this street and
     take up space and wear what I like
     and go as I please as any man. I am
     not the problem, you're the problem.
     Don't you ever look at me, or any
     woman, that way again.

Guard is too stunned to say anything. Other
WOMEN of various ages, dressed in Indian and
Western clothes, start emerging in solidarity
from behind gates and cars and shadows and
begin walking toward him. Realizing he will
soon be surrounded, Guard starts to run.
A WOMAN, carrying a basket of potatoes and
onions, hurls one at him, then another, and the
other women rush to join in. A potato hits him
in the head. He falls, gets up, keeps running,
disappearing into the night as the women stand
watch.

As soon as Noreen finished this scene, she knew it was ridiculous, a Bollywood simplification in which problems had shallow roots and were easily solved. Still, it made her feel better, to channel her indignation into words, fill a blank screen with imaginings, even if simplistic and formulaic.

She was writing again.

Noreen had been working on the terrace so she wouldn't disturb Kabir. A servant's family was sleeping on a roof across the back alley, their straw cots lined up in a row. One of the boys had been coughing, and now he sat up, hacking out phlegm as his mother rubbed his back. This boy's lungs in twenty years, she thought. But wasn't that the sickest joke of all, the toxic subtext to every Delhi scene; all of them, villain or hero, young or old, broken or whole, breathing themselves to death.

thirty-one

Air Quality Index: 215. Very

Unhealthy.

HARI RETURNED TO SEA and Noreen went home to spend a little time with her mother. Ruby told her to stay with Kabir, that she'd be fine, but Noreen didn't like the thought of her eating ice cream alone at midnight. Even if her mother wasn't in love with Hari, it had to break her heart a little. Noreen's own turn was in less than three weeks, and she didn't know how she'd recover. Her mother's path to healing was more straight-forward: jokes, joints, dancing, movies, retail therapy—Noreen could tolerate a day of shopping if it began and ended with good food. They bought too much, ate too much, made up a goodbye song for Hathi Blingbling to the tune of "We Wish You a Merry Christmas."

We will miss you, Hathi Blingbling
We will miss you, Hathi Blingbling
We will cry gold tears

She thought of Kabir often, wondering where he was and what he was thinking and wanting to kiss that soft spot between his neck and shoulder. So this was also love, to feel the constant tug of the beloved, to wish yourself in two places at once. Though she didn't regret being with her mother, the intensity with which she longed for Kabir made her fear that her love for her mother had somehow become less. When she confessed this to Ruby, Ruby said, "Love isn't like the eggs in your ovaries; it's not a limited commodity. You need more, you make more."

On Noreen's last day before returning to home base, she was drinking her 5:00 p.m. cup of chai and perusing the headlines. She preferred to do this in the evening because she found it easier to swallow the inevitable bitter pills.

TWO MUSLIM MEN TRANSPORTING BUFFALOS LYNCHED BY COW VIGILANTES. INDIA EXPLORES NEW TRADE AGREEMENT WITH CHINA. THREE ARRESTS MADE IN GANG RAPE OF 3-YEAR OLD, VICTIM REMAINS IN CRITICAL CONDITION. JNU PROFESSORS PROTEST PROPOSED CHANGES TO HISTORY CURRICULUM. NEW AAMIR KHAN FILM BREAKS BOLLYWOOD RECORD.

Ruby set her phone down over Aamir Khan's face. It was open to a photo from the EDP, her mother in profile, reading the karaoke machine instructions. "Camille sent me this."

"It's nice."

"You don't see it?"

"See what?"

Ruby zoomed in on the lower half of her face. "Look at my jaw. That's my mother's jaw."

"What's so wrong with having Naani's jaw?"

"She has a frowny jaw! Even when she's smiling, she's frowning. That's not me. Hell, I smile when I ought to be frowning."

This wasn't true; her mother frowned quite a bit, less so at people, but at her phone, at the newspaper, after a disappointing bite.

"I suppose I should be happy it's a firm jaw," her mother continued. "We have good genes that way. Though my days of Botox are starting soon."

"I thought you swore never to get Botox."

"I did," Ruby said. "The trouble is, everybody's doing it. So, at a certain point, if you don't do it too, you get older, while everyone else stays frozen at fifty-two for a good ten years."

Noreen turned the page to an op-ed titled *Rohit Chopra's Most Challenging Role Yet: In This New MeToo World, Our Favorite Bollywood Lothario Casts Himself as a Victim.*

It was a sign.

"What?" Ruby said. She'd been standing at the mirror near the front door, massaging her jaw with the pads of her fingers while opening and closing her mouth.

"What what?"

"You let out a small but distinct gasp."

"I did?"

"You did."

Noreen closed the newspaper. "Why was Dad a Pakistani Lothario?"

Her mother flattened her palms to her cheeks. "What?"

"I overheard Divya Auntie call him that once, a long time ago. This whole thing with Kabir's dad, it's made me want to know more about mine. I mean, I know he was a big cheater and he hit on Divya Auntie and he slept with two of your work colleagues he met at the holiday party, but did he engage in any MeToo level behavior? I want, no, I *need* to know the most despicable thing he did."

Ruby nodded and took a deep breath. Noreen had been worried about upsetting her mother, but she seemed almost relieved. "You sure about this?"

"Yes. I've been meaning to ask you for a while now, but I was waiting for the right time, but there never is a right time, is there, to ask something like this." Noreen held up the newspaper. "Then I saw the word *Lothario* in the paper, and I figured it was a sign."

"Makes sense. I'm glad you asked. With MeToo and what's going on with Kabir's dad, I've been wondering if you've been wondering. It's definitely the right zeitgeist for this kind of conversation." Her mother tied her hair into a ponytail, extended her arms overhead, cracked her knuckles. "Let's walk."

Along the park's boundary wall, between a parked Mercedes and Lexus SUV, a driver sat on a plastic chair, reading a Hindi newspaper and scratching his balls. It was splendid weather, and the semal tree in one corner of the park was a sight to behold. When Noreen had moved here, the tree was starting to shed its leaves. By her first kiss with Kabir, nearly all of its leaves had fallen. The first time they had sex, a few green buds had appeared on the bare branches, and, while she'd been staying at the barsati, these buds had grown long and pink. The day Adi Uncle left, one of the buds at the top of the tree bloomed. Other buds quicky followed, unfurling into fleshy five-petaled flowers, each one a fiery, sumptuous red. Now, in early March, the tree was close to full bloom. In the mornings, birds flocked to it to drink nectar and sing. She'd been waking up early, drinking coffee on the terrace and enjoying the morning show. There was a second concert in the evenings, although right now the birdsong was competing with a mustached uncle dressed in a crisp white kurta pajama and breathing "Test, test" into a microphone as a group of mostly old folks gathered around.

Noreen and her mother joined the dozen or so people who were running, jogging, or strolling the perimeter path. The park, Kabir had explained to her, was based on the Mughal charbagh design, which meant it was divided into quadrants. This evening, each quadrant hosted a different activity. There were the old folks near the semal tree, and a father bowling a cricket ball to his young son, yelling, "Chin up! Head forward! Eye on the ball! You can't hit something you can't see!" In the third quadrant, a group of neighborhood girls and boys played badminton without a net, in the fourth, three aunties sat a bench with a thermos of chai, chatting and eating rusk while a husband and wife in matching teal tracksuits exercised on the body-powered elliptical machines.

After they'd completed one round in silence, her mother began to speak. "So. The worst of it. Your father was involved with a variety of women in a variety of ways, but the worst of it were the girls—well, they were women, technically, twenty-one, twenty-two. He liked them right out of college, new to the city, attractive, skinny, white, though one of them was desi."

"He met them online?" Noreen asked.

"Not many people were online back then. No, he hit on them at bars, when he was out alone or with his friends. He'd tell them he was a filmmaker, that he had helped found the Dubai film festival, say he was looking for an actress for his next film."

"And the girls fell for it?"

Ruby waited to answer until after they'd passed a pair of aunties clutching small weights as they power walked, one auntie saying to the other in Hindi, *I don't know who she thinks she is . . .*

"Your father could be convincing, and charming. And he was stylish and handsome. I think the girls felt flattered this 'director' was interested in them. He'd court them for a month or so, and then tell them he had to go back to Dubai for some film festival stuff, ghost, and move on to the next one."

"That's gross," Noreen said. She was both disgusted by what her father did and slightly relieved that it had not been something even worse.

The gathering of old folks, which included Geeta Auntie, had formed two concentric half circles around the uncle with the microphone. The uncle had a female assistant next to him, a tough-looking auntie in a peach lace shalwar kameez and red Nike high-tops.

"In hindsight, I could see how he played me from the beginning, like he played those girls, but while it was going on, I was clueless," Ruby said. "I believed him, I believed the things he said. For a long time, I was ashamed—how could I be so stupid? You think you're too smart to ever be hoodwinked like that, until it happens to you."

The father and son had switched roles, the son bowling, the father tapping the cricket bat to the ground and saying, "Watch what I do." Raju was pushing Yash Uncle in his wheelchair to join Geeta Auntie and the other retirees.

"You can't blame yourself," Noreen said.

"Oh, I don't anymore. But it took years of therapy to get there. Now if I could only resolve my mommy issues."

The badminton kids had ended their game and were heading catty-corner to where the uncle with the mic had begun leading the group in a stretching exercise: arms up, head back, side to side.

"You think he's changed?" Noreen said.

"I couldn't say."

"I would not mess with Leila if I was him. She owns like four hundred stilettos."

Ruby laughed. Noreen stopped, took both of her mother's hands. "I'm sorry you had to go through that."

"Oh, Nor-bear . . . I mean, that's very sweet, but it was so long ago. And if I hadn't married your father, I wouldn't have met the love of my life."

"Who?"

"Tammy, who else? You, silly!"

Noreen grinned. "I love you too, Mom."

The group was doing breathing exercises now, raising their arms as they inhaled, bringing their arms back to their sides with a *HO!*

"I don't have to go back to home base today," Noreen said. "I can stay another night with you."

"Are you kidding? You've been counting the minutes till you see Kabir."

HO!

Noreen started to protest, and Ruby touched her cheek. "I have dinner plans with Pooja and Camille. Go see your man. I'm sure you want to process this with him. Your days with Kabir are numbered, while we'll have lots of time to talk this through later."

HO!

She did want to see Kabir, curl up in his arms, tell him everything. "Are you sure? Because it's true I'd like to see Kabir, but if you need me—"

"Then I will let you know. And Camile is supposed to be picking me up in . . . twenty! I should go get ready."

"Mind if I do another round?"

"Hug first."

They embraced, moving out of the way of the power-walking aunties. The uncle said into the microphone, "It is universally acknowledged and scientifically proven that laughter is the best medicine," and then threw his head back, his belly shaking as he laughed HA! HA! HA!

By Noreen's second solo approach, the laughter yoga had begun in earnest, and the group had expanded to include the badminton kids and some middle-aged aunties and uncles, everyone clapping in sync, crying *HA HA HA!* as they thrice-clapped left and *HO HO HO!* as they thrice-clapped right.

Next they swayed from left—*HA HA HA*—to right—*HO HO HO*. As Noreen passed them, Geeta Auntie called out for her to come join. Noreen's initial reaction was *No way* but then Geeta Auntie gave her a big wink and mouthed, *Aa jao, na,* and Noreen thought, *Why the hell not?*

She weaved her way toward Geeta Auntie as Laughter Uncle instructed them to tuck their hands into their armpits, move their arms like birds' wings, and cry out *VERY GOOD VERY GOOD YAAAY!!!*

As Sonia Khala liked to say, in for a penny, in for a pound. Noreen took a deep breath and started flapping her arms, hollering, *"VERY GOOD VERY GOOD YAAAY!!!"*

"Now thrice-clap to each side!" Laughter Uncle said.

HA HA HA. HO HO HO. HA HA HA. HO HO HO.

"Now, swing your arms all the way down, and as you come up, laugh! Husso! Husso! Laugh! Laugh! Dil khulke husso! Let all problems go!"

Geeta Auntie, whose limberness at seventy-eight was an inspiration, swept her arms down and came up chortling. Everyone, including Noreen, was cracking up, bellowing, roaring. Laughter Uncle had to keep reminding them of the accompanying motions, to shake out their arms, shake out their legs, shake it all out.

Soon, they were so caught up in laughter that they stopped following instructions. Noreen rolled on the ground laughing so hard her stomach hurt, Geeta Auntie guffawed as she swayed, a grinning Yash Uncle moved his head in slow figure eights. One auntie rose and fell in tandem with her laughter's dramatic crescendos. One uncle was on his back, bicycling his feet in the air as he giggled.

Laughter Uncle let them go wild for a few minutes, then guided them back down, until they were standing upright, and relatively quiet.

"Very good," he said. "Now relax your jaw, relax the limbs. Yes, yes. Now wag your heads. Now stick your tongue out and exhale the buri hawa, let all the bad air out, then share your good energy by high-fiving each other with a HA!"

Noreen wagged, stuck out her tongue, exhaled her bad air, gave high-five *HA!'s* to Geeta Auntie and friends, who were all in cardigans even though it was seventy degrees, then to an auntie in yoga pants, her hair tied up in a fluffy red scrunchie, and an auntie who'd come straight from work, her heels on the grass next to her. She was about to hit up the badminton kids when Laughter Uncle switched it up again.

"Now, last time!" Laughter Uncle said. "Arms down one, two, three slow slow, then say *HA HA HA!* Arms up one, two, three slow slow, now say *HO HO HO!*"

Noreen moved her arms down slow slow.

My dad is a lying, manipulative, con artist jerk.

HA HA HA!

Noreen moved her arms up one, two, three slow slow.

And my mom is such a strong person.

HO HO HO!

Down, one, two, three, slow slow.

Twenty-one-year-old girls, new to the city.

HA HA HA!

Shit, new move.

"Fly!" Laughter Uncle was saying. "Fly free as a bird! Let out all your heavy air! Use your wings! Open your heart! Cool your mind! Now say VERY GOOD, VERY GOOD, YAAY!!!"

Noreen stuck out her chest, flapped her wings.

My dad *sucks*.

VERY GOOD

My mother is *amazing*.

VERY GOOD

I want Kabir.

YAAY!!!

thirty-two

Air Quality Index: 191.

Unhealthy.

THE FIRST THING SHE noticed upon entering the café was the goateed young man in the corner reading *The Palace of Infinite Salt* by Inder Chaudhury. Noreen wasn't planning on finishing it. At least for now, it was impossible for her to separate the art from the artist, to not read Kabir's father into the condescension and misdirected anger of the male protagonist, even as she was moved by his beautiful meditations on grief. She'd arrived early, browsed the bookstore below the café, bought an anthology of women's writing in India from 600 BC to the present, and had only just sat down when she heard a woman say, "Have you talked to Meena?"

The auntie who'd spoken had short, spiky blue hair—an unusual sight in Delhi, even more unusual on a woman her mother's age.

"I haven't seen her since the news broke," the auntie across from her replied. She wore peacock feather earrings and a red scarf printed with flowers and lizards that reminded Noreen of a sarong her mother had bought in Thailand. "I heard she went to some ayurvedic spa in Kerala."

"Achcha? When the going gets tough, the tough go to a spa in Kerala."

"Can you blame her?" Peacock Auntie asked. "I'd want to run away too."

Blue Hair lowered her voice, but Noreen was close enough to hear. "Inder is lucky nothing else has come out."

Peacock Auntie pushed aside the gooey slice of chocolate cake they'd been sharing and leaned across the table. "Kyun? What do you know?"

"Come on. Everyone knows he had a full-on affair with another young research assistant some years back."

"But they had an open marriage then, na?"

"Yes, but they had a rule—no one more than ten years younger."

Peacock Auntie snorted. "Itna stupid. Who would trust a man with that rule? And anyway, how many male artists have slept with their young assistants? It's practically part of the job description."

Too bad her father hadn't been an artist; all the twenty-one-year-olds, without the duplicity.

"Inder has always been a cocky bastard, but I do feel bad for him," Blue Hair said.

"I caught him staring at my breasts once. I said, Inder, my eyes are on my face, not my chest."

The aunties chuckled.

"Noreen."

She startled at her name, her book falling with a thud to the floor. As Kabir bent to one knee to retrieve it, Blue Hair said, "Kabir, beta! It's been so long."

Kabir nodded. "Hi, Bhavna Auntie. Hi, Prerna Auntie. How's Dunda?"

"Oh, Dunda is dandy," Peacock Auntie said. "He's studying chemical engineering at MIT. Can you believe two artists gave birth to a chemical engineer? And he's not a dunda anymore—too many American donuts and bagels and fries."

"It's good he's doing engineering; he'll always have a paycheck," Blue Hair said. "How is your work going, Kabir? We've been eagerly awaiting your first film."

"I still remember when Kabir and Dunda drew Asterix and Obelix all over my grant proposal," Peacock Auntie said.

"They did?" Blue Hair said.

"Yes, and I didn't have time to reprint the whole damn thing, so I sent it in aise hi. And I got the grant!"

They both laughed, a little too hard.

"How are your parents?" Peacock Auntie asked Kabir.

In the moment that followed, Peacock Auntie ate a chocolate curl off the top of the cake, Blue Hair toyed with her teacup, and Noreen reached for Kabir's hand under the table.

"They're both well, thanks," Kabir said.

"Tell Meena I'll call her soon," Peacock Auntie said.

"You two carry on, then," Blue Hair said. "We have some shopping to do."

The aunties stood up, wearing crocodile smiles. "So nice to see you, Kabir," Peacock Auntie said as Blue Hair waved with her fingers.

Kabir smiled back, asked Peacock Auntie to give his regards to Dunda.

"They were talking about my father, weren't they?" Kabir said after they'd left.

"How did you know?"

"From Prerna Auntie's face. She'd have that same look when she'd finished all the sweets and had to tell Dunda there were none left."

"But you were so nice to them," she said.

"How else should I be?"

She loved Kabir for his unflappable politeness, made even more remarkable given the daily aggressions one faced living in Delhi, but worried he might get an ulcer from being so nice. She worried, too, about his tendency toward lying low and wallowing. Sometimes you needed to release it, stand on a rooftop and scream, shake your fist at the world. Whip your hair. Exhale the bad air.

"Hey," she said. "You wanna get out of here? You were

planning on taking me to that ruin you love tomorrow, but why don't we go now?"

"Yeah?" Kabir said, his eyes a little brighter now. My sweet boy and his ruins, she thought. What would he wander if he ever came to America?

"Let's do it."

"Noreen Mirza, you are a woman after my own heart, you know that?"

Yes, she thought. I do.

thirty-three

Air Quality Index: 186.

Unhealthy.

JAHANPANAH, THE FOURTH CITY of Delhi, was established in 1326–1327 by Sultan Muhammad bin Tughluq, also known as the "Mad" Sultan. The city's name means "Refuge of the World." Begumpur Masjid was the main mosque of Jahanpanah. It once had sixty-four domes, and its sizable main courtyard measures 60,000 square feet.

The traffic came to a noisy standstill near the Green Park metro station. Noreen avoided eye contact with the steady flow of beggars, not that it mattered; even through the glass they sensed her foreignness and headed straight for her. The hawkers did too, first a wide-eyed boy selling wilting roses, then a man carrying a stack of pirated books. Though she knew she shouldn't encourage him, she couldn't resist reading the eclectic assortment of titles, top to bottom: *The Da Vinci Code, How to Win Friends and Influence People, Crazy Rich Asians, Shantaram,*

Half Girlfriend, The Alchemist, The Hunger Games, One Hundred Years of Solitude, Harry Potter and the Philosopher's Stone, The Palace of Infinite Salt, Fifty Shades of Grey, My Name Is Red, The Fault in Our Stars, Immortal India, Mein Kampf, and *The Book Thief.*

She was about to point out the disturbing juxtaposition of the bottom two books to Kabir, when he got a phone call.

"Kabir here. Lotte! What a nice surprise! Are you in India? Mumbai? Any plans to come to Delhi? Okay. Yes, tell me. Yes. Yes. Understood. Sounds good. So nice to hear from you, Lotte. Cheers."

Noreen shook her head again at the hawker, who'd kept waving *The Da Vinci Code* at her, which she tried not to take personally. The traffic began to move, and Kabir shifted into gear.

"Who's Lotte?" she asked.

"A Dutch girl I know. I met her two years ago when I helped out on a documentary they were shooting—one week on the Indian railways. She's back, working on a segment about Pamela Shergill for Dutch TV."

"Who's Pamela Shergill?"

"A B-list Bollywood celebrity. They're shooting in Delhi in a few days and want me to be an assist."

"You're going to do it, right?"

"Of course. The firangs pay well, and on time. And Lotte is lovely; it'll be nice to see her."

She pictured a Dutch woman, leggy, six feet tall, delft blue eyes and tulip lips. Though she recognized the futility of retroactive jealousy, she still felt its sting every time Kabir mentioned a girl from his past.

"You should come hang out on set," he said. "If you'd like."

"I'd love that," she said.

Kabir parked the car and they entered the dusty, winding lanes of the urban village of Begumpur. Inside cramped rooms, women crouched over stoves frying onions and garlic while children raced in and out of the open doors, past old men and the occasional old woman smoking beedis on the threshold. They turned a corner and stopped at the wide stone steps that led up to the massive, domed gateway of Begumpur Masjid. Four young men with oil-slicked hair were hanging out on the top step, and Noreen adjusted her scarf to cover her chest.

They walked through the gate's arched passageway and entered a vast and empty prayer courtyard of such majestic proportions that she rubbed her eyes as though it might be a dream. The courtyard had arched arcades on three sides, topped with black domes.

"How many people could fit in this courtyard?"

"Ten thousand, easy," Kabir said.

"I'm officially awestruck," Noreen said.

"Come," he said. "I'll take you to one of my favorite spots."

As they crossed the courtyard, Kabir giving her a tour, she thought of Sonia Khala, how much she would have loved it here.

She'd adored Islamic art and architecture, the domes and the courtyards and the fountains and the precise and loving attention to the minutest of details, and though Noreen had marveled at the Alhambra like everyone else, only in Delhi did she feel she understood the intrinsic beauty of Islamic design. Take this place. It had lost all the dressings that Kabir now helped her imagine, the sixty-four shining white domes, the elegant calligraphy in the prayer hall, the turquoise tiles and the silk carpets and the play of light and shadow from the lamps that once hung in the arched collonnades, their gilded glass decorated with Quranic verses. That this masjid, stripped to its blackened bones, a shadow of its former self, could still inspire such awe simply from its shapes, ratios, and proportions, was a testament to the aesthetic and mystical power of Islamic architecture.

They stopped in front of the mihrab, the niche that signaled the direction of Mecca. The red sandstone and white marble decorating the arched niche were a welcome contrast to the darkened ruins. On either side of the mihrab were long arcades. As Noreen observed the one to her left, she felt the pull of the passage's sacred geometry, a series of pointed archways designed to draw the eye down its symmetrical path, toward a final doorway filled with soft, gentle light. As she looked upon this luminous doorway, she saw that Sonia Khala was there, and understood, in the depths of her heart, that somewhere beyond this doorway, this liminal threshold between their world and the infinite, the hidden, the eternal, the light, her aunt was at peace.

At last, a message from her aunt, not through a dream but a passage.

Noreen started to cry.

Kabir, who'd been standing a few feet away to allow her space, took her in his arms.

The young men from the masjid steps came through the gate running. Noreen and Kabir moved apart and began to head back across the courtyard. The boys climbed on each other's backs, photobombed each other's selfies, their laughter escalating as Noreen passed.

Noreen stayed quiet on the ride home. She wasn't ready to put it to words, to limit it, give it borders. To think, she'd visited beautiful churches and masjids and temples all over the world and never felt the presence of God. But there, of all places, inside a vast and ruined masjid inside a crowded village inside a polluted city, God had found her.

thirty-four

Air Quality Index: 94.

Moderate.

NOREEN TOLD RUBY ABOUT it the next afternoon
as they hung out on her bed and listened to music. Thankfully,
the sad white people music that had been on repeat post Hari's
departure—Portishead and Elliott Smith and Cigarettes After
Sex—had been replaced by qawwali and Afrobeats. Right now,
they were enjoying a playlist of bands from Mali, Tinariwen and
Ali Farka Touré and Amadou & Mariam.

"It felt like a message," Noreen said. "That, yes, there is so
much more to this world beyond what you can see, and also that
Sonia Khala had become light. At least that's my interpretation
of what I was feeling. What do you think?"

"I think it sounds lovely. I think if you felt Sonia Khala, it
means she was there."

"Really? You used to be such a skeptic."

"So did you," Ruby said. "Man, Kabir's taken you to some amazing places."

"He really has."

Her mother walked to the balcony door. She opened it, leaned her shoulder into the wall, crossed one ankle over the other, lit her joint. "And your feelings about your dad? Have you been interpreting those?"

"Not really. I've got two weeks until I have to say goodbye to Kabir, so I've kind of pushed everything else aside. Brace yourself, because it'll all hit me when I go back home. How are you? Have you heard from Hari?"

Initially, her mother tried to pretend she wasn't disappointed when she checked her phone and there was no word from Hari. When Noreen pointed out that if you check your phone every five minutes, you're bound to be disappointed, she'd kept it in her drawer, but this only meant when she checked it an hour later and there was still nothing, she was even more disappointed.

"He messaged two days ago to say he was watching this incredible bioluminescence."

"Like what?"

"He said the entire ocean was illuminated, from the ship all the way to the edge of the horizon, as far as the eye could see. I asked for a photo and he refused to take one because he said a photo would never do it justice."

"Hmmm."

"It's fine," Ruby said. "I always knew he was married to the sea. And even if he wasn't, we never would have lasted."

"A wise woman once said, the hurt will fade and you'll understand he came into your life for a reason, and it's better it ended when it did."

Ruby smiled. "Very wise indeed."

They heard the muffled vibrations of Ruby's phone.

"Could it be El Capitán?" Noreen said.

"Check."

"It's Naani. Should I answer?"

Ruby stubbed the joint on the balcony floor and answered the phone, saying salaam to Azra's cheek and ear. A thick gold filigree earring in the shape of a question mark curled around her slightly stretched earlobe.

"Tum log kya kar rahe ho?"

"Just chilling, Naani," Noreen said.

"Achcha. What else?"

"Nothing too interesting," Ruby said. "Finishing up my big report for work."

"What will it say?"

"Well, it's about fifty pages of clear and succinct writing sprinkled with some requisite jargon, in which I evaluate various projects and outcomes and explain how it's all very complicated—can you move the phone so we can see your whole face?"

"Better?"

"Yes."

"I have some news." Azra disappeared for a second, replaced by a dark leather sofa, then returned, a mug in her hands. "Imran is moving to Seattle to be close to his parents."

"Makes sense," Ruby said. "Imran Bhai is a widower with two young boys."

"He has a girlfriend there, too, someone he went to high school with."

It was weird to think of Imran Khalu with someone other than Sonia Khala, but it was bound to happen. Sonia Khala had even given him her blessing. She told him, just because I'm dead doesn't mean you should die alone.

"It's been almost two years since Khala died, Naani," Noreen said. "He has to move on."

"But so soon? Another woman raising Sonia's sons? We don't even know her. And the boys will see Imran's parents all the time but what about me? How often will I get to see them? I can't go stay with Imran and his new wife. And long flights aren't so easy for me anymore. What if they don't visit me? I'll barely see my own grandchildren."

"Imran Bhai is a good guy," Ruby said. "He'll make sure the boys have a relationship with you. No one can replace you. You're one of a kind."

"It won't be the same."

Ruby and Noreen exchanged glances. What was there to say?

Of course it wouldn't be the same. Of course it was unsettling to think of another woman raising the twins who had Sonia's eyes. Of course Azra would see her grandchildren more if her daughter were still alive. Of course the twins would be closer to the grandparents they saw every week than the ones on the opposite coast. And Imran Khalu was a good guy, but he could only take so much of Azra, even with the exalted position of son-in-law. Sonia had often brought the twins without him.

"It's going to be okay," Ruby said.

"No, it's not," Azra said.

"Yes, it is," Noreen said, with more force than she'd intended. "I know it's difficult, but the twins will still love you, I promise. Very soon they'll be old enough to fly alone and come visit us. Imran Khalu won't have a problem with that."

"Maybe." Azra sighed. "Achcha suno, don't forget to buy me a pashmina—plain black but finest quality. And take a local with you—the minute you open your mouth they'll rip you off. Neither of you know how to bargain."

"Mom's actually pretty decent," Noreen said.

"I learned from the best," Ruby said. They said khuda hafiz to Azra, and Ruby fell back on the pillow, the phone screen down on her chest. "Sometimes I wish she could understand that the biggest obstacle to her being close to Amir and Sohail might be *her*."

Noreen lay on her belly next to her. "Yeah, I think that ship has sailed."

"I know. It's sad."

"But you can't change anyone else, so I guess it is what it is."

"Oh, Nor-bear."

"What? I can tell whatever you're going to say next is going to make me want to hug you and gag at the same time," Noreen said.

Ruby caressed Noreen's cheek with her thumb. "You know, when they handed you to me after you were born, and you looked up at me with that little wrinkly old man alien face, I made you a promise. I said, I promise to be the kind of mother you will never dread coming home to. And that promise has carried me all these years, that promise has made me a better person. Loving you is the best part of me."

"Wow. Hari leaving and all that Elliott Smith has made you super senti."

They laughed, then Noreen said, "I'm sorry, though, that you can't talk to Naani the way I talk to you."

"Ah, that's okay," Ruby said. "It is what it is."

thirty-five

Air Quality Index: 212. Very Unhealthy.

WHEN NOREEN TURNED ONTO the residential street in Lajpat Nagar, she could tell which house it was from the crowd forming outside. She called Kabir but he didn't pick up. A few months ago, she would have hung back, but now she squared her shoulders and elbowed her way through, catching snippets of conversation in Hindi.

Do you know which celebrity it is?

I heard it was Huma Qureshi.

I heard Radhika Apte.

Wasn't she in Haider?

No, no, that was Shraddha Kapoor.

I heard Abhishek Bachchan is coming.

I think he's a terrible actor.

He's okay, but he'll never surpass his father.

When she finally reached the gate, a burly guard barred her

from entering. "Shooting ho rahi hai," he told her. "No entry."

Someone knocked on the gate from inside. The guard opened it, and Kabir instructed him to allow her in.

"Sorry," he said, "I only now saw your message. We're wrapping up."

They'd finished filming the scene in which Pamela Shergill brings them to her childhood home and talks about her modest upbringing. The film equipment was set up at one end of the garden, two cameras and a large furry microphone and a white board on a stand that Kabir explained was called a reflector, used to reflect the best light on the interview subject.

At the garden's other end, Pamela Shergill pouted at a large mirror held up by a young female assistant in an oversized flannel shirt. Her red leopard print jumpsuit was unzipped enough for a tease of cleavage, a rhinestone belt cinching her narrow waist. Loose curls with honey-brown highlights spiraled down her back, a diamond Om necklace sparkled at her neck. Another young female assistant flitted around clutching a clipboard, acting harried but not doing very much.

The crew—Lotte, Saskia, and a guy named Luuk—were standing around drinking chai in clear plastic cups. Lotte had very dark brown hair and eyes, was even more beautiful than Noreen had imagined, and wore a silver wedding band.

"There's a ton of people outside," Noreen told them after exchanging hellos. "Some press, too."

Lotte rolled her eyes and lowered her voice. "I overheard Pamela's assistant call the press to tip them off that we were coming. She told them Abhishek Bachchan might show up to make sure they got a good crowd. Then, when we arrive here, Pamela points to the crowd and says to us, 'I know it's part of being a celebrity but it's so exhausting to be followed by so many people everywhere I go.'"

"Turns out Pamela Shergill is a B-list diva," said Luuk.

"Shocking, isn't it?" Kabir said.

In Delhi, at 5'10" Kabir was often one of the tallest in a room, but both Lotte and Saskia were taller by an inch or two, Luuk towering over them all. It must be extra challenging, Noreen thought, to be a Dutch little person.

"So what's the next scene you're filming?" Noreen asked.

"Pamela supports a women's shelter for victims of domestic violence, so we are heading there next." Lotte glanced at her watch. "We should leave jaldi jaldi. We're already behind schedule."

"Nothing on this shoot has happened on schedule," Saskia said.

"India is great but always late," Noreen said, and was pleased when the Dutch crew laughed.

Then Pamela started shouting.

"What do you mean, you didn't bring it?"

The assistant cowered in front of her, hugging the clipboard to her chest. "Sorry, ma'am. That particular outfit hum Bombay mein chhor ke aaye. But we brought the blue dress as per your instructions."

"But the blue dress is too glamorous for visiting the shelter!" Pamela said. "For this I need my Anokhi kurta and jeans—I have to look casual but smart, like a celebrity of the people and for the people."

Lotte checked her watch, shook her head, and crossed the garden, the rest of them following a safe distance behind. "Pamela, sorry, we are on a tight schedule and we should get going."

"Yes, but they've forgotten my outfit."

"Actually, ma'am," said the assistant wearing flannel, "I've just now spoken with the director of the shelter and she said there can be no filming there."

The crew exchanged glances.

"Kya matlab?" Pamela said. "What do you mean, no filming?"

"Pamela madam," Flannel said, "aisa hai ki the shelter is in a secret location."

"So we will do all the filming inside the shelter," Pamela said.

"You see the women, because they are in hiding from their husbands, they cannot be filmed either," Flannel explained. "It's for their safety only."

Pamela palm-slapped her forehead. "Tum ko yeh baat abhi pata chali! Only now you discover this? Do you see the incompetence we have to deal with in India, Lotte?"

"Yes, yes I do," Lotte said.

"Well, there's no point in going to the shelter now." Pamela glared at her two assistants.

"But ma'am," Clipboard began, "the women at the shelter have been so excited to meet you. The director said they've even prepared a—"

"Tum pagal ho gayi ho kya? Is your brain not functioning properly?" Pamela snatched the clipboard, which had nothing attached to it, and threw it to the ground.

Flannel and Clipboard cowered as Pamela, almost as tall as Lotte in her stiletto boots, came a step closer. "I am not going to sit in an hour and a half of traffic to go to fucking Ghaziabad if I cannot be filmed at my own shelter. What do you think I am, a charity case?"

Noreen laughed.

She hadn't meant to, not out loud, at least, but she did, and now Pamela Shergill had done a 180 and was looking right at her, her breasts heaving against the pleather, her heels sinking into the grass as she strode toward Noreen.

Shit.

Pamela paused a few feet away and tucked her thumbs inside her rhinestone belt. "And who are you?"

Noreen stood straighter. "Me?"

"Yes, you."

"I'm a comedian," Noreen said. Where the hell that came from, she had no idea, but it felt good.

"Comedian?" Pamela said. "You think you're very funny?"

"I didn't say I was a good comedian."

A few snickers.

"Lotte, who let this comedian on set?" Pamela said.

Lotte folded her hands behind her head. "Hey, Pamela, let's call today a wrap, shall we? We'll skip the shelter and pick up tomorrow morning at the Oberoi."

"But what do we do about the shelter? People must know the good work I do for women."

"Tomorrow we'll film you talking about all of your good charity work," Lotte said. "It's a wrap, everyone! Let's pack up."

Pamela flashed Noreen a dirty look and went back to Flannel and Clipboard.

"Sorry," Noreen said to the crew, craning her neck to look each of them in the eye.

"No worries," Lotte said. "At least you brought some levity to this nightmare. Time for a drink. Kabir, how about a beer at 4S, for old times' sake?"

"Sounds good," Kabir said. He turned to Noreen. "Comedian?"

"Yeah," she said. "Don't know where that came from."

"From here," he said, placing his hand over her heart. "Where else?"

All this rajma and chole talk brings me to Rule Number Four: When living in South Asia, try to have a nice bathroom. You'll be spending a lot of time there. Because butter chicken goes down fast and comes out slooow. My toilet seat isn't the best, it slides around and the plastic is cheap, you know, the kind that leaves a big red imprint on your ass after you get up. I'm starting to worry it's permanent. People will ask me, Noreen, what did you bring back from Delhi? Well, let's see . . . a Banarasi sari, a pashmina shawl, and an ass like a rhesus monkey.

thirty-six

Air Quality Index: 139.
Unhealthy for Sensitive Groups.

ALL SHE COULD REMEMBER about the dream was that it began with her father and a young blonde in pigtails holding hands and blowing bubbles as they roller-skated around a mall in Delhi, and ended with Noreen opening her Moleskine notebook and finding a letter to her from the jinn.

"A letter from the jinn?" Kabir said when she told him. He'd swiveled the desk chair to face her, his computer on his lap. "What did it say?"

"I woke up too early to find out. All I can remember is it was written in runes, but it was English. How long have I been asleep?"

"Almost an hour."

"Why didn't you wake me?"

Kabir closed his laptop. "I was enjoying the view."

She'd been napping half-naked, and when she sat up Kabir made a low sound in his throat.

"What?"

"You look stunning in this light. Mind if I photograph you?"

Now that Kabir was applying to MFA photography programs next year, he'd started shooting again. This was the second time he'd asked to photograph her. The first had been in Purana Qila, the ruins of the sixteenth-century fort where the Mughal emperor Humayun fell to his death down the library stairs, and she was so self-conscious she'd kept laughing into her hands. But here, in a post-nap haze in bed at home base, she felt more relaxed in front of the lens.

"Go ahead," she said.

He walked over to the curtains, opening and closing them to adjust the light until he was satisfied. "Perfect."

"No tits," she said.

"No problem." He crouched and started to shoot, directing her to tilt her chin this way or that, rest her hand there, here.

"Turn a little bit on your side. Excellent. Now curve your right arm over your head."

"No way," she said. "I haven't shaved my pits in two days! Nobody wants to see that."

"It's beautiful—the shape, the shadow."

"In what world is armpit stubble beautiful?"

"You think beauty comes from being flawless?"

"No. But—"

"Do you trust me?"

"Yes." She lifted her arm, rested her head against her elbow, turned her face as Kabir said, "Now look at the camera and think, I am perfectly imperfect."

I am perfectly imperfect.

"I am a writer."

I am a writer.

"And a lover."

And a lover.

"And a comedian."

And a comedian. But was she a comedian? That remained to be seen.

"My jokes are like lotuses."

She laughed, stuck her tongue out. He took one last photo, put his camera aside, and jumped on top of her, kissing her collarbone, cheeks, lips.

"Can I see?" she asked.

"I shot on film," he said.

"Is film really that much better?"

"To me it is. I like the tangibility of developing your photos. It's almost meditative. And also unpredictable. You don't get that with digital."

"Pretentious," she said.

He raised his eyebrows. "I'm ready for my MFA, then. Did you find what you needed in the market?"

"I did. Speaking of jokes like lotuses . . ." She showed him the photo of the flyer she'd taken that morning. He read it aloud.

HEY, YOU!

YES, YOU!

GOT JOKES?

ANNOUNCING OPEN MIC COMEDY NIGHT

EVERY FRIDAY AT DEPOT!

SIGN UP AT WWW.DEPOTDELHI.IN

"Did you sign up?" he asked.

"Yup. I got the last available slot for Friday."

"Your second-to-last night in Delhi?"

"Why not go out with a bang? Or a bomb."

"You won't bomb," he said. "Wow, Noreen. That's brilliant."

"What it is, is crazy. Doing stand-up is my worst nightmare. My dream's always been the writers' room, not the stage. But ever since I told Pamela Shergill I was a comedian, I've been thinking."

"About what?"

"All these experiences in Delhi, they've helped me realize that, aside from love, of course, writing and making people laugh are the things that light the lamp of my heart. If you can laugh about something, then it can't totally destroy you. So, I'm diving in headfirst." Noreen threw up her hands. "Stand-up comedy, baby! Even if it's only this once."

"You're going to be great."

"You have to say that."

"You make me laugh all the time."

She pressed her finger to the Milky Way swirl in his stubble. She'd already told him it was hers forever, and he'd laughed and agreed. "That's different. Truthfully, I'm a little nervous about you being there."

"Me? Why?"

"Abby was super into this poet named Pete, and they started dating and everything was going amazing, until he showed her his poetry. And she thought it was so terrible—irredeemable, she called it—that she had to break up with him. She said his art was so bad it crushed her love."

"What are you getting at?"

She picked up his camera, centered his face in the viewfinder, zoomed in on his eyes. Around his lovely light brown irises was a thin ring, the color of espresso. They were called limbal rings. She had them too, hers almost black.

"What if you find my stand-up irredeemable?"

"Impossible!" Kabir said.

He was being sincere, but that didn't mean her fear wasn't valid. She took a photo of him, parted lips, slightly offended Bambi eyes, then put the camera away.

"Think about it," she said. "Maybe you can hate the artist and still love their art. But if you hate their art, can you love the artist?"

"I could never hate your art. And it's the act of getting up there and doing it that's the most important."

She folded her arms. "Even if no one laughs?"

"All that matters is that we put our heart into it and give it our best."

Noreen smiled. "You telling me to practice what I preach?"

"Yes. And I don't care if you get zero laughs or a hundred. You could stand up there, frozen the entire time, and though I'd feel for you, because I know that wasn't what you wanted, I'd still be your number one forever fan. The simple fact of you standing in front of that microphone will make me . . ."

"Make you what?" she said.

He paused. "Incredibly proud."

He'd meant to say something else; she was certain of it. Was it love? But then why didn't he go ahead and say it?

Sometimes, when she was eager to tell Kabir something, she imagined her telling, and his response, and the anticipation of sharing it with him became almost as exciting as the thing itself. Even the shittiest of subjects, like learning about her father, Lothario to the new girls of the city, became less dire inside his arms. But *love* was the only word she'd been too nervous to utter, even in his arms, even after sex. She'd never said "I love you" to anyone she wasn't related to or best friends with. It was so consequential and serious and if unrequited could come swinging back to shatter your heart.

And if he did reciprocate, then what? I love you, I love you too, goodbye?

"You're too kind," she said. "When I win my Academy Award, I'll be sure to thank you for your support."

He held her arms over her head, sucked softly on her lower lip. She reached for his erection, wishing she could make love to him a hundred more times in these last days, however many it would take to imprint her touch and taste and breath and lips and skin into the memory of his body, so that after she was gone it would yearn for her, as she would for him.

thirty-seven

Air Quality Index: 208. Very Unhealthy.

NOREEN WAS WALKING BACK from the park when two young boys, squatting and laughing on her neighbor's roof, hurled a water balloon that burst in front of her, drenching her feet. One of the boys picked up another balloon, and she hurried through the gate of her house. Geeta Auntie was on the patio, her engraved silver paan box open in her lap.

"They got you," she said, gesturing at Noreen's soaked sandals.

"Isn't Holi day after tomorrow?" Noreen said.

"The pranks begin a full week before, nowadays. Aao, baitho. I'll make you a paan." Geeta Auntie smeared some white chuna and a little bit of red katha paste on the heart-shaped betel leaf in her palm. "When is Ruby back from Rajasthan?"

"Three days." Her mother had gone with Pooja and Camille on an abbreviated version of their Rajasthan tour.

"Where is Kabir taking you for Holi? Remember you must be in a safe place with people you know."

"We're going to a party at his friend's house," Noreen said.

"Good. Don't go walking on the streets on Holi, and never go anywhere alone."

The spring festival of Holi was celebrated by consuming bhang, a form of marijuana, throwing colored powders on one another, and generally transgressing boundaries. Camille and Pooja had explained that, in North India at least, heavy marijuana ingestion plus transgression meant blitzed men thinking they had carte blanche to harass and grope women. Pooja had told them there was even a famous Holi phrase, Bura na maano, Holi hai, which translated into, "Don't take offense, it's Holi."

Noreen pointed at the newspaper on the empty chair next to Geeta Auntie. "Did you read about what happened at Delhi University?"

Geeta Auntie grunted. "Bastard hooligans."

Yesterday, two Delhi University students had left their all-girls college campus to have lunch at a nearby restaurant and were hit with water balloons filled with semen. After it happened again later that day, the college ordered that, for their own protection, the female students be locked inside their hostels from 6:00 p.m. the night before Holi all the way through to 6:00 p.m. the day of. Female college students across Delhi, along with some of their teachers, responded with protests, holding signs saying NO HOOLIGANISM ON HOLI and WE DO TAKE

OFFENSE and SUPPORT GENDER EQUALITY.

"Locking the girls up isn't the answer, though," Noreen said.

"Correct," Geeta Auntie said. "They should lock up the boys, so the girls can be free."

"Ideally, they shouldn't have to lock up anyone."

"Is it much better in America?"

"In some ways yes, in others no."

The maali, who'd been pushing a wheelbarrow of soil across the garden, stopped to spit in the grass. Judging from its dark red color, he'd been eating Geeta Auntie's paan too.

"Speaking of boys, have you told Kabir that you love him?" Geeta Auntie asked.

"Auntie!" Noreen was embarrassed, but also touched, that Geeta Auntie wanted to know. She was going to miss these sessions of Geeta Auntie real talk. When she returned to America, no one would ask about her motions.

Geeta Auntie clucked her tongue. "Why not?"

"I've been waiting for him to say it first."

"Your whole life will you wait for boys to do things first?"

"No, of course not."

"Then?"

"I don't know," Noreen said. "I'm leaving now, so what's the point?"

As they'd been talking, Geeta Auntie had been adding careful, precise amounts of toasted coconut flakes, fennel seeds, dried rose jam, aniseed, chopped dates, and cardamom powder to the betel leaf. The secret to good paan, she'd told Noreen, was in the proportions. Too much or too little of any one ingredient would throw the balance off.

"It used to be," Geeta Auntie said, "when someone went to America, it was like they were going to another world. Now, there is not so much difference between moving to America and moving to Chennai."

"I wouldn't need a visa to visit Delhi if I were moving to Chennai," Noreen said. "It's easier for a Martian to come to India than someone with Pakistani heritage."

"Haan, main yeh *Veer-Zaara* maamla bhul gayi. But I have a solution. Build a time machine, go back to 1946, and stop the Partition of India. Simple."

Noreen laughed. "I'm on it. All I need is some aluminum foil, copper wire, and a pair of tweezers."

Chuckling, Geeta Auntie folded the betel leaf into a triangle. She pierced it with a clove, handed it to Noreen, picked up the paan she'd already made for herself.

"Happy Holi," she said, tapping her paan against Noreen's.

"Happy Holi." Noreen had not learned to enjoy paan, but she had learned how not to make a face after chewing.

"It makes me so happy you like my paan," Geeta Auntie said. "Whenever the German tenant saw me with my paan box, he'd start running like he'd seen a ghost."

thirty-eight

Air Quality Index: 156.

Unhealthy.

VARUN'S HOUSE WAS BOTH charming and dilapidated, a one-story colonial-style bungalow with high ceilings and blue window shutters and a lovely veranda that opened onto a large grassy lawn dotted with trees. The guests, mostly young and Indian and dressed in white, greeted them with such enthusiastic "Happy Holis!" that Noreen asked Kabir if they were already high.

"Anticipatorily, yes. Come, I'll show you the colors."

In one corner of the lawn, dozens of large steel plates holding mounds of brilliantly hued powders had been laid out across two large tables. Varun's father worked in the civil service, which was how they had this lovely old bungalow, and his mother was in textiles. Each year, she made the Holi colors from natural ingredients, the pink from beetroot, the blue from hibiscus, the yellow from turmeric, the green from henna, and the yellow-orange, which was the traditional color of Holi, from the tesu flowers that bloomed in March.

"They're all so stunning," Noreen said. "It does come off, right?"

Kabir laughed. "Ears and fingernails can take a while."

Next to the tables were buckets containing both clear and colored water. "What are those for?" she asked.

"So you can fill water guns and shoot people."

She understood why Kabir had told her to seal her phone in a plastic bag.

Noreen excused herself to pee, walking through the bungalow's double doors into an airy foyer decorated with two woven chairs and a carved table. Several closed doors led into other rooms, and one had a taped, handwritten sign saying SUSU HERE with drawings of two men at urinals, their arms around each other's waists, and a woman on the toilet, applying lipstick in the mirror of her compact.

On her way out, she stopped at the food table on the veranda to survey the offerings: samosas and syrupy fried dumplings, fried kachoris and pakoras. She piled some snacks on a plate and returned to Kabir. He was talking to Tara, who was swinging on a wooden jhula tied to a tree branch while rubbing almond oil on her face, forearms, and scalp. The oil helped the colors come off, but Noreen didn't dare because the one time she'd tried her mother's argan oil her entire face had broken out.

"Noreen!" Tara said. "You've really never played Holi? I

thought all the goras played it now in the States."

"Color wars or whatever you call it? Never played. And it definitely wasn't a community holiday. My grandparents were like, we don't do that, that's a Hindu thing."

"That's historically inaccurate," Kabir said. "Traditionally, Muslims in India have celebrated Holi. My naani always played growing up. The Mughal emperors hosted huge Holi parties. Under Emperor Shah Jahan the other name for Holi was Eid-e-Gulabi."

"Pink Eid? Yeah, my grandparents definitely didn't celebrate that one." Noreen held out her plate. "Anyone want some pakoras?"

"Did you have any?" Kabir asked her.

She gestured at the pakora in her hand. "I had a bite of this one, why?"

"They might be special pakoras."

"What?"

"Pakoras made with bhang."

Noreen nearly dropped the plate. "I thought you drank bhang!"

"That's the most common way to consume it," Kabir said, "but people also make edibles. Let me taste it. Yeah, definitely special. How much did you have?"

"Only a small bite." Noreen frowned and ran her tongue over her molars.

"You'll be fine, then," he said.

"You sure you don't want to try?" Tara asked. "It's Holi, everyone will be high. Even them up there."

She pointed at the bungalow's roof terrace, where Varun's parents, his mother wearing sunglasses and a white cotton caftan, his father dressed in a white safari-style suit, were laughing with some other adults. There were a few old people up there, too, including a little old lady in glasses that Kabir said was Varun's naani. She remembered Varun mentioning her, how she used to be a principal of a girl's school and would still correct Varun's English grammar.

"Are you telling me Varun's naani is also going to drink bhang?" Noreen asked.

Tara laughed. "Yes, she always has a little."

Noreen wondered if she ought to imbibe—when in Rome, if you couldn't even do what the naanis were doing, then what did that say about you? But she knew herself; she'd fall into a bhang hole and they'd find her curled up in fetal position underneath the snack table, eyes squeezed shut as her thoughts spiraled too dark, too deep.

"So they all get a little high and play Holi up there?" Noreen said.

"Yes, a kinder, gentler version," Kabir said.

"Then they sit around laughing," Tara said, "and eat a big, yummy lunch, then they shower and take a long nap."

Chilling with Varun's naani sounded more appealing than getting doused by water guns, but she needed to stick with her generation and share in Kabir's Holi experience. Wasn't that the point of being in a safe space? All the fun with none of the groping.

Kabir went to the bathroom and Varun and Yasmeen came over. It was the first time Noreen had seen her without her backpack, though she still stood with her thumbs tucked under phantom straps.

Tara snatched the white feather boa from Varun's neck. "I'll put some nice color on this," she said, and headed toward the tables.

Noting the plastic water bottle in Varun's hand, Noreen said, "Hey, can I have a sip of that?"

"Of course," he said. "Happy Holi."

"Thanks." Generally, the custom here was to not let bottles touch your lips but instead tilt your head back and pour the drink into your open mouth. Noreen had yet to master this skill. She managed to only spill a tiny bit but took in more than she'd intended. She walked over to the boundary wall, swishing the water around her mouth with vigor to dislodge any lingering bits of bhankg pakora, then spat into a bush.

"Hey!" Varun said when she returned. "Did you spit it out?"

"I think she might not know, Varun," Yasmeen said.

Noreen wiped her mouth. "Know what?"

"That was molly water," Varun said. He made a sheepish face, cradling his fists to his mouth.

The water had tasted a little weird. "Are you serious?" Noreen said. "Is nothing safe on Holi?"

"Bhang puts both me and Varun straight to sleep so we have a tradition of doing MDMA on Holi instead," Yasmeen said.

Noreen looked around. "Where's Kabir?"

"He hasn't come back from the toilet," Yasmeen said. She brought the jhula to a stop, gestured for Noreen to sit beside her.

"I only swallowed a little," Noreen said.

"You'll be fine, then," Varun said, though the look he exchanged with Yasmeen told a different story.

"I can't make a fool of myself," she said. "Me and drugs, not friends."

"It'll be okay," Yasmeen said. "We're here, and Kabir is with you."

"Kya hua, guys?" Kabir said as he walked up to them. "Why all of a sudden so serious?"

"I unintentionally had a sip of molly water," Noreen said.

"Shit. Who made it, Yasmeen or Varun?"

Varun raised his hand. "Guilty."

"How many grams did you put in it?" Kabir asked.

"Bhai, meri philosophy hai ki if you're going to do it, then you do it right. When Noreen asked me for my water, how was I to know she didn't know?"

"You could have made sure first," Kabir said.

Not wanting to be a source of friction between them, Noreen decided she had to play it cool. Also, maybe if she played it cool, she'd actually *be* cool, and it would all be fine.

If Naani ji on the roof terrace could have a little bhang, surely Noreen on the lawn could have a little MDMA and live to laugh about it tomorrow.

It was all going to be okay.

"Guys, chill," she said. "I only had a little bit, and maybe it'll be fun. Maybe this is Fate saying, 'Girl, nice try staying sober on Holi! If the pakoras don't work, we send in the molly water.'"

Varun rubbed his belly as he laughed. "She's damn cool, Kabir. You're a fucking bastard, you know that?"

"You mean lucky bastard," Kabir said.

Yasmeen threw her hands over her heart. "Kabir and his sweet dialogues! Can you please find me a boyfriend who speaks as meetha as you? You should see the boys on Tinder. Why can't there be a Sweet Boys Only version of Tinder?"

"He is pretty sweet," Noreen said, smiling at him. Was she already high? She didn't know what to expect, if she'd even done enough to feel anything. Varun might have a point; if she was going to do it, she might as well do it rather than spend the rest of the day in an anxious state of am I or aren't I? She needed to channel her mother, who, in her twenties, had partied around the world, dancing on drugs at jungle and beach raves.

"Happy Holi, everyone!"

Ankita's hair was loose, her feet bare. She'd tied her white sari a few inches off the ground, her smooth stomach glistening from oil.

Noreen looked down at her white kurta pajama, one size too big.

Now she'd really have to play it cool.

Be cool, Noreen, be cool.

Ice ice baby.

"Noreen accidentally had a little of my water," Varun told Ankita.

"Your famous Holi molly water? Consider it a rite of passage, Noreen," she said.

Varun beamed. "Would you like some?"

"No, thank you, I'll pass," Ankita said. "But is there the rose petal bhang lassi you had last year? That stuff was damn good."

"I've kept some aside especially for you," Varun said.

"Hey, me too, please!" said Tara, who'd returned triumphant with a boa in shades of brilliant blues and pinks. She draped it around Varun's shoulders, styling it to her satisfaction.

"The lassi's inside the house; come with me," Varun said.

Yasmeen went with them and Kabir took her place next to Noreen. Together, they kicked their feet, propelling the jhula upward. A tall guy sporting mutton-chop sideburns and aviator sunglasses walked through the gate with a machine-style water gun.

"We can leave," Kabir said. "I don't mind. I do this every year."

"But I don't," she said. "And . . ."

She was about to say, and we may never, again.

"Well, I'll stay sober enough to drive at a moment's notice," he said, "so anytime you want to leave, say the word."

"What word?"

"You mean like a code word?"

"Yeah," Noreen said. "What's our code word for GTFO?"

"How about . . . marvelous?"

"Marvelous? Subversive. I like it. And also, I'm sorry."

"Sorry kyun?"

"Now you can't get fucked up on Holi because of me."

Kabir laughed and kissed her. "You are my best trip, Noreen Mirza."

"Ahhh. So cheesy. And you're the profile of the month on Sweet Boys Tinder."

"You love it."

"Are you kidding?" She pretended to lick her hands. "I'm like, more, more. His mattress may be hard, but his words, his words are soft feathers, a pillow for my weary head."

He laughed. "Sunny's bed is very hard."

"*So* hard. Even my spine is like, I don't need to be this straight."

"I love the little dialogues in your humor," Kabir said.

"What?"

"Like you told us what Fate said, and now your spine. You know, your anthropomorphic asides."

She'd never noticed that about herself until he said it.

A catchy Bollywood hit boomed through the enormous rental speakers. People started dancing, everyone happy and garrulous and laughing. Then Mutton Chops, having loaded his machine gun with purple water, started spraying people, and the Holi play began, the revelers racing to fill water guns and grab fistfuls of colored powder from the tables.

Even from the jhula, it was impossible to avoid it. People tossed powder on them as they sprinted past, and once they had to duck from water gun cross fire, though this was nothing compared to the players, now drenched head to toe in color. "Rang Barse," the classic Bollywood song about Holi, came on and the party turned even more raucous, the dancing beginning in earnest. Kabir started bopping his head and Noreen insisted he go dance out the song.

So far, so good. She was definitely high but thoroughly enjoying the spectacle of Holi, the cloudbursts of vivid color, the brilliant powder whirlwinds spinning off the ground like psychedelic Tasmanian devils.

She saw Ankita dance toward Kabir, performing a sexy Bollywood move that Noreen could never pull off, her sari beetroot pink and her face turmeric yellow, her hair parted with a thick streak of purple. They were both good dancers, a joy to watch. Kabir, she noted, maintained a cordial distance—poor guy, she really scared him with their first fight. How could she have been so mean to someone she loved so much?

God, she loved him so much.

She lost sight of Kabir in the crowd. As the song began to transition, she found him again; he was dancing his way back to her, his chest soaked in scarlet. Seeing the bottle of water in his hand, she realized she was parched. When he handed it to her and said, "Regular water," she wanted to get up and hug him, but she didn't trust herself not to fall.

Then Varun and Yasmeen came to check on her, arm in arm, smiles plastered across their green faces. Yasmeen had a lovely amoeba of primary colors across her abdomen.

"Noreen!" she said. "How are you feeling?"

"I actually feel pretty good," Noreen said. "But I don't want to move."

"Don't move, then," Varun said. He was holding a rosebud, and as he drew the rosebud along the inside of her forearm, every nerve ending in her arm awoke with a quiver.

"Wow," Noreen said. She repeated what he'd done, except with her own hand, savoring the way her skin tingled.

"Chalo, we're going to dance," Yasmeen said. "We wanted to check in and say we love you both."

"We love you too," Noreen said. And she did love them, truly. They looked out for each other, took care of Kabir.

"That rosebud felt so good against my skin," Noreen said. "So did my own fingers."

"That's the molly."

"If you touched me, I might explode."

Kabir grinned. "Do you want to try?"

"Yes." She offered her hand, closed her eyes as their fingers intertwined.

"Good?" Kabir asked.

"It's like, my entire body's melting into this touch," she murmured. "I don't even know how to explain it."

"Don't explain. Feel."

She closed her eyes for a bit, rode the warm, soft waves of pleasure. The dancing had slowed, joints were being passed around. Nearby, two girls were eating pakoras. Though she'd been peckish when they'd arrived, she couldn't even think of food now. She did, however, have to pee, but that meant getting up and walking across the lawn, the locking of doors and the removal of clothes.

Kabir accompanied her. After the first few steps, she settled into her vertical state, reasoning that she couldn't be that messed up if she could hold a straight line. Up on the roof terrace, the adults were splattered with color, their hearty laughter punctuated with handclaps. Naani ji was wearing a captivating smile. Noreen wished she could tell her how truly captivating her smile was. She did tell Kabir, who agreed.

They made it to the bathroom.

"You need me to come in with you?" Kabir said.

"I'm good," she said.

"Okay. I'll be right here on the veranda."

She fumbled with the double knots in the drawstring of her

pajama. After she finally managed to untie it and sit on the toilet, she proceeded to have the most amazing susu of her life. Even rinsing herself with the bidet spray felt blissful and erotic. The sink was speckled green and pink and orange. She ran the water, watched the colors swirl and disappear.

Gorgeous.

There was a knock on the door.

"One sec." She wiped her hands on the color-streaked hand towel and opened the door.

"Hey," Ankita said. "Kabir told me you were in here, so I thought I'd check on you. All well?"

"Yeah. I'm good."

Ankita was so elegant and accomplished. In the passion of the moment, Noreen felt it imperative she know this, so she grasped Ankita's supple, turmeric arm and said, "I admire you so much. That report you did on TB hospitals, so brave. And the one about female trafficking in Haryana, I got angry and teary-eyed reading it. Sometimes I think, laughing is good and all, but it's not going to change the world. But you, you're hot and you're changing the world."

"You're very sweet," Ankita said. "Though comedians can make a difference, too. When a society is no longer allowed to make fun of itself and its leaders, things get really scary. Do you know some comedians here are too nervous to even say the prime minister's name? Promise me you'll go back to America and always take the piss out of your government. Do it for me."

Noreen pledged on her heart, with both hands. "Pukka I will. I'll do it for you."

"So sweet! You're too much."

Somewhere deep down, a small voice said, *Yes, you really are too much*, but she ignored it, because she was nothing if not a fount of love and goodwill, gushing out of her with a force beyond her control.

"Hey." Kabir stepped into the foyer. "All well?"

"All well," Noreen said.

"I'll go pee," Ankita said. "See you out there."

As Noreen and Kabir walked back toward the jhula, she squeezed his hand. "I'm really sorry about your dad."

"And I'm sorry about yours. But we're both going to be okay."

"And our dads?"

"Not our responsibility," he said.

"Or our fault."

"Correct."

Correct. She was going to miss Indian English. And hearing Hindi and Urdu every day.

"I'm going to miss you so much," she said, and stopped walking.

"Is everything okay?" he asked.

"There's something I have to tell you. I can't keep it inside anymore."

"Go ahead."

Cue music, cue lights, cue fountain.

And action.

"I think you're so amazing, Kabir. When I'm with you, I feel like the best version of myself. You have such a beautiful heart. I love you. Like, capital L Love you. And I don't know if it's wise to have kids, climate change and all, but I could definitely have your babies. They would have your eyes and your kind smile and my sassy mouth—can you imagine?"

She paused, realized what she'd said.

I love you. Please impregnate future me.

He had to be flipping out.

She gathered the courage to look at him. He was smiling, probably so that he wouldn't freak her out with how freaked out he was.

Behind Kabir, a guy dumped a bucket of water over a girl's head, her high-pitched scream ringing in Noreen's ears. It was all too much, she was too much. She needed to go somewhere quiet.

"Marvelous," she said.

"Let's go."

"I'm sorry I'm making you leave early." She was truly and deeply upset for ruining his Holi. Also, if she put her tongue between her front teeth, she could feel them chattering. Was that normal?

He took her hands in his. "Noreen Mirza. I love you too."

She gasped. "You do?"

"Are you really that surprised? You couldn't see it on my sleeve?"

"No. I mean, yes and no. I guess part of me thought if you loved me, you'd tell me."

He turned her hands over and massaged her palms with his thumbs, a sensation so sublime it almost didn't matter what he said. Almost. "I hesitated because you were leaving, and I didn't want to put pressure on you, on us. And it seemed like we'd made this silent agreement not to talk about it. I should have told you. I'm sorry."

"No! Don't be sorry. You're so sorry all the time. I should be sorry. I'm the selfish one in this relationship—you really love me?"

"I started to fall in love with you when we were lying on the grass after running from the jinn," he said.

"I love you so much, you have no idea," she said.

"Sometimes I look at you and my heart catches its breath," he said.

The music paused as whoever was playing DJ cued the next song.

"If it's Bryan Adams, I swear to God," Noreen said.

Kabir laughed, and she laughed, and Noreen didn't even realize what song came on next because Kabir kissed her, sending ripples of ecstatic heat down her body.

The clitoris had eight thousand nerve endings.

She pulled away. "Home base at once, please."

He grinned. "After you, madam."

Hell if she would ever do this again, but she would be forever grateful to the molly water, because of which Kabir and she were off to have I love you sex. Thank you, molly water. Thank you, Allah. Thank you, Hazrat Nizamuddin. Thank you, Ganesh. Thank you, Mother Earth. Thank you, Jinn. And, of course, *Thank you, India.*

thirty-nine

Air Quality Index: 113.
Unhealthy for Sensitive Groups.

HOLI NIGHT, TIRED AND sober and lying in Kabir's
arms, Noreen couldn't sleep because her mind kept returning to
Ankita. She shifted to the other side of the bed. Kabir's chest
was damp where her head had been. They'd taken bucket baths
when they'd gotten home to wash off the color, another after sex.
Using a Q-tip to clean color from another person's ear was its
own kind of intimacy.

It's been a marvelous day, she told herself. In this moment,
you have everything you want, Kabir and you, together, in love.
It's perfect.

Then why couldn't she trust it?

Kabir stirred, and she coughed to wake him up.

"You awake?" He turned to face her, traced her collarbone.
"What are you thinking?"

"How did Ankita know I want to be a comedian?" she said.

"I told her," he said.

It made sense; she knew they were in touch.

"How often do you two WhatsApp?" she said. "Every day?"

"It varies. Sometimes we're not in touch for days, a week, sometimes we message once or twice a day." He propped himself up on his elbows. "Does that upset you?"

"A little."

"You know we're only friends."

"I know," she said.

"Do you want me to stop communicating with her?"

"No! Definitely not." What was she doing? She'd started this conversation with no actual purpose, except maybe self-sabotage. Maybe this was her legacy of paternal abandonment; instead of getting into shitty relationships, she'd get into good relationships and turn them shitty.

"Did I do something wrong?" Kabir said.

"No. It's me, I'm the one that's wrong." She buried her face in the pillow. "I was so happy and now I don't even know why I'm saying what I'm saying. And deep down I'm blaming my dad but is that true or is it a cop-out?"

"Hey, hey." Kabir kissed the back of her head. "Slow down. Sit up. Talk to me."

Growing up, she'd seen her mother pace when she had to make a big decision or work something out in her head. Noreen preferred to do her deep thinking on the couch but now she got up and, naked, paced the length of the room from Shiva to Shabana Azmi and back, as Kabir watched from bed.

"I think I'm feeling weird because, number one, I did drugs, so there's that, and number two, we've officially told each other we love each other, which is awesome, but in a few days I leave India, probably forever. And I guess I'm also nervous about doing stand-up, and I haven't been thinking about my father but it's clearly coming out in other ways, and the Ankita thing, it's not actually her, it's what she represents—whoever you're going to fall in love with next."

"Why are you thinking about this now? What was it Adi Uncle's mom used to say?"

"Remember the past, look to the future, but live in the moment. The thing is . . . love is scary."

"And why is that?"

Noreen leaned against the wall next to Shabana Azmi, looked down at her feet, wiggled her toes. There were still flecks of yellow and pink in the bed of her toenails.

"Because it can hurt you so much," she said. "As romantic as it turns out I am, I've watched my mom and her friends nurse each other's broken hearts enough times to also be a realist. If we stay half a world apart, eventually you'll meet someone else. You *should* meet someone else. But even the thought of it sends a pain shooting through my heart. And it's not only that."

Kabir looked up at her with such tender concern that a different kind of pain shot through her chest. "What else scares you?" he said.

"When someone you love dies, it shifts your perspective; not only can the people you love hurt you, they can also die on you. But I tell myself I can't let this fear stop me, because if you don't love others, if you don't let love in, if you keep your heart dark, you might as well be dead, right? Wow. From Ankita to death." She shook her head. "Sorry! I didn't mean to ruin this perfect day."

"Noreen, it's still perfect," Kabir said.

"Perfectly imperfect?"

"Exactly.

Noreen collapsed on the desk chair, drained from the bite of bhang and the sip of molly and the unexpected confessions. "You know, if you'd asked me even six months ago, I would have said I'm not the jealous type, but look at me now, jealous of someone who doesn't even exist yet."

Kabir shrugged. "Well, it's also a good thing, right, that you can surprise yourself? It means you're not static, that you can change. And as for the future . . . who can say?"

"Cannot predict now, need more prosecco."

"What?"

"It's something Adi Uncle says."

Kabir moved the stool in front of her and sat down, resting his head in her lap. She smiled at him, ran her fingers through his hair. There was a soft bite mark on her inner thigh from when he had been teasing her earlier.

"The future is that you're starting college in August, a whole new adventure," he said. "I'll apply to some MFA programs in America, but who knows where I'll end up? If I save up enough money, maybe I can visit."

"My mom says the only thing you can predict about the future is that almost nothing happens the way you expect."

"She's right."

"I don't want to leave you," she said.

"I don't want you to leave."

He noticed the bite mark, kissed it.

"Kabir?"

"Yes?"

"Maybe we can change, but what about our fathers? Can they?"

"I don't know," he said. "Now that my father's out of the news cycle, I'm hoping he'll start to reflect. And I was again thinking about Adi Uncle's advice. When I'm old, I want to look back and know I tried my best to help my father change, to understand."

"But what if the person he hurt the most was the person you love the most? What then?"

He leaned back and looked up at her. "As in your father? Honestly, Noreen, I don't know. Only you can answer that. But I do know you don't need to answer it anytime soon."

Now and then, a memory of Sonia Khala would come to her. When this happened, it was intense but also comforting: since she could no longer make memories, it meant the day had not come when there was nothing new left to remember. Sonia Khala had flown out for a four-day weekend, all by herself, which made it extra special. Noreen had skipped school Friday, something Sonia Khala would never let her own kids do, and the two of them had gone into the city, up to Central Park. When Sonia Khala was in med school, she liked to visit the Conservatory Garden. She enjoyed returning places; she'd visited the Alhambra three times. She said even if the place hadn't changed, you'd see it with new eyes, because you were different than the last time, and the time before that. That morning, it'd been raining, but by the time they reached Central Park, the sun was breaking through the clouds. They'd passed a busker, singing an old folk song. He had a lovely voice and it was a lovely song, about life passing by and thinking something's been left behind. When the song ended, Sonia Khala thanked him, and since she'd given her last dollar to a homeless woman on the subway, told him she'd go to an ATM and be back. They returned quickly: even after decades in California, Sonia Khala still walked like a New Yorker, but the busker had gone. They looked at the bench where he'd once been, and, in near unison, sang the same line.

And there'll be time enough for thinking come tomorrow.

forty

Air Quality Index: 225. Very Unhealthy.

NOREEN, WHO'D SPENT THE last two hours on Ruby's bed, brainstorming jokes while her mother packed and repacked, was discovering how much she sucked at punch lines. Nikhil, who ran the open mic comedy night, told her she'd have five minutes for her set, though he never cut people off till the eight-minute mark, which seemed like an eternity anyway. Writing jokes was an art, of course, that required a regular practice of writing and thinking and rehearsing, and she was only starting out. She tended toward longer narratives, which might contain amusing moments or funny bits of dialogue, but few punchy jokes. It seemed easier to get an audience to cry in five minutes than to keep them laughing.

"Hey, did you see the video of Sohail pulling a dupatta out of a hat? He's getting pretty good at magic," Ruby said.

"Mmmm," Noreen said.

"Are you even listening?"

"Do you think I should do a bit about my Brazilian wax?" Noreen said. "I read that starting out the easiest jokes are usually personal."

"Can't get more personal than a Brazilian wax," her mother said. "But if it's funny, why not? You have a punch line?"

"Welcome to South Delhi, where it takes four people to change a light bulb and two to wax your crack."

Ruby laughed. "Not bad."

"Are you really okay with my talking about my crack in front of an audience?" Noreen said.

"Even if I wasn't, I'd want you to do it."

"Why?"

Ruby shrugged. "Because it's who you are. And because I know the minute you tell a kid they can't do something, they want to do it even more."

"Here's meri philosophy," Noreen said. "If I'm doing this, this thing that terrifies me, then I want to do it. I want to be the girl who goes there. Like Margaret Cho. I want to talk about my body, and sex. Not only about those things, but you know. Like, I'm probably going to use the word *vulva* Thursday night."

"*Vulva*'s an excellent word." Having failed at folding a maroon-and-gold sari the first time, Ruby shook it out to try again. "And I'm the one who taught you to use the proper terms for your genitalia so I should be proud. Does that mean you're doing the Brazilian wax bit?"

371

"I don't know. I'd have to introduce the light bulb joke before. And set it up by talking about how labor is so cheap here that it leads to gross inefficiencies."

Noreen closed her notebook and hung her head off the bed. Months of shopping lay in piles around the room: shawls, scarves, saris, earrings, bracelets, embroidered dinner napkins and pillow covers, leather juttis, ayurvedic creams and lotions, a Madhubani painting they'd bought for Adi Uncle, lac bangles and handmade puppets from Rajasthan, assorted trinkets for relatives and friends, and some gifts that would stay: a Chanderi sari for Sarita, an embroidered shawl for Geeta Auntie.

"The Mirza girls need a caravan," Noreen said.

"When we add up all your stuff, we'll probably have four suitcases. We're only allowed one suitcase each. We're going to pay baggage fees up the wazoo. Thanks, United."

"How do you greet a drag queen doing downward dog?" Noreen said.

"How?"

"Namaslay."

"Ha! That's funny."

"Yes, but not original, not the punch line, at least."

"So add more of your own twist," Ruby said. "And remember it's an open mic night at a rando South Delhi bar; I don't think people are expecting Kumail or Mindy."

"Kumail Nanjiani is Pakistani, so he wouldn't get a visa. The closest he'd get to doing stand-up in India is yelling it through a bullhorn across the Wagah border."

Ruby laughed. "See? I've already laughed twice in one minute of talking to you."

"It doesn't count, you're my mother."

Ruby, unhappy with her latest fold, flung the sari out again, the pallu caressing the wall opposite before fluttering onto an open suitcase. "Speaking of visas, you never told me what you and Kabir decided. About the future."

"You mean, capital *F* Future?"

"That's the one."

"We're going to stay in touch, obviously. Since it could be another year, at least, until we see each other again, it doesn't make sense to put a label on it. I'll be starting freshman year, and Kabir will be busy. He's moving in with Tara and Yasmeen and will have to do the freelance hustle to pay his rent, and he's starting therapy—his first appointment is Monday—and dealing with his parents and working on his photo portfolio."

"That's very mature of you two," Ruby said. "I'm impressed."

"That's because it's not going to fully hit me until I'm on the plane. Then I'm going to turn into Devastated Girl with Daddy Issues."

"Do you think there's a cape for that?"

Noreen laughed. "Hey, let me help you." She got up off the bed and picked up both ends of the pallu.

"Thanks. And here's something you'll be happy about."

"What?" Noreen said.

They met in the middle, folded the sari once, moved apart.

"Guess what I've decided to do when we get back?"

"Give Zumba another chance?"

"Ha! Never. I've decided to sign up for one of those online dating apps," Ruby said.

"Really?"

"Yes. Even though Hari and I wouldn't have worked long-term, being with him was so nice it inspired me to put myself out there. The world is full of possibilities, and anyway you're going to be gone soon and I'll have a lot of free time."

"I think that's great," Noreen said. They folded the last section of the sari, and Noreen took it from her mother to smooth out a crease.

"Good, because you're writing my profile."

"We'll write it together," she said. "All right. I pronounce this sari folded to the best of our abilities. I gotta go. Abby brainstorm session in five."

"Enjoy," Ruby said. "Hey."

Noreen turned back from the door. "Yes?"

"How many men does it take to change a light bulb in South Delhi?"

"Four," Noreen said. "One to take the bulb out, one to stand on the chair, one to turn the chair in circles, and one to tell them they're in the wrong house."

forty-one

Air Quality Index: 91. Moderate.

DEPOT WAS A LONG narrow room with a bar on one side and eight small round tables with wooden chairs on the other. A mirror ran the length of the bar, above which were tiny yellow and red bulbs that blinked DEPOT on and off. The mic had been set up in the center, and there were people at every table, thirty-two in total, eight of whom were there for Noreen: Kabir, Ruby, Camille, Pooja, Yasmeen, Tara, Varun, and Geeta Auntie. The open mic started late, and Noreen was too nervous to talk, drink, or even hold Kabir's hand. There were four comics on the roster, and Noreen was last.

Nikhil, the emcee for the evening, had a thick beard, a baritone voice, and woolly chest hair that formed a curly choker around his neck. He greeted the audience, warming them up with a few jokes about being hirsute. Then he said, "Tell me, who of you thinks that, generally speaking, men are funnier than women? Show of hands. Come on, we're in a safe space."

Varun winked at them, Tara elbowing him in the stomach as he raised his hand.

"Well, sir," Nikhil said, "prepare to be shamed because tonight we have four, yes, one, two, three, *four* lady comics who are going to prove you wrong! We only had women sign up this week, so please put your hands together for the first Unofficial Ladies Only Open Mic Comedy Night at Depoooooot!"

The first comic had short hair and wore ripped jeans and a white tank top with a marijuana leaf across the front. She was hot, her set not so much, only two of her jokes landing.

My ex-boyfriend was such a pothead narcissist that he'd only pass the joint to himself.

The second comic was better; even when her jokes weren't funny she earned some chuckles for her deadpan delivery.

I want to talk about my childhood. I wasn't being bullied enough, so my parents got divorced. They also pushed me into bisexuality; they kept telling me to keep my options open.

The third comic was so nervous her voice shook, some of her jokes so visceral Noreen could feel the audience squirming.

Men are such assholes. Most are real creeps. But I've figured out a way to deal with the creeps—if a man says something creepy to you, you say something creepier. If he says, your hands look so soft, you say, thanks, I use them to slowly castrate goats in the lab.

By the time Nikhil took the mic to introduce her, Noreen had relaxed a bit; at least she wouldn't be the worst performer of the night.

"A round of applause for Bhavna, everyone! Remember, every Friday night at Depot, good jokes, good times. Tell your friends. Not only is tonight all women but it's also international, because our last lady of the night comes to us all the way from New Jersey. It's her first time doing stand-up, so please, put your hands together for our newbie Jersey girl, Noreeeeen Mirza!"

Newbie Jersey girl? And why did he have to keep calling them lady comics? It was kind of a dick lead, but no time to dwell, the show must go on. Kabir nodded *you got this*, and her mother gave her two thumbs-up, and Geeta Auntie had her right fist raised *go go*.

She went to the mic, stood in the small spotlight.

Noreen had been worried that she'd freeze, but being in front of the audience actually calmed her. There was something free-ing about the point of no return. You've come all this way, it's your kismat to see it through. As Sonia Khala would say to her kids: Bismillah and do your best.

Bismillah.

"Hi, everyone. My name is Noreen, and it's true, this is my first time."

forty-two

Air Quality Index: 119.
Unhealthy for Sensitive Groups.

LAST DAY IN DELHI, day of dread. But when she looked into Kabir's eyes at the first light of dawn, she vowed she'd try to live this day in the moment, and definitely no crying until the end.

They took an auto through smog so thick it muted the sun and transformed concrete high-rises into smoky silhouettes. From a distance, people looked ghostly. Only when they came close did their bodies take form. A boy around thirteen, pushing a fruit cart, the pomegranates and oranges and long, skinny green grapes coated in fine gray dust. A newspaper wallah riding his cycle at a leisurely pace, his basket full of folded papers. A beggar with no legs wheeling himself along the side of the road. A malnourished woman at a construction site, carrying bricks on her head.

Nizamuddin was beginning to buzz, the juice center at the entrance serving up glasses of fresh sugarcane. At least half the food and prayer scarves and rose petal stalls lining the lanes to the dargah were open for business, though the shopkeepers were chilling, finishing their chai. A few called out, *Madam, see this, Madam, buy these roses*, but didn't push beyond that. Ahead of them, two young men walked hand in hand. A teenage boy on a scooter, gelled hair and a shadow of a mustache, came barreling around a curve from the other direction, forcing the two young men apart and Noreen and Kabir to one side. She adjusted her dupatta and they walked the rest of the way without incident, stopping to leave their shoes at the dargah entrance.

She was back.

This early in the morning, the dargah of Hazrat Nizamuddin was quiet and at peace. Walking here, she'd seen one other woman, with her husband and son, but inside the dargah there were a dozen or so women, and enough space for everyone to go about their business undisturbed. A woman brushed her teeth in the corner. A man in a crooked purple beret sat with his head in his hands. Two women shared a samosa. A bearded man with a red shawl and melodious voice was singing "Aaj Rang Hai," a poem by Amir Khusro and song number seven on Sonia Khala's qawwali playlist.

Verily there are signs for those who reflect.

Kabir joined the short line to enter the tomb and Noreen stepped onto the tomb's platform. A man in a gold-sequined skullcap read a Hindi newspaper, his legs extended in front of him. An old woman was sleeping, her younger companion reading a Quran taken from the shelves that lined one wall of the tomb.

This time, Noreen had a clear path to an empty jali. She pressed her forehead to the marble.

Dear Haẓrat Niẓamuddin, please bless Sonia Khala's soul, and everyone else I love, and the world, too, if you don't mind. Not sure it's going to last long without some divine intervention. Sonia Khala was a huge fan of yours. She wanted to come here herself, but never got the chance, so I'm here in her stead. I tried to do this once before, but that didn't go as planned, so now I'm back. I'm a poor substitute for her devotion, though I did feel touched by the divine in the ruins of Begumpur Masjid. And I am on a journey. I don't know if I'd call it a spiritual journey, but all journeys are that, too, aren't they?

Kabir told me a lot of lovers come to you, in real life and in Bollywood, to ask you to remove obstacles in their path. There are a fair few obstacles for Kabir and me: distance and visas and our age and even our dads. Please help me trust that if we are meant to be together one day, we will. Is Fate really a thing, Haẓrat Niẓamuddin? Sorry. I can ask a lot of questions sometimes. When I was young, my nana used to call me "Miss Question Mark." All right. One last prayer for Sonia Khala, and I'll leave you in peace.

After reciting Sura Fatiha, she tied the thread to a side of one of the screen's six-pointed stars. She considered chilling on the platform for a bit, but the dargah was getting busier so she went to find Kabir. Reading the question in his eyes, she smiled and nodded her head and he clapped his hands. Mission accomplished, they went to celebrate with a big dosa breakfast.

The uncle at the table to their right paid his bill and left his newspaper behind. Kabir picked it up and said, "Oh good!"

"What?"

"The two guys who tried to assassinate Dara Khan have been arrested."

"Thank God," Noreen said.

"Now let's see if they actually serve any jail time."

"What else is happening?"

Kabir summarized the rest of the news for her. Two Christian men beaten to death by mob after refusing to recite "Jai Shri Ram." A police constable had been arrested for raping a six-year-old girl. A famous Bollywood director cast #MeToo accused star Rohit Chopra in his upcoming film, citing "innocent until proven guilty."

"So basically a typical day," Noreen said.

"Seriously." Kabir folded the paper, offered it to the uncle eating idlis to their left.

"Do you think it's going to get better? Not only here, but America, everywhere."

"I don't know," he said. "I was thinking last night, there is so much bad energy in the world, maybe I should write to the assistant who accused my father. I don't want her to think no one in my family gives a fuck. But then I considered what Ankita said, that she could publish the letter and it could seem like I'm incriminating my father. What do you think? And is it egoistical of me to assume I can make it better?"

"I don't know, it's complicated," Noreen said. "But I don't think you should do anything before talking stuff through with your therapist."

"This therapist is going to get an earful."

Noreen laughed. "I think that's the point."

The day of his first appointment, she would be gone. They would not meet at home base, he would not tell her about it over jalapeño chicken burgers, she would not hold him in her arms. Instead, they would speak through rectangles.

They walked back to the barsati. Creepy Guard was kindly absent today; there were some things about Delhi she would not miss. Kabir had gotten Sunny's record player fixed as a thank-you for letting them stay. They flipped through the crates, decided on an album of Raag Khamaj, a late-night raga sung by Ustad Rashid Khan. "Wrong time, right mood," Kabir said as he dusted it off.

After they made love and napped, Kabir said he had something to show her. Noreen pulled on her shirt and Kabir's boxers, opened the curtains, and took the folder from his proferred hands. Inside was a slim stack of photos, 8 x 10 black-and-white portraits of his naani.

She arranged the photos across the desk. Kabir and his naani had the same emotive, honey-brown eyes. In one photo, she was on a park bench and three butterflies, two spotted, one striped, had gathered on a low-hanging tree branch, only a few inches from her face. She was looking at them like she recognized them, like they were old friends. In the distance, farther down the path, an auntie wearing headphones and a pollution mask was power walking.

In another photo, she was on the roof terrace, bundled in a shawl on a wooden cot, staring into the distant smog as their maid Charu braided her thinning hair. Kabir had told her she spent quite a bit of time on this cot; though she refused to wear a mask and they worried about the pollution, she became distressed if she stayed too long inside. In Noreen's favorite photo, she was lying down on the cot, a small cube speaker near her head. Her right arm was lifted in the air, moving to the music, and she was smiling, lost inside some happy memory. In the glass wall of the solarium, you could see her reflection.

"What was she listening to?" Noreen said.

"An old Mohammed Rafi song—'Badan Pe Sitare Lapete Huye.' She kept asking me to bring the speaker closer and closer, and then she got lost in the music. I couldn't believe it; she remembered almost every word. She sang along and after I took this photo, she said to me, 'You show-off, you love it when the girls admire your dance.' She must have thought I was my grandfather. I've no memory of him; he died when I was a baby, but apparently he knew how to cut a rug."

"Kabir, these photos are wonderful," Noreen said. "The way you shot them, they're so intimate and moving. No one else could have done it like this."

"I don't think I can ever show them," he said. "They're so

personal, and she's not in a position to give me permission."

"You could use them for your portfolio, though," she said.

"Yes. There's one more." He opened the top desk drawer and took out another photo. "It's my gift to you. If that mean girl from summer camp got a load of this . . ."

"What? Let me see."

Noreen, in bed, under the muslin blanket, her shoulders bare, one arm curved along the pillow. The light hit her at a diagonal, her armpit a shadow within a shadow. Both her eyes were illuminated.

She had never seen herself look so happy. And, judging from her small, wicked smile, also on the cusp of some joke.

"Kabir, I love it," she said. "I love the way you see me."

"That's who you are," he said.

And when she left him for America? What then? How would she find home? It didn't matter; she would not trade her time here with him for anything. It was already so much a part of her that she couldn't imagine any other version of Noreen except the one who'd fallen in love with Kabir.

She kissed him. Earlier, they'd made love with all the urgency of the end; now she wanted it soft and slow, but it wasn't time yet. Sex would have to wait until they'd returned from the jinn.

forty-three

Air Quality Index: 124.
Unhealthy for Sensitive Groups.

Dear Jinn,

Well, it's been a moment. Kabir told me jinn are supposed to live far longer than humans, so for you it must literally feel like a moment. And while time has also flown for me, so much has happened. I should start by saying thank you, since my question to you about my father received its answer. Now is not the right time. I haven't even processed it all yet, to tell the truth, so maybe send me good vibes for that. Kabir's starting therapy and going to talk to his father soonish, so please also send him good vibes for all of that, and in general. My mother is returning to America energized and more hopeful about love—if you have any power to send a loyal and kind and funny man her way, I would be very grateful. Not sure if you have any contact with the dead; if so, please send Sonia Khala our regards. It sounds like Amir and Sohail are about to start a whole new chapter, but Mom and I will be there for them, and Nana and Naani too.

As you can see, humans are making a hash of the world. A

humble request to save humanity. Ha! Sorry, but it's so bad I'd be remiss not to ask this of all gods, jinn, and saints. I'm sure you've been seeing how hateful the rhetoric is becoming, here and everywhere. Is the jinn world as complicated as the human one? I can't imagine anyone destroying themselves as we are. And also, I forgot to ask Hazrat Nizamuddin to bless the woman I saw whipping her hair at Princess Jahanara's tomb. If she hasn't found peace yet, maybe you could help her, too.

To end on a happier note, I did stand-up, and got a couple laughs (even from strangers!). Not sure I'll make a career out of it, but I've been writing every day, and it feels great. I can't believe I was away from it for so long. I realized not writing makes me more depressed, that I need to keep on, even when I think I have nothing good to say, especially then. Not that I'm depressed now—I'm happy, writing, in love. But the idea of not being with Kabir—if only we were jinn, we could fly to each other. Do all jinn fly? Are jinn big romantics? Who isn't, deep down? I'm sure you must understand my pain. I know there are no easy answers for this, and that the only answer is to see it through, step by step, moment by moment. Ultimately, though, I've decided that if you can face your demons and end up laughing more than you cry, then you've lived a good life.

Here's to all of us, human and jinn, finding our way home.

Take care and go in peace.

Until next time,

Noreen Mirza

forty-four

Air Quality Index: 99.

Moderate.

IT WASN'T THAT SHE didn't feel all the same things in the underground altar—the pain and the longing and the grief and the hope and the despair, a brief history of human anguish huddled in the dark—she did, but she was different than the time before. This time, it wasn't the emotions that overwhelmed her but the smoke. They stayed long enough to whisper their words and leave their letters, and for Noreen to tell Kabir, "Thank you, for bringing me to the jinn."

"Thank the jinn, for bringing us together," Kabir said.

"I already did."

"So did I."

Together, they stepped out of the dark and walked back through the light-spliced passage hand in hand. The shrieking of the bats was as loud as she remembered, but this time, she could look at them without fear.

The sun was beginning to set. As they crossed the park, half the sky went dark with thousands of small birds.

"What's happening?" Noreen said.

"The rosy starlings are returning north," Kabir said.

Every person on the grounds of Firoz Shah Kotla stood transfixed by the starling murmuration; the birds, who had been flying as one, now moving apart and together again, shape-shifting with seamless grace and intuition, a figure eight, an hourglass, a strand of DNA, a dove, a wing, a whirlwind.

Then the starlings flew away, and people returned to prayers and leisure, and it was time for Noreen and Kabir to leave the ruins, for a last meal of kabobs, and a long journey home.

I read somewhere that for each thing that is true about India, the opposite is also true. I'd add that for each thing you might not like about India, you will find something to like as much, or more. I hope, though, that all the hate we're hearing in public discourse doesn't tip that balance, and I mean this not only for India, but for my home country, and the whole world. Jokes aside, these months in Delhi have been some of the best of my life, and that brings me to Rule Number Five: When you return to America, your lungs may be grateful, but your heart will be incredibly sad.

That's my set, everyone. Thank you for listening, and have an amazing rest of your night.

Acknowledgments

It took a village to write this book. My deepest gratitude to:

My editor, Rosemary Brosnan, for believing in this project and for your wise and patient guidance as this book journeyed from one kind of jinn to another.

My agent, Ayesha Pande, for your support and encouragement and for taking a chance on a new writer many years ago.

The wonderful team at Quill Tree Books/HarperCollins: Veronica Ambrose, Jessica Berg, Almeda Beynon, Jacqueline Burke, Shannon Cox, and Courtney Stevenson for all of their dedication and hard work.

Samya Arif, for the marvelous cover.

Jahaan Shah, for setting the Mirza Girls to music. Sunaina Coehlo, Jall Cowasji, and Avi Kabir, for helping bring it to life.

The Vanderbilt Creative Writing Program, especially Lorraine Lopez, Justin Quarry, and Nancy Reisman. The Iowa Writers' Workshop. USIEF and the Fulbright Program in India.

Dorland Mountain Arts Colony and Rockvale Colony for the Arts, for a quiet space to write.

David Arnold, Kendare Blake, and Manjula Menon, for taking the time to read in a world that can seem so short on time.

Mira Ram for being the landlady with the mostest. Sunita James and Nisha Advin, for running the house and taking such good care of my children while I completed a draft of this book.

Tomiko Peirano, for our trips down memory lane, a few of which made it into the book. Lynn Berger, for your Dutch insights and general loveliness.

Captain Nagendra Vikram Gahlot, for your sea stories. Neil Chadha, for the pomegranate.

Amaar Abbas, Anindita Ghose, Biba Saxton, Mandakini Gahlot, Rosalyn D'Mello, and Vikramaditya Singh, your warm Delhi welcome was all a new girl could ask for.

Carissa Cascio and Stephanie Ham for being my village during the pandemic.

Christine Rogers, for being the best auntie in Nashville. Kevan Peden, for your excellent taste in love songs.

Melissa Chadwick and Cynthia Kueppers, for making the West Coast the best coast.

Nicky Dodd, Olivia Dar, and Punit Jasuja, meeting you three beautiful people made my Delhi life next level. Here's to a lifetime of adventures, all over the world.

Nabil Ashour, you mock me. Keegan Finberg, for book recs and the bike rescue. Diyari Vazquez, for being the best date to a Delhi wedding. Abeer Hoque, wherever this life takes me, I'll be always be your baby. Taniya Kapoor, for lighting up my life. Rahim Rahemtulla, I love you, Nizar.

Maneesha and Suveesha, for being two awesome buas. Ashu Bhai for the mutton.

Aman, New Mexico forever. Dipali and Vinod, for their support across continents. Team Dadi-Dadu forever.

Shahina and Iqbal, for instilling a desire to see the world and for being the world's greatest Amma and Nana. Mona, for looking out for your little sis and introducing me to The Smiths.

Anand, Lillah and Inaya, you know it's true. (Everything I do) I do it for you.

Thank you, Reader, for spending time with this book in a tumultuous world. However near or far your journeys take you, may the light in your heart guide you home.